Sèvres Protocol

DAVID LEE CORLEY

DEDICATION

I dedicate this story to my son Justin Michael Corley. He is
my first born and one of the smartest people I know. It
never ceases to amaze me how much knowledge he has
about the most obscure subjects that don't seem to be
related but are in his mind. I will never fully understand
him but I love him dearly.

ACKNOWLEDGMENTS

I would like to thank Antoneta Wotringer for her excellent book cover design. She is truly an artist with a unique sense of style. I would also like to thank JJ Toner for proofreading. He is by far better at spelling and grammar than I and an author himself.

NOTE FROM AUTHOR

This is a work of fiction based on historical events. It is not history. To create a coherent story and to satisfy the need for brevity I found it necessary to combine characters and create fictional events. In such cases I did my best to remain as genuine as possible to the events and true to the nature of the characters as I saw them. Many of the character names in this story belong to real people. This was done to allow the reader to research the true stories behind these people if they wish.

I also want to make note that the entire story is divided into two books. There were two military campaigns during the Suez Crisis. The first was the Israeli campaign called Operation Kadesh. The second was a British and French campaign called Operation Musketeer and Operation Revise. As much as I tried to keep it to just one book, there was too much interesting material and I wanted to give the reader a thorough view of these important historical events. This book covers Operation Kadesh and the sequel covers Operations Musketeer and Revise. Both campaigns overlapped and therefore both books overlap somewhat. I separated events into two stories so the reader will find some backtracking in the beginning of the second book. The dates in both books are as accurate as I could make them while still telling a cohesive story.

I hope you enjoy the story as much as I enjoyed writing it.

"War is the failure of diplomacy."

John Dingell

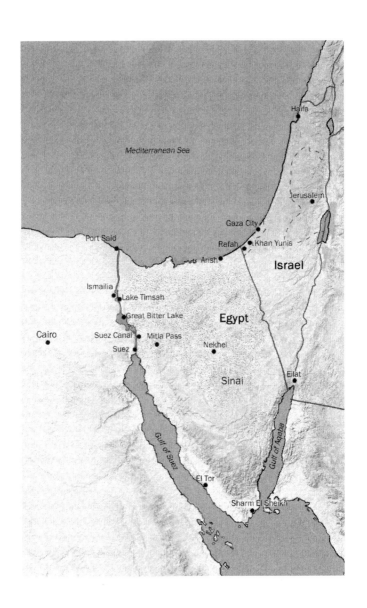

PROLOGUE

February 28th, 1922

After three years of armed rebellion, Egypt gained its independence from Britain. As a condition of independence, the British maintained the right to defend international interests in Egypt, namely, the Suez Canal Company. The company was owned by British and French investors. It operated the canal and collected tolls from passing ships. None of the revenue went to Egypt, one of the poorest countries in the world.

As industry grew and oil was developed in the Middle East, the Suez Canal became more crucial to European countries rebuilding from the devastation of World War II. To keep the vital passage open the British established the world's largest military base in the Suez Canal Zone. Eighty-eight thousand British troops were station on Egyptian soil. The base exceeded the ten thousand troop limit allowed by the 1922 agreement. The Egyptians objected to the British intrusion and demanded that the British leave. Britain ignored them and Europe turned a blind eye.

Then came Nasser...

ONE

November 23, 1954 - Suez Canal Zone, Egypt

The night air was hot and the Suez was still. The moon in a cloudless sky reflected off the water. Two British soldiers manned a machinegun surrounded by sandbags. It was one of hundreds of outposts flanking the canal. "I've gotta pee like a race horse," said a private.

"You just said you were thirsty," said a corporal.

"I am. I'm thirsty and I've got to pee. The water runs right through me. I think it's got bugs in it."

"Wait until the end of our watch."

"I can't. It hurts. I'll pee in the corner if I have to."

"Like hell you will. All right. Go and pee. Just don't do it too close. Your urine smells like curry."

The private climbed over the sandbags and walked toward the canal. The corporal kept a sharp eye out. The desert was flat except for the canal. The private unbuttoned his trousers and urinated into the canal. "Oh, that's just wrong," said the corporal shaking his head in disgust.

The canal was narrow. Only one hundred feet across at some points. The size of the ships that passed through the canal was increasing, especially the oil tankers. Traffic was becoming a problem. Ships were lining up at the canal entrances in both the Mediterranean and the Red Sea.

The three hundred European pilots that navigated the canal preferred the daylight so they could clearly see the red and green buoys that marked the way. One poorly executed maneuver could ground a ship and block the canal for weeks, or even months. If that happened, Europe would suffer. There would be fuel shortages. Industry would grind to a halt. Jobs would be lost. The Suez Canal Company would be deprived of its precious tolls.

The Egyptians would feel nothing. They derived no benefit from the canal. They did not share in the tolls since the Egyptian government was forced to sell their share of the Suez Canal Company to the British in order to shore up their failing banks. The British were only too happy to purchase the shares and take over the operation of the canal. They helped Egypt in its time of need, and now Britain was reaping the benefits. This was capitalism at its finest.

The British Army base in the canal zone was massive – the largest military base in the world. Home to eighty-eight thousand British soldiers, it was their job to protect the canal against terrorists and foreign invaders. Their presence caused tension with the Egyptian Nationalists. Times were changing. The Egyptians were no longer willing to follow the British lead when it came to international politics. The Egyptian leaders had their own agenda and were determined to see it realized.

The private finished up with two taps and re-buttoned his trousers. He pulled out a pack from his pocket and lit a cigarette with his lighter. "Hey. Be careful. You'll give away our position," said the corporal.

"Right-o," said the private taking another puff and dropping the cigarette in the canal.

The private turned and walked back toward the corporal. The corporal saw a flash on the opposite bank. The private's head exploded followed immediately by the crack of a rifle shot. The bullet had entered through the back of his skull, broke into multiple fragments and exited through the front taking most of the private's face with it. It was a dum-dum bullet, outlawed by international conventions but often used by Egyptian raiders.

The corporal swung his machinegun around and opened fire in the direction of the flash. The roar of the machine gun echoed off the canal banks, its flashing muzzle lighting up the surrounding area. He saw three more flashes from the opposite bank before his own head exploded and he fell dead on to the sandbags.

Two Egyptian raiders rose from the desert floor in

front of the outpost. They signaled the three snipers on the opposite bank and ran to the dead British soldiers. They emptied the soldiers' pockets of all valuables, picked up their rifles, spare ammunition and the machinegun, and disappeared back into the darkness.

January 23, 1955 - London, England

Gamal Abdel Nasser, the soon-to-be president of Egypt, crossed over the River Thames on Westminster Bridge riding in the back of a Rolls Royce. He was accompanied by his Foreign Secretary and Egypt's ambassador to Britain. His bodyguard, armed with two large caliber revolvers beneath his suit coat, rode beside the driver, also armed. There had already been several attempts on his life by the Muslim Brotherhood. Nasser badly wanted to be the leader of the Arab world. The Muslim Brotherhood had other ideas, and Nasser wasn't taking any chances, not even in London.

Nasser had been born into a middle-class family. His father managed a post office. His mother died when he was a teenager and it affected him deeply. He was smart and charismatic. He was an avid reader and observer. As a teenager, he observed the unfairness of the Egyptian class structure. Studying the problem on his own, he became convinced that British colonialism was at the heart of the injustice. He vowed to see the British leave his country forever.

After witnessing protestors and police clash in Manshia Square, he joined the demonstration without knowing its purpose. He was arrested and detained for a night before his angry father bailed him out. In November 1935, he organized and led a student demonstration against British rule. Two students were shot and killed. Nasser was wounded when a police bullet grazed the top of his head, and his name appeared in the newspaper for the first time, labeling him a political activist. He kept a clipping of the article in his wallet for the rest of his life.

In 1937, Nasser joined the military. In the academy, he met Abdel Hakim Amer and Anwar Sadat who would become important advisors to Nasser during his presidency. The three discussed the corruption prevalent throughout the administration and were determined that justice should prevail, even if it meant overthrowing the monarchy. Nasser, clear-thinking, passionate and energetic, became the unspoken leader of the miniature cabal. He devoted himself to his military career and rose quickly through the ranks, even though his political connections were few and far between. Armed with unshakable confidence and charisma, Nasser was a natural leader. He and his two friends sought out young military officers with strong nationalist sentiments who supported some form of revolution, and expanded their secret organization.

When the British withdrew from Israel in 1948, King Farouk sent his armies into the newly-formed Jewish nation with the intention of wiping it off the face of the earth. Nasser saw his first military action as part of the 6th Infantry Battalion. The invasion was a disaster. Nasser's unit was surrounded by Israeli forces in Faluja but refused to surrender. The Egyptians took a beating from the Israeli artillery and Nasser was wounded. The siege lasted over a month before the Egyptians finally turned Faluja over to the Israelis. When he returned home, Nasser became a national hero for having withstood the Israeli bombardments. Nasser had lost the battle but in the end he had won in peace. A lesson learned and remembered.

In 1948, Nasser tried to form an alliance with the Muslim Brotherhood but soon discovered that the religious principles of the Brotherhood clashed with Egyptian Nationalism. He abandoned his efforts and formed his own organization calling it the Association of Free Officers. Nasser was elected president of the Free Officers. He recruited more officers for three years stating that the association's only goal was to restore Egypt's reputation and glory. On July 22, 1952, Nasser and the Free Officers executed a coup d'état against the monarchy, and overthrew King Farouk. General Mohamed Naguib was named the first president of the new Egyptian Republic. Nasser was named vice-president. Within two years, Naguib became wary of Nasser's ever-increasing popularity and, with the help of the Muslim Brotherhood, attempted to have Nasser assassinated. The assassination failed. Nasser, backed by the military, arrested Naguib and became the acting head of state until elections could be held, elections that Nasser was sure to win as his popularity soared.

Big Ben chimed. Two British police officers patrolled the area on white horses. Artists stood by their easels and painted Westminster Abbey. *It is all so damned quaint,* Nasser thought as he stared out the window of the Rolls. *A facade of civilization.*

Nasser liked London. Everyone obeyed the rules. The streets and parks were clean. The buildings were tall and stately. The bridges were well maintained with a fresh coat of paint each year. Even the rivers and canals flowed green and smelled sweet. It was a far cry from his own capital – Cairo.

Even he had to admit that Cairo was a cesspool compared to London. The streets were crowded with millions of peasants that had nowhere else to go, and traffic was impossible. Garbage was stacked on the few sidewalks that had been built, and the people defecated in the alleys and parks. There were no public toilets. The Nile, the lifeblood of Egypt, was brown and smelled sour. Cairo was an old city and the foundations of many buildings were cracked. It was not without its charms, though. It had the pyramids, after all. But even the ancient monuments needed repair before they crumbled to dust. The Egyptian Museum held many of the world's greatest treasures and artifacts. But the streets were not safe. Only the bravest of tourists visited Cairo.

Nasser understood why the two cities were so different. Egypt was one of the poorest countries in the world and Britain one of the wealthiest. The British had stolen the wealth of her colonies for centuries and given little in return. Egypt knew this all too well. Not long ago Egypt had been a British colony and toiled under its master's whip. Even after Egypt had won its independence, Britain continued to steal Egyptian wealth by refusing to share in the lucrative tolls from the Suez Canal. *It's all so misguided*, thought Nasser. *The British wear patent leather shoes while most Egyptians walk barefoot.*

The driver turned right after crossing the bridge and headed into Whitehall. He pulled to a stop in front of number 10 Downing Street. Nasser waited patiently as his driver and bodyguard got out and surveyed the area. When he was satisfied it was safe, the driver opened the back door and Nasser emerged. He was tall, at six foot, but seemed taller because of his broad shoulders. His hair and mustache were coal black and his face was long. He straightened the jacket on his tailored grey suit. He was greeted by Selwyn Lloyd, the British Foreign Secretary and his assistant Patrick Dean. Nasser had not expected that the Prime Minister would greet him personally. That would have offered Egypt too much respect. Nasser knew the game well and would play it their way for a few moments longer. It started to rain. The driver pulled out an umbrella and covered Nasser while allowing himself to get wet from the big English raindrops. They moved into the building.

Nasser sat quietly on a couch sipping his tea. He was not interested in making the first move. That would be left to Sir Anthony Eden, the British Prime Minister, sitting across from him in an easy chair.

Eden was a conservative; the handpicked successor to Winston Churchill. He was highly intelligent and well-organized, often serving as a secretary for powerful leaders who became his mentors. He spoke five foreign languages. He had learnt French and German as a child, learnt Turkish from a teenage friend and studied Arabic and Persian while at Oxford. Eden had served as a second lieutenant in the King's Royal Rifle Corp. Commanding a platoon on the Western Front during World War I, Eden won the Military Cross for saving a badly wounded sergeant under fire, something he made little mention of during his political career. At twenty he became the British army's youngest brigade major. He was an author, and collected impressionist paintings. He was an extraordinary man at the pinnacle of his political career.

Egypt was a thorn in Eden's side. The treaty that gave Britain the right to protect Egypt's commercial interest was almost at an end. Eden could not understand why a country like Egypt would not want British protection. It was no longer a colony and paid nothing to Britain for the privilege. Britain's only interest was in keeping the canal open and functioning properly. The Suez Canal was a commercial interest owned by investors who had a right to collect profits on the money they had invested. This had nothing to do with Britain being an ally of Egypt and continuing to guide the young democracy in its international endeavors. What could Nasser possibly have to lose by accepting Britain's friendship?

Eden suspected that Nasser was posturing for power. By defying the British, Nasser would look strong to the other Arab leaders. Intelligence reports had revealed that Nasser wanted to become the leader of a new Arab federation made up of other Middle Eastern and North African countries. There were other leaders such as Jordan's King Hussein and Saudi Arabia's King Saud who were jockeying for the same prestigious position. Both King Hussein and King Saud were far more pro-western than Nasser, and therefore favored by the British.

Eden had requested that Nasser and he speak alone so they could have a 'frank discussion.' This was the first time the two had met and both men were keen to assess their counterpart. The two leaders sat in Eden's office. It was an impressive room. The cloth on the furniture and drapes were of the finest fabrics, the photos and paintings on the wallpapered walls steeped in history, the obligatory painting of the new Queen Elizabeth II hanging prominent in the center. A framed photo of Winston Churchill sat on Eden's credenza. *It must be hard,* thought Nasser. *Living in Churchill's shadow.*

"I know you are anxious to discuss the distribution of canal tolls but first I should like to discuss these continued rebel attacks on our troops in the canal zone," said Eden. "The situation has become intolerable and must be dealt with immediately."

"I agree," said Nasser.

"Very good. I was hoping you would see it my way."

"Of course. What other way is there?"

Eden smiled at Nasser's veiled snip and continued, "I believe the best way to proceed is a joint action between our two intelligence services. Once we root out the perpetrators, we can send in the army to deal with the problem."

"Which army?"

"British forces. We understand that your resources are stretched to the limit and we do not wish to put any more of a strain on Egypt. Besides, our troops are well versed in civilian uprisings and know how to deal with this sort of thing."

"Very kind of you," said Nasser. "I would like to propose a different plan to deal with the problem."

"Of course. I am all ears," said Eden, a bit taken aback that his plan was not accepted without question.

"Leave," said Nasser.

"Excuse me."

"It is time for British troops to leave Egyptian soil. Once you are gone the problem will cease to exist."

"You can't be serious."

"Oh, but I am."

"We have a treaty."

"Which you violated by exceeding the ten thousand troop limit."

"The expanded troop levels were necessary to protect the canal against Axis forces."

"Perhaps. But World War Two came to an end over ten years ago and your troops are still in Egypt. In fact, the numbers have increased to eight-eight thousand, I believe."

"Egypt is not capable of protecting the canal."

"I assure you it is and will. It is ours and we protect what is ours."

"I am not prepared to dispute the ownership of the canal. We have agreed that it is Egypt's. But we also agreed that Britain has the right... no... the obligation to protect it."

"Yes. Thank you. Now leave."

"We are not going to just leave as you say."

"Oh, but you will."

"Why would we do that?"

"Because it pleases you."

"I assure you it does not."

"It will. When enough blood has been shed, you will leave of your own accord."

"Are you threatening war with Britain?"

"War? There is no need for a war."

"Then what is it you plan to do?"

"Nothing," said Nasser, confident. "If I do nothing the Egyptian rebels will pick off your soldiers one by one and you will not even see them coming. They are excellent marksmen, as you well know. Egypt will achieve its goals by doing nothing to stop them."

"You have a moral obligation to patrol your lands."

"Egypt is a big country with vast deserts and wastelands. Our army cannot possibly be everywhere at once. As you say… our resources are stretched thin."

"This is blackmail."

"This is justice. Egypt is fed up with the British. You have refused to share in the revenue from the canal. You have treated us, your hosts, as second-class citizens. You have disrespected our authority over our own land. The people have grown to resent your presence and it is they that are asking you politely to leave. Soon, they will insist."

"We are well-armed."

"Not well-armed enough, I fear. You have eighty-eight thousand soldiers stationed on Egyptian land. We are twenty-one million civilians that can easily overwhelm your army, not to mention create an international travesty should you choose to resist them by force. It is time to leave, Prime Minister."

"I don't know what game you think you are playing or what you hope to achieve, but British troops are not leaving the Canal Zone."

"Then our conversation is at an end," said Nasser, rising.

Eden was stunned that Nasser would call an end to their meeting after having traveled so far. Nasser had said what he came to say. There was no need to stay and watch Eden boil over like a tea kettle too long on the stove. Leaving their well-publicized meeting early would be seen as an insult to the British. Insulting the British gave Nasser power and power was the thing Nasser craved most of all.

Eden stood outside of 10 Downing Street with Lloyd and Dean and watched as the Rolls Royce carrying Nasser pulled away from the curb and drove down the street. "I truly despise that man," said Eden with a snarl. "He will be crushed under his own ambition."

August 12, 1955 - Jerusalem, Israel

In his office in Jerusalem's Givat Ram, David Ben-Gurion, Israel's prime minister, greeted Shimon Perez, his Defense Minister. Isser Harel, Israel's spymaster was also waiting in Ben-Gurion's office. Perez gave Harel a polite nod instead of the traditional hug and cheek-kisses. It was the best Perez could muster. Harel knew Perez didn't like him. He wasn't alone. Too many secrets and not enough sharing was the general complaint among the Knesset cabinet members. As head of both Shin Bet - Israel's internal security service, and Mossad - Israel's intelligence agency, Harel wielded considerable power. He reported only to Ben-Gurion which made others envious, including Perez. They sat, and iced tea was served.

"Tell him," said Ben-Gurion to Harel.

"The Egyptians are negotiating a large weapons purchase from the Soviets through Czechoslovakia," said Harel.

"Jets?" said Perez, concerned.

"We believe so."

"We are fucked if Nasser gets jets before we do. He will attack without delay."

"And if he does?" said Ben-Gurion.

"We will lose our air force," said Perez. "There will be nothing to stop his tanks from crossing the border."

There was a long silence in the room.

"Others will join him?" said Ben-Gurion.

"If he gets jets… probably," said Harel. "They'll wait until he wipes out our air force then… Syria for sure. Kuwait and Jordan are possibilities, maybe even the Saudis."

"My god," said Ben-Gurion. "Will the French side with us?"

"Maybe. They've got their own problems with Algeria."

"The British and the Americans?"

"The British will want to stay out of it, especially if the Saudis and Iraqis get involved. They need the oil. The Americans will follow the British lead, as always."

"Then France," said Ben-Gurion.

"Maybe," said Perez.

"Go. Talk to them, Shimon. Quietly," said Ben-Gurion. "We do not want Nasser to see us in a panic. It will only encourage him and the others."

April 7, 1956 - Paris, France.

Tom Coyle sat in a hospital patient's room browsing through a newspaper. He couldn't read it. It was in French and he didn't speak French beyond a few social niceties. But he liked the photos and tried to piece together what the articles were saying. The lead story was something about the last British soldier leaving the Suez Canal Zone. Coyle knew this because the photo above the story showed a British soldier boarding a landing craft filled with soldiers.

In the bed beside Coyle lay Colonel Marcel Bigeard, asleep with tubes running in and out of his body. He had been shot in the back by an assassin while out jogging along the Mediterranean in Algiers and flown to Paris for treatment. The bullet missed his heart by a fraction of an inch... again. Bruno, as everyone called him, stirred.

Coyle walked to the doorway and peeked out as if looking for someone. He walked back to the bed and leaned over Bruno. Bruno's eyes slowly opened. Coyle's face hovering above him was not what he was hoping to see. "Where am I?" said Bruno.

"In heaven. You're dead," said Coyle.

"Really? Why do I hurt so much if I am dead?"

"Penance for your sins."

"Ah. That explains it."

"Seriously. Why are you still alive? You've been shot in

the chest twice in less than a year and survived. That's not normal."

"I do not have time to die. Where's Brigitte?"

"She went for coffee. She'll be upset that she was not here when you woke."

"She will blame you."

"Probably."

"Life is just. Is my nurse cute?"

"No. Life is just."

"Did they catch the woman with the bicycle… the one that shot me?"

"They captured the bicycle, but not the assassin."

"A shame. She was quite attractive."

"And a bad shot."

"No. Her aim was true. I am like a bear. It takes more than one bullet to kill me."

"Apparently."

A paratroop commander, Bruno was considered by many to be the healthiest man in the French army. He exercised daily for two to three hours.

Brigitte Friang entered carrying two coffees. "You are awake?"

"Coyle poked me until I woke," said Bruno.

"He's lying," said Coyle.

"I would hope so," she said.

"Is one of those coffees for me?" said Bruno reaching up with a groan.

"Not until the doctors give their okay," said Brigitte. "Should I get your nurse?"

"Not yet. She will kick you out."

"Okay," said Brigitte with a smile.

"Besides, Coyle told me she was really beautiful, and I wouldn't want to distract him."

"He's lying again," said Coyle.

"I know. I saw her," said Brigitte. "A face like a mule."

"Then it is true. God is punishing me," said Bruno.

The nurse entered. Bruno was surprised. She was far

from ugly and had a trim figure. "You are awake?" she said. "I'll get the doctor."

"Maybe you could adjust my pillows first?" said Bruno.

"Of course," said the nurse leaning over him, her breast inches from his face.

"Shift must have changed," said Brigitte with a shrug.

"Yes. The shift," said Coyle.

Bruno was in pain but happy.

May 2, 1956 - Cairo, Egypt

It was early in the morning when Ben Bella traveled to Cairo International airport in one of the Egyptian government's limousines. He was a legend and treated like royalty in most of the Arab world, but was a wanted man in his own country of Algeria. As one of the top leaders of the FLN movement, the French had a price on his head. The Arab people saw the bounty as a badge of honor awarded to Bella for resisting the Western nations. He lived in Cairo under the protection of Nasser, who supported the FLN in their war of independence against the French.

The war had dragged on for two years with heavy losses on both sides. The constant stream of bombings and drive-by shootings in Paris had a particularly devastating effect on the French public, who treasured their café culture. There was genuine fear of sitting at a café and enjoying a coffee. One never knew when the person at the next table was going to place a bomb and excuse themselves to go to the restroom.

The French had had enough and were offering peace talks with the FLN in Rome. Bella had been selected to represent the FLN. His mind was clear. He knew that the FLN would accept nothing less than full independence from France. There could be trade agreements, cultural exchanges and even some say so in the protection of the

European colonists that called Algeria home, but the Algerians wanted their nation back and they were going to get it.

When Bella arrived at the airport, the plane that the Egyptians had chartered for him was already fueled and waiting. He and his entourage of five FLN bodyguards would be the only passengers. They boarded immediately and the plane took off.

The plane reached the northern coast and headed out over the Mediterranean Sea. Still a hundred miles from the Italian coast, two French Mystère fighter-bomber jets with external fuel tanks under their wings pulled up alongside the plane. The pilot in one of the jets contacted the plane's pilot by radio and informed him that the plane was to follow the two jets. When the pilot protested, the jet pilot simply said, "Follow us or we shoot."

The plane followed the two jets as they changed course and headed west. The pilot was concerned about the plane's fuel consumption but realized that the French probably knew how much fuel the aircraft was carrying and would have planned accordingly.

The co-pilot went back and informed Bella and his bodyguards what was happening. Bella knew immediately that he had been set up. The French could do nothing while he remained in Egypt under Nasser's protection. Now, they had him. The French had no interest in negotiating with the FLN. Bella considered making a stand after the plane landed but knew that the French would be only too happy to kill him and his men there and then. He was not afraid to die but he didn't want his bodyguards hurt. He knew they would fight to the death for him. If he lived, there would be international outrage at the manner of his capture over international waters. In prison, he would become a living symbol of French cruelty and injustice. He abandoned his plan to fight and informed his men that he would give up.

The plane was forced to land at Nice airport. Bella and

his men were immediately taken into custody by French Army Intelligence. It was a huge loss to the FLN. Bella had planned most of the major attacks against the French. He was a hero and his leadership would be missed.

In Paris, the news of Bella's capture was celebrated. People felt safer with the notorious Bella in custody. Many went out to dinner at their favorite restaurants. The FLN set off three bombs that night to honor Bella and to remind the French that the war was far from over. The French bled.

May 8, 1956 – Paris, France

Brigitte sat staring out the window at her office in downtown Paris. She was the only journalist at the magazine that had an office. It was one of the perks that Damien, her editor, used to keep Brigitte from considering employment offers from other magazines or newspapers. She didn't like how it looked to the other reporters, but she had to admit it was nice. The bullpen where the rest of the journalists worked was a maelstrom of clacking typewriters and overly loud phone conversations, not to mention the ever-flowing river of gossip.

Half the battle of writing an article was figuring out the angle, and Brigitte was on the verge of discovering the angle for the series she was going to call "The Café Wars." Her phone rang and she answered it. Brigitte recognized the voice on the other end of the line. It was a gate attendant at the international airport and one of Brigitte's informants.

"Shimon Perez," was all the man said.

"What is Israel's Minister of Defense doing in Paris?" said Brigitte.

"And even more interesting... why is he traveling without his usual entourage of bodyguards?"

"No bodyguards?"

"Not that I can see, but one never knows with the Israelis."

"Sounds like a man that doesn't want to be recognized."

"I think maybe yes. At any rate… I thought it might be of interest to you," said the man.

"It just might," said Brigitte. "I'll send you something if it pans out."

"Merci," said the man and he hung up.

Brigitte thought for a moment. She couldn't make any sense of it, but thought it was worth investigating. She grabbed her coat and purse on her way out the door.

Shimon Perez sat across from Maurice Bourgès-Maunoury, France's Minister of Defense. Perez had become Director-General of Israel's Ministry of Defense at the age of twenty-eight. He was the protégé of David Ben-Gurion, Israel's founding father, and was considered one of his country's greatest orators. Even though France was Israel's biggest supporter, Perez was still cautious.

"We are surrounded on all sides by our enemies," said Perez.

"Israel has always been surrounded. What you need are fewer enemies," said Bourgès-Maunoury.

"What we need are weapons. The Arabs are arming themselves."

"Where are they buying their weapons?"

Perez knew he could not reveal what he had learnt from Harel about the Czechoslovakian arm sales. "The black market. Weapons left over from World War II," he said.

"Piecemeal relics. More rust than metal. I would hardly concern myself."

"You do not have them pointed at you. We do. I am telling you the Arabs plan to attack Israel."

"They always plan to attack. They are Arabs. They say

one thing and do another."

"I don't think so. Not this time. Nasser is whipping them into a frenzy. The only thing stopping them is that they still squabble amongst themselves. Once that ends, they will unite and try to wipe out Israel."

"Ah, Nasser. At least we can agree on one thing. He is a menace."

"He wishes to unite the Arabs against the western powers. And he helps the Algerians in their bid for independence. He helps the FLN."

"The FLN and others, yes."

"He is a thorn in your side?"

"Yes… and yours," said Bourgès-Maunoury.

The French minister remained quiet for a long moment as if considering. It was an act. He knew exactly what he wanted to do and what he wanted Perez to do. "Perhaps you are right. Perhaps we should sell you arms."

Perez was surprised by the sudden change in attitude. The Western nations had been united in their efforts to restrict arms sales to all nations in the Middle East. *Why the sudden change of heart?* thought Perez. He was confident in his ability to put forth a good argument, but this was too easy. He decided to probe a bit. "What types of weapons?"

"What do you need?"

"Everything."

"Then you shall have everything."

"Fighter jets?"

"They would be part of everything, would they not?"

Perez was again stunned. Israel had been pleading since its inception for modern weaponry to defend itself.

"Beware of Greek's bearing gifts," said Perez.

"It is hardly a gift. You will still have to pay for the weapons," said Bourgès-Maunoury.

"And what of the Tripartite Declaration?" said Perez referring to the agreement between the U.S., Britain and France to limit arms sales to Israel.

"What about it? I don't see any need to publicize your

weapons purchase from France."

"You would have us hide the shipments from the Americans and the British?"

"I would have you only tell them what they need to know which is exactly what you have always done."

"Why is France being so generous?"

"We are a friend to Israel. We like it when our friends survive and thrive."

"You do not want us going to the Russians or the Chinese."

"The thought had crossed our minds but there is more too it," said Bourgès-Maunoury.

"Such as?"

"A message."

"For Nasser?"

"You are very perceptive. His meddling in France's affairs is not appreciated."

"That is one hell of a message."

"It is meant to be. He must understand there are consequences for helping the FLN and the other underground Algerian organizations that seek to harm France."

"Interesting diplomacy. And if the Americans and the British find out?"

"See that they don't. It would not bode well for either of our nations."

"I shall make a list of the weapons we require."

Bourgès-Maunoury opened a folder on his desk. He pulled out a typed list and handed it to Perez. "I was thinking this might be a good start," he said.

Perez read down the list. "Yes. A very good start. You are prepared to sell us the listed items?"

"Yes," said Bourgès-Maunoury. "It has already been cleared with the Prime Minister and the required members of Parliament."

Perez contained his elation. It was a very good day for Israel.

"There is one other thing I wish to discuss," said Bourgès-Maunoury.

"Of course," said Perez.

"Have you ever considered invading the Sinai?" said Bourgès-Maunoury.

"You are serious?"

"Let's just say I am curious… for the moment."

Perez's mind was racing. What was Bourgès-Maunoury up to? The invasion of another country was not a subject for casual conversation.

"Israel could achieve many objectives by invading Sinai. It would give Nasser a bloody nose. He and the other Arab leaders would think twice before attacking Israel," said Perez.

"I thought as much. Maybe you should consider it more aggressively and get back to me."

"As you wish. I will bring it up with the Prime Minister on my return," said Perez.

"Have a safe flight," said Bourgès-Maunoury rising to escort him out.

Perez walked out of the French Defense Ministry. His head was spinning. Hundreds of questions whirling around in his mind. Brigitte was waiting with a photographer. "Minister Perez, what are doing visiting our Defense Ministry?" said Brigitte.

"I am not answering any questions at this time," said Perez.

"With whom did you meet? Was it Minister Bourgès-Maunoury?" said Brigitte refusing to let up. "What did you discuss?"

A sedan pulled up to the curb. Perez moved toward it. The photographer snapped a photo of Perez as he was getting into the back of the sedan. "That was not smart," said Perez.

Two Mossad agents jumped out of the sedan and

grabbed the photographer by the arms. "The camera," said one of the agents.

The photographer refused and received a punch in the gut. He fell to the ground clutching his stomach. The agent took the camera, opened the back and ripped out the film. "This is France, not Israel. You cannot do that," said Brigitte.

"File a complaint with our embassy," said the Mossad agent as he pulled out his bill fold and peeled off several U.S. dollars, tossing them to the ground in front of the photographer. "For the film. Sorry about the cheap shot."

The two Mossad agents climbed into the sedan and it sped off. "Fucking Nazis," said Brigitte kneeling to help her photographer, curled up in a ball on the ground.

TWO

May 20, 1956 - Brussels, Belgium

Sir Anthony Eden sat with Dwight Eisenhower – the American President – in the lounge at NATO headquarters in Brussels. They had just finished a meeting with the heads of state to discuss the growing Soviet threat and the new Warsaw pact. Eden had asked Eisenhower for a few minutes after the meeting for a private conversation.

Eisenhower did not trust Eden, but he did respect him. Winston Churchill had always been a force to be reckoned with when Eisenhower was given the command of directing allied forces in the invasion of Europe during World War II. Eden was Churchill's right-hand man and therefore often charged with delivering bad news to Eisenhower. It was not a pleasant task and Eisenhower knew it. When it was finally time for Churchill to retire from public life, Eden had been asked to fill his shoes, so to speak, and that was not a minor task.

Britain was one of America's oldest allies and a key player in the new NATO alliance. America needed Britain and Britain needed America. It was that simple. The two countries had a special relationship and neither took that responsibility lightly. But just because they needed each other did not mean that they always agreed. Britain was still an empire with colonies around the world. America had fought a revolution to be freed from that empire and was naturally supportive of other countries that sought their freedom. Britain's leaders understood the sentiment but also saw it as somewhat of a betrayal. Britain and America were allies and allies were supposed to support each other through thick and thin. America was not holding up its part of the bargain when it criticized Britain for continuing its imperialistic traditions.

Eden was a nationalist. His focus was on Britain, not

the world or even Europe. There were times when Eden had a holier-than-thou tone in his voice that sounded very much like a father lecturing a child, especially when he was dealing with third world nations. Even so, Eden was a respected diplomat and a strong spokesman for any cause he chose to support. He was the elected leader of one of the world's greatest powers and, like Churchill, a force to be reckoned with.

Eisenhower knew that Europe would need to remain united if it was going to fend off Russian aggression and the communist threat. He just wasn't sure Eden was the right man for that particular job. Eden had a reputation for being inflexible once he started down a path and a tendency to piss people off. Eisenhower also knew that one does not get to pick one's friends in the world of diplomacy. One way or another, Eisenhower would need to find a way to deal with Eden.

Eden liked Eisenhower, and he trusted him. Eisenhower was a man of principle and had an easy-going manner about him. He was intelligent and well-organized, much like Eden. However, Eden did not respect Eisenhower the way others did. Eden had heard Churchill complain about Eisenhower too many times to think otherwise. He knew Eisenhower could be indecisive and he saw that as a flaw especially in international politics. Eden believed that Eisenhower got too much credit for his role in leading the invasions of North Africa and Europe during World War II. By some historians' recollection, it seemed like Eisenhower had won the war single-handedly. Eden knew otherwise. He had lived through the German blitz on England. He had been with Churchill when all seemed lost. If Britain had given up hope, America would probably never have entered the war and the world would have been lost to the fascists. It was Britain, not America, that anchored the allied effort and it was Churchill, not Eisenhower, that stood against the Nazi storm. Historians were often fooled by a good story and a popular figure.

Eden believed Eisenhower could be convinced into changing his mind on a matter. He had seen Churchill do it. Eisenhower was not the stalwart leader that everyone believed. He could be cautiously manipulated.

Drinks were served and the two leaders conversed politely, enjoying their scotch and smoking cigarettes, until Eden decided it was time to get down to the business at hand. "I know it's been a long day, but I feel it is most urgent that we put a stop to Nasser's rhetoric against the Western allies," he said.

"I don't believe his issue is with the West as much as it is against the colonial powers, namely Britain and France," said Eisenhower bluntly. Eden and Eisenhower knew each other well and neither felt obliged to shield their feelings on any matter.

"Perhaps," said Eden. "But the result will be the same if he continues to push the Middle East towards the Soviets."

"What makes you believe he's moving toward the Soviets?"

"One of our MI6 operatives has discovered that Egypt plans to purchase a large quantity of Soviet built weapons from Czechoslovakia."

Eisenhower's expression sharpened on hearing the news. "How reliable is your source?" he said after taking a moment to consider.

"Quite," said Eden.

"That is disconcerting."

"I am glad you share our concern."

"What do you have in mind?"

"Perhaps it is time for NATO to play a bigger role in the protection of the Suez. God knows what will happen if it falls under Soviet control."

"I think we're getting ahead of ourselves. Besides NATO has its hands full right now. Still, I think it's important that Nasser be sent a message. He must choose between the Soviets and the West."

"I agree," said Eden pretending to analyze the options. "What about the funding of his Aswan Dam project?"

"We have already agreed to fund it. America does not welch on its financial commitments."

"The same goes with Britain. But the Egyptian economy is slackening because of Nasser's social programs. Both our countries could slow funding of the dam until the Egyptian economy recovers. I believe it is within our rights under the existing agreement."

"That would piss Nasser off."

"And send him a message."

Eisenhower considered the idea carefully, then said, "Alright. Let me talk to my treasury secretary and see what we can do. I'll get back to you shortly."

July 19, 1956 - Cairo, Egypt

Nasser was furious as he marched through the halls of his presidential palace, trailed by his entourage of ministers. "This is an outrage. They committed the funds and now they pull them back like a cheap magician," he said.

Nasser suddenly stopped as if a thought had occurred to him. "Get me the plans for the nationalization of the canal."

"Such an action would surely destroy any hope of foreign investment in Egypt," said his finance minister.

"Perhaps, but if we have the toll revenue from the canal we won't need foreign investment. We can fund the building of the dam ourselves. It may be a worthwhile tradeoff," said Nasser. "We should consider all options for the sake of the people. We need that dam."

The Aswan Dam would be the largest dam in the world. It would provide badly needed power to Egypt and irrigate hundreds of thousands of acres of farm land. It was Nasser's biggest promise to his people, and he planned on seeing it come to fruition no matter the cost.

July 20, 1956 – Algiers, Algeria

Faris Guerouabi was a longshoreman at the Port of Algiers. He operated a forklift. He was also an informant for the FLN. He would identify weapons shipments as they were unloaded from the ships and transferred to trucks for delivery to French army bases. When he spotted a load that looked interesting, he would go to the dispatch office and look up the destination on the schedules that hung on the wall. He would place a call on the public pay phone to his FLN handler and tell him which route the arms were most likely to take, and when.

The French counter-intelligence unit knew that Guerouabi was an FLN informant. They had turned him when he was caught smuggling opium without the proper tax stamp, earlier in the year. He did not hold up well under torture and gave up every contact he had with the FLN within the first hour. He also agreed to inform for the French when required. Today was one of those days.

Two French soldiers kept watch as an arms shipment was loaded onto six army trucks. One of the longshoremen loading a crate accidently dropped one end. It crashed down on the asphalt and the wooden box split open. Several rifles tumbled out in clear sight of anyone that might be looking. The soldiers cursed him for an idiot and told him to load the rifles back into the broken crate. He did so. The longshoremen finished up and closed the back of the trucks.

It was all a very clumsy show that had been preplanned for over a week. French counter-intelligence wanted to ensure that Guerouabi's cover was not blown. If everybody saw the weapons in the shipment nobody could be pinpointed as a snitch. Guerouabi thought it was a stupid idea, but he was not in any position to bargain, so he went along with it. He called in the weapons shipment just as he always did and hoped his friends in the FLN did not take the bait.

It was early afternoon when the truck convoy left the port. The column of vehicles was led by a jeep carrying the officer, a French lieutenant, in charge of the convoy. At the rear of the column was a Panard armored car holding a crew of four and armed with a 75-mm cannon and three 7.5-mm machineguns. The lieutenant was informed by his commander that there was a high probability of ambush, but he was instructed not to inform his men of the intelligence. The lieutenant was noticeably jumpy. The men in his unit suspected he'd had too much Turkish coffee of which the lieutenant was fond.

It took several hours to travel through Algiers because of the heavy traffic. In some parts of the city the roads were not good and there were often bottlenecks usually caused by a stubborn donkey, a herd of goats or a jackknifed bus. This was normal, and the soldiers used the extra time to smoke cigarettes and share pictures of girlfriends or wives from home. Nobody was overly concerned about security. There was little chance of the convoy being attacked while it was in the city. The fighting would need to be close quarters and the rebels were not fond of confronting the well-armed French at close range.

When the convoy finally reached the outskirts of Algiers it was late afternoon and the sun hung low in the sky. The convoy was heading west which meant the sun was in their eyes, not an ideal situation for spotting a potential ambush. The lieutenant was concerned about driving through the hills after dark. His temper was short, and he pushed his Algerian drivers to go faster.

He had orders to radio in his position every fifteen minutes once he left the city. He didn't understand why his commander did not give him more of an escort if he knew the odds of an ambush were high. He was told that if his convoy was attacked, he and his men were to hang on until help arrived. That was foolish, he thought. It could take hours for reinforcements from Algiers to reach him and his men. He wished he was inside the armored car at the rear of the column and not riding point in an open jeep.

As the convoy drove up a slope, the rebels attacked. The first shot hit his driver between the eyes, killing him instantly. The lieutenant grabbed the steering wheel and kept the jeep on the road. He couldn't reach the gas pedal or the brake with the dead driver still in the seat so he pushed him out of the jeep. His corpse tumbled off the road into a ditch. The lieutenant had no time to feel remorse for the soldier. He was fighting to stay alive. As more bullets shattered the windshield, he slid behind the wheel and floored the gas pedal. The jeep lunged forward but the speed did not increase much. It was going uphill and had a small engine. He barked out commands to his radio operator riding in the back, "Send our position and tell them we are under attack."

Several bullets hit the jeep's radiator. Steam poured out from under the hood. It would be just a matter of a minute or two before the engine seized. *Then we'll really be in a world of shit,* thought the lieutenant. *If we stop moving we're dead men.* "Get that damn armored car to the front," he said to the radio operator.

The armored car was having its own problems and was in no condition to help. An RPG, fired by a rebel hiding behind a boulder, had taken out one of its back wheels. To the driver's amazement, the vehicle still had power and could maneuver. The three machineguns rattled off rounds as they searched for targets. Tracer rounds illuminated the fading light. Another RPG hit the flank of the armored car and it toppled over on its side. The crew scrambled for the hatches to get out. They knew what was coming. A third round hit the belly of the vehicle and the gas tank exploded, killing everyone still inside. The flaming wreckage of the armored car blocked the back of the convoy, making a rearward escape impossible.

"I think the armored car just took a hit," said the radio operator looking to the back of the column. "Yeah, it's gone."

"Ah, fuck," said the lieutenant.

The engine on the jeep seized and the vehicle decelerated quickly to a stop. "Damn it all to hell," said the lieutenant. "Any word from H.Q.?"

"They say they're sending help," said the radio operator.

"Any indication as to how long?"

"They didn't say."

"Would you consider asking them or do you need my foot up your ass?"

"I'll ask."

The lieutenant gave a hand signal to the drivers of the convoy to stop and dismount. They were fucked if they stopped and the lieutenant knew it, but he had little choice. If the rebels had RPGs they could pick off each truck at their leisure. Each truck had a French soldier riding shotgun. The Algerian drivers were also given rifles, but the lieutenant had little faith that they would be anything more than cannon fodder. *Still, the more guns the better in a situation like this,* he thought.

The truck crews dismounted and sought cover under the vehicles. The lieutenant saw what they were doing and immediately knew it was a bad idea. An RPG would not only take out the truck but the defenders beneath it. He shouted to his men to get out from underneath the trucks and to find cover elsewhere. Some did. Some didn't.

The mujahideen rebels that they faced were well-trained fighters and the lieutenant wished he could switch sides. It was all too easy for them. Now that the convoy was immobilized, they could take their time. All they needed to do was to keep the French soldiers and the Algerian drivers pinned down. The rebels had no intention of destroying the trucks. They could consolidate their forces on a portion of the convoy and pick off the riflemen opposing them one by one. They would roll up the line and kill everyone in less than an hour. The convoy and its precious cargo would be theirs for the taking after that.

The lieutenant had all but lost hope when he heard the heavy thump-thump-thump of helicopters approaching. He looked up. At first, he couldn't see anything, but the sound grew louder.

The first French helicopter gunship, a Sikorsky, appeared from over a hilltop. It was followed by three more. They were part of Bruno's strike force. They had been following the convoy at a distance like an airmobile mousetrap waiting to spring. The Sikorsky gunships did a flyover to assess the situation.

It was enough to strike fear into the Mujahideen. They knew the French gunships and the destruction they were capable of inflicting. Some of the veterans broke and ran. They had no intention of facing the gunships' cannons, rockets and machine guns. Better to run and take one's chances before it was too late.

The Sikorskys banked hard and flew back around. The second pass unleashed hell on the mujahideen that were brave enough to stand and fight. Anyone not hidden behind a large boulder died. Rockets first, then cannons. The machineguns followed with a raking barrage. The survivors broke and ran.

The truck drivers and the French soldiers cheered. The lieutenant wanted to cry but held back his tears. He was an example after all… and a hero. *There will be medals,* he thought.

Bruno and his paratroopers had already disembarked from their troop transport helicopters behind a hill. The helicopters had flow away so as not to give away Bruno's position. He had predicted the direction the mujahideen would flee once their lines broke. He was right on the money. The French held their fire until dozens of mujahideen had flooded over the hilltop. Then the paratroopers opened fire on Bruno's signal.

The mujahideen were completely surprised and twenty fell dead in the first few seconds of the battle. Others ran towards another hilltop until they saw a large airplane flying overhead and sixty-five parachutes floating down directly in their path.

It was Coyle flying his C-119. He found the backdoor of the mujahideen escape and slammed it shut with a load of paratroopers. It was a proven formula that Bruno and he had devised.

For the rebels the situation was hopeless. The mujahideen threw down their weapons, kneeled and put their hands in the air. The French paratroopers swept in and took them prisoner. They would be a treasure trove of intelligence once they had been interrogated.

It was early the next morning before Bruno and his men made it back to the airfield outside Algiers. Coyle was waiting for him as the helicopters landed. "Your new mousetrap worked out well," said Coyle. "How did you come up with it?"

"They never should have shot me. I had time to think while lying in my hospital bed," said Bruno.

"How are you holding up?"

"I am a bit sore but it is just a matter of time and exercise."

"You speak from experience."

"I do. I am getting good at being shot."

"You might not want to make it a hobby."

"Yes. Yes. I agree. It would be a bad hobby."

"How did you get the army doctors to release you from the hospital so soon?"

"I started doing pushups and squats in the morning. They said I was disturbing the other patients."

"Interesting strategy. Are you up for a coffee and

croissant?"

"Yes. Yes. But I need to eat my raw onion first."

"Now that's a nasty habit."

"I just survived a second bullet to the chest. You might not want to lecture me on what is healthy and what is not."

"I can't argue with that."

"Would you like an onion? I have plenty."

"I'd rather take the bullet."

"That is why you fly planes and not jump out of them, Coyle. You are soft."

"No. Just sane."

They laughed and walked off in search of coffee and croissants.

July 22, 1956 – Cairo, Egypt

Nasser stood over a conference table studying the drawings of the Suez Canal. Mahmoud Younis, an Egyptian engineer, explained how the canal worked. "The canal is not a canal in the traditional sense. It's more like a river or waterway between two seas. There are no locks required in the canal since the water levels between the Red Sea and Mediterranean are almost identical.

The shores of the canal are too narrow to allow two-way traffic, therefore we use a convoy system. Thirty-eight ships sail one way one at a time through the canal then the direction reverses and thirty-eight ships sail in the opposite direction. It takes twelve to sixteen hours for a convoy to pass through the canal.

The ships sail in the center of the canal since that area is the deepest. At night or when there is fog, buoys guide the way. There are four control towers that monitor the convoy's progress and spacing. The ships need a half kilometer of water between them to navigate freely. Even then if a ship should need to stop it can take one and a half kilometers to slow to a full stop. Since only one ship can fit in the canal's deepest channel, there is little room for error once a convoy starts moving."

"What if there is an accident?" said Nasser.

"It depends on how serious the accident. If two ships collide but stay afloat there is no serious harm to the canal. But if a ship runs aground it can block the canal and prevent any ships from passing."

"How long does it take to clear a ship that has run aground?"

"A day at the minimum. But a ship that runs deep aground can require a dozen tugs to pull it free and that can take a week or more."

"What happens if a ship sinks?"

"That is the worse-case scenario. If a ship sinks in the deep channel it could block the canal for months. The only way to remove a sunken ship is to refloat it if the damage is not too bad. Otherwise, it must be cut into pieces by underwater divers and pulled out using cranes on barrages. As you can image, that is laborious and costly."

"I see."

"That's why we use pilots to take control of the ships as they make their way through the canal. They know the canal inside and out. They become the captain of each vessel while it is in the canal zone."

"How many pilots are there?"

"About three hundred."

"And how many are Egyptian?"

"None… that I know of."

"Well that is not good. We'll need to train some… quickly. You seem to know a lot about the canal."

"I am an engineer."

"You work for the canal company?"

"Yes. I work on the dredging team."

"Good. You will be the new chief engineer and head of our new canal company."

"Wait… What?!"

"Smile. You're being promoted."

"But there is so much I don't know."

"I suggest you learn quickly. Your country needs you. Don't fuck up my canal. The new company will need a name. Something that reflects authority. See to it."

"Yes, your excellency."

"Now... How exactly do we take control of the canal?" said Nasser.

"There are four control points. One is at Port Sayid on the Mediterranean. Another is at Port Suez on the Red Sea. There are two more that control traffic on Great Bitter Lake and Lake Timsah. Headquarters for the Suez Canal Company is in the city of Ismaïlia on Lake Timsah. If you control those points you control the canal."

"Very well. I want you to draw up plans for taking control of the canal on my command. How many men will it take? What type of weapons will you need?"

"But I have no military training."

"Of course not. You're an engineer. What does a general know about taking and operating a canal? This is your job. I am confident you will not fail me," said Nasser with a smile.

Younis was not so sure, and thought he might heave his breakfast after Nasser left.

July 26, 1956 - Alexandria, Egypt

Nasser loved giving speeches. His blood ran hot as the crowds cheered. He was an excellent orator and the people loved him. They were his base of support. They kept him in power.

Nasser's speech in Alexandria was critical. The people were gravely disappointed after the news that funding for the Aswan Dam project had been cut off. They were losing hope that their miserable lives would change. Nasser needed to remind them of their destiny and revitalize their dreams. He also needed to work the name of the original builder of the Suez Canal into his speech. The name was the code word that signaled the teams that Younis commanded to seize control of the canal. Nasser waited two hours into the speech before saying the name of Ferdinand de Lesseps.

July 26, 1956 – Suez Canal Zone, Egypt

On hearing the code word over the radio, Younis and his teams of engineers stormed the control points and headquarters of the Suez Canal Company. Younis had decided not to use professional soldiers but rather the engineers that he knew and trusted for the operation. He knew it was a risk, but he also knew that he needed the British engineers and pilots to continue operations until the Egyptians could be trained. Younis was concerned the Egyptian army might be too heavy-handed in dealing with the foreigners, many of whom were British.

The management team of the Suez Canal Company knew Younis. When Younis and his men stormed into the headquarters, the CEO thought it was a bad joke. It wasn't. Younis had orders from Nasser to shoot anyone that got out of line. That was the last thing that Younis wanted but he would do whatever was necessary to carry out Nasser's orders. It didn't take long before the CEO knew Younis was serious. It wasn't the pistol in Younis' hand that finally convinced the CEO that he was serious… it was his eyes. He ordered his managers and security guards to stand down. "You are making a big mistake, young man," said the CEO.

"You could be correct, sir, but it will be an Egyptian mistake," said Younis.

It only took thirty armed men to take control of the Suez Canal. It was a bloodless affair and no shots were fired. Younis did his best to reassure the British engineers and pilots that they were not in danger as long as they cooperated and committed no acts of sabotage against the canal. The engineers and pilots were outraged but did not resist. They believed it was just a matter of time before British troops arrived and retook control of the canal. It was too important an asset to leave in the hands of the Egyptians.

July 26, 1956 - Alexandria, Egypt

At the end of Nasser's speech in Alexandria he announced that Egyptian forces had just seized control of the Suez Canal. The crowd went wild and broke out in a spontaneous celebration that last several days. Nasser loved it.

July 27, 1956 – Washington D.C., USA

In the White House, Eisenhower stood over his desk, looking down at a map of the Suez Canal and surrounding area. John Foster Dulles, the U.S. Secretary of State and his brother Allen Dulles, the Director of the CIA, were with the president.

"I can't believe Nasser thinks he can get away with this," said Eisenhower.

"He needed to do something after losing the funding for the Aswan Dam project. He was losing political support," said Allen Dulles.

"That was a bad call on my part," said Eisenhower. "I never should have cancelled the funding. I left it to the British to control the situation with Nasser and Eden's just made a big mess of it."

"We should have seen this coming," said Allen Dulles.

"We did. We just didn't think it was a high probability," said John Dulles. "We made a calculated guess and we were wrong."

"Alright. No use crying over spilt milk. What are our options?" said Eisenhower.

"Unfortunately, Nasser is holding most of the cards at the moment," said John Dulles. "He controls the Suez."

"Military interdiction?" said Allen Dulles.

"No," said Eisenhower. "We can't keep solving every problem with a war. We need to solve this diplomatically."

"I am sure the British are furious," said Allen Dulles. "Eden hates Nasser."

"I agree. Eden is a loose cannon when it comes to Nasser. If he gets involved any more than he is it will just make things worse. That's the last thing we need," said Eisenhower. "What about the U.N.?"

"Everyone is condemning the Egyptians except for India and the Arab nations, oh and the Soviets of course. They are naturally concerned but recognize Egypt's right to control its own land. Canada is somewhat neutral."

"Good. The Canadians could be of use as a mediator. Cooler heads must prevail. We don't need another war, especially not with things already overheating in Hungary," said Eisenhower.

"What if we put together a conference of users of the Suez Canal?" said John Dulles.

"Another conference? What will that solve?" said his brother.

"Maybe nothing, but we cannot be seen as impudent. We have to do something," said John Dulles.

"A conference of users is not a bad idea," said Eisenhower. "They are the ones that will be paying the tolls for their ships. They could threaten a boycott. It would show Nasser he could face consequences if he does not behave rationally."

"Do you really believe Nasser fears a boycott?" said Allen Dulles. "The Suez is the only alternative to the long way around the Horn of Africa. Nasser knows it and so does everyone else. I doubt there will be much of an appetite for a boycott."

"Apparently, Nasser fears very little. I don't like what he did, but I admit it was ballsy," said Eisenhower. "I agree with John. We've got to do something before this thing spins even more out of control. I don't want the Soviets to gain any more influence in the Middle East than they already have. God help us if Egypt becomes a Soviet satellite state."

"Nasser is an opportunist, not a communist," said John Dulles.

"Yet," said Eisenhower.

"Nasser wants to be the leader of the Arab countries. He can't do that if he's a communist. The Arab leaders would never stand for it," said John Dulles.

"There is no telling what Nasser will do. We gave him a three-million-dollar bribe to join MEDO and he took our money but failed to join," said Allen Dulles. "He is not someone we can trust, no matter what."

"Well, we are going have to start trusting someone in the Middle East or the Soviets are going to fill the vacuum," said Eisenhower. "John, let's try the conference idea and see what sticks. Allen, I want you to increase our reconnaissance flights over the Suez and Egypt. I want to keep a sharp on what Nasser is doing."

"Yes, Mr. President," said Allen Dulles.

July 28, 1956 – Adana, Turkey

At the newly-constructed Incirlik US Air Base in Turkey, Gary Francis Powers performed a preflight check on his U2 reconnaissance aircraft before suiting up. His preflight check was more a habit than a necessity. There was an entire team of mechanics and engineers that maintained and watched over the U2s. The aircraft were an essential reconnaissance tool in the Cold War and one of America's closest held secrets.

The U2 was designed by the engineering wonks at Lockheed's Skunkworks. She had massive wings and a long narrow fuselage. A single Pratt & Whitney turbojet engine achieved speeds of five hundred miles per hour and carried the aircraft up to her operating altitude of seventy thousand feet. The plane was difficult to fly and, because of the low-profile cockpit and small landing gear, almost impossible to land without a chase car providing a second set of eyes to instruct the pilot by radio when he had touched down on the runway. The fuel in both wing tanks had to be perfectly balanced to prevent the wings from tipping to one side or the other and dragging on the runway. The engineers nicknamed the aircraft "Dragon Lady" because she was extremely unforgiving to the pilots that flew her.

Powers would put on his spacesuit before his scheduled flight and pre-breathe one hundred percent pure oxygen for one hour before take-off. The oxygen helped drive out nitrogen from his bloodstream and prevent decompression sickness during and after the mission.

There were few pilots capable of flying the U2. Powers was one of the best. He knew the risks if he was ever shot down and captured. The CIA had offered him and the other pilots a suicide pill containing liquid potassium cyanide. It would cause death in ten to fifteen seconds once taken. Most of the pilots declined to carry it on their missions after one of the pilots mistook it for a piece of candy and almost killed himself while prepping for a flight.

Once he was ready, Powers would be escorted to the aircraft and helped into the cockpit. The spacesuit made every movement seem clumsy. He would wear the suit and fly the plane for up to twelve hours at a time depending on the mission.

The aircraft had multiple types of instrument packages that could be placed into her belly pod. Once the mission was completed, the instrument package would be retrieved by CIA operatives and the image and data analyzed in a top-secret facility within the airbase.

Today was a simple mission. Photography. His orders were to fly over the Suez Canal Zone and take high resolution photos of the canal and the surrounding area. The Egyptians would probably never even know he was there. Once he completed his primary mission, he was to fly back over the Sinai and photograph various strategic points of interest, including the Israeli border.

He climbed into the cockpit and the engineers sealed him inside. The cockpit was partially pressurized to the equivalent of twenty-eight thousand feet which helped with temperature and icing of the windshield.

The plane was towed out of its hanger and pulled to the end of the runway. Once the tow vehicle was clear and the tower radioed its okay, Powers fired up the engine and rolled down the runway, gaining speed.

He liked flying the Dragon Lady. She was a challenge. He liked the feeling of being special. A hero, even if nobody knew it. *I am the dragon master,* he thought as he took off into the early morning sky.

September 14, 1956 – Suez Canal Zone, Egypt

The majority of the British engineers and pilots had stayed on with the Suez Canal Authority and the canal continued to operate smoothly. The British had claimed the Egyptians would fall flat on their faces and traffic in the canal would evolve into a log jam if it wasn't for the British employees.

Nasser knew that the British needed oil. He was counting on it. The British could not afford for the canal to be closed or even slowed without facing serious fuel shortages and a recession in their economy. Nasser was playing for time while Younis trained his Egyptian engineers and pilots to take over the entire operation.

On September 14th time ran out. Three hundred British and European pilots walked off the job without any notice. Traffic in the canal halted abruptly with no one to guide the ships.

Nasser was furious. The British were once again playing games with the lives of Egyptians. He ordered Younis to keep the canal working no matter the cost.

"It is not a matter of cost, your excellency. It is a matter of safety," said Younis. "Our pilots are simply not ready. Most have only had rudimentary training on how to navigate the canal and operate the vessels."

"We have no choice. If the world sees that we cannot operate the canal then the British will be proven right and the U.N. will demand an international authority to operate the canal," said Nasser. "Chief Engineer Younis, you must get those ships moving…now."

Nasser hung up the phone and Younis was again feeling nauseous. After a few moments of uncertainty, he realized that his country was counting on him, his crew of engineers and young pilots. He would throw up later. He told his assistant to place the personnel folders of all the pilots on his desk immediately.

He spent the next hour going through the files, examining each of the pilot's background and test results. He settled on a twenty-six-year-old that had scored exceptionally high in his engineering classes at Cairo University. His name was Ali Nasri. He called the training supervisor and ordered him to have Nasri report to headquarters immediately.

Nasri arrive thirty minutes later. He had been training to navigate an old freighter in Lake Timsah when he received a notice that the chief engineer wished to see him. He thought he was in trouble. He was right.

Younis explained the situation and informed Nasri he would be the first Egyptian in history to navigate a freighter through the Suez Canal. It was a great honor. Nasri went to the toilet and threw up.

A speed boat carried Nasri to the freighter and pulled alongside. He climbed the pilot's ladder and boarded the ship. The captain of the ship asked what the hell was going on. Nasri informed him that he would pilot the ship from this point forward. The captain looked very worried and asked, "Have you ever piloted a ship this size before?"

"No," said Nasri.

"Have you ever piloted any ship before?"

"By myself… no."

"This is insane."

"This is Egypt and if you want your ship to proceed through the canal you will turn over your bridge to me. Otherwise, your freight can rot."

The captain thought for a long moment. It was tradition that the pilot was responsible for the vessel while it was under his command and if the ship was sunk or ran aground the pilot, and not the captain, would be blamed. It didn't seem to make the captain feel much better. Still, Nasri was right. Egypt controlled the canal and supplied the pilots. If Nasri was selected to pilot his ship, the captain had no choice but to accept. He stepped out of his captain's chair and away from the ship's controls. "You have the bridge," he said.

"Thank you," said Nasri.

He looked at the control panel and realized he had no idea how to operate this ship. The ships he had trained on were old pre-war freighters. This ship was new. It didn't even have a steering wheel to operate the rudder. The ship was controlled by thrusters. The crew on the bridge stared at him waiting for orders. He turned to the first mate and said, "Take her into the channel."

"Aye, master pilot," said the first mate, who in turn gave orders to the crew on the bridge to get the ship underway.

Nasri didn't want to just stand there so he stepped to

the window and peered through his binoculars as if searching for something. The crew cast off the ship's lines, releasing the vessel from the pier.

The ship began to move. Nasri took a deep breath and tried to relax. The crew seemed to know what they were doing. He knew most of the way through the canal and what he didn't know he could use the buoys to guide him… he hoped. *Allah, don't let me run her aground,* was his silent prayer.

As the vessel sailed into the channel, Nasri looked over at the shore. There were a dozen Egyptians cheering, including Younis. Nasri took heart. *I can do this,* he thought. *With God's help, I can do this.*

Hour after hour, the Egyptians held their breath and waited, especially Nasser. He received reports every thirty minutes on the ship's progress. There was nothing he could do but hope and pray. All of Egypt's dream were held within the bridge of that ship.

After fourteen hours, the vessel cleared the mouth of the canal and entered the Mediterranean Sea. Nasri turned the bridge back over to the captain. "That was some damn fine piloting, son," said the captain, feeling like a proud father.

"Thank you," said Nasri.

He climbed down the ladder and entered the pilot's boat. Tears welled up in his eyes. It was over. He had not embarrassed his country. He thanked Allah and planned on going to the nearest mosque in Port Said for his evening prayers.

As the boat approached the pier, Nasri looked out the boat's windshield and saw thousands of Egyptians on the concrete pier and thousands more on shore. They were cheering wildly. Nasri was a national hero.

Eden was livid. Nasser was elated.

THREE

September 29, 1956 – London, England

The British commonwealth was totally unprepared for the nationalization of the Suez Canal. At 10 Downing Street, Eden was unhinged. Many in Parliament, including several in his own party, blamed Eden for antagonizing Nasser by shutting down the funding for the Aswan Dam project. Immediate action was demanded. But there was little Eden could do short of sending British troops back into the canal zone and seizing control once again. That was not a good option. The international community was displeased with Nasser's actions but few wanted to see Britain return to its imperialistic heavy-handedness. Eden was stuck.

A few days after the nationalization of the canal became formalized, Eden received a request from the French ambassador. The ambassador and General Maurice Challe - Deputy Chief of Staff of French Armed Forces – wanted to meet with Eden in private, away from the office, to discuss the Egyptian situation. Eden was curious. He invited them to a weekend lunch at his country estate outside of London. They accepted.

October 14, 1956 – Buckinghamshire, England

Chequers Court or Chequers as it is commonly known was the country house of the Prime Minister of the United Kingdom. The 16th century manor house is in Buckinghamshire at the foot of the Chiltern Hills. It sits sixty-five kilometers north west of central London. Nobody is sure where Chequers got its name but many suspect it came from the chequer trees that grow on its grounds. Others believe the name came from the coat of arms of the original owner which featured the chequer board of the Exchequer. It didn't really matter but it made for a nice bit of trivia during afternoon tea.

Chequers was a tranquil place to relax from affairs of state and to entertain foreign dignitaries when privacy was required. It was a criminal offense for anyone to trespass on the estate and it was heavily patrolled by British security forces.

Eden was giving the French Ambassador and General Challe a tour of the estate's greenhouse when Challe offered a unique solution to the current state of affairs of the Suez Canal nationalization. "We have developed a strategy that could benefit both Britain and France," he said.

"You have my undivided attention," said Eden.

"Israel will attack Egypt through the Sinai and threaten the Suez Canal. Once the Israeli forces occupy the entire Sinai including the east bank of the Suez Canal, Britain and France will demand an immediate ceasefire. Nasser can never accept a ceasefire with Israeli troops on Egyptian soil. It would be political suicide. He will refuse. Britain and France will be forced to intervene to force the two antagonists apart and to protect the canal from damage. Our joint troops will occupy the canal zone and give Egypt a good throttling as punishment for taking over the canal in the first place," said Challe.

Eden was shocked by the boldness of the plan but also intrigued. "What makes you think the Israelis would go along with such a plan?" said Eden.

"The Israelis are anxious to get at the Egyptians before they receive the balance of their arms shipments from the Czechs. They want to hit Nasser while he is still weak. Give him a bloody nose, degrade his military and erode his support with the generals."

"…and the people I would imagine," added Eden.

"The Israelis will also be sending a message to the other Middle Eastern countries not to fuck with Israel unless they want their own armies destroyed."

"Interesting… But one can never trust the Israelis. They have little concern for international politics beyond their own self-interests."

"In this case, their interests are our interests."

"I can see that but what makes you so sure they will accept a ceasefire when the time comes?"

"The Israelis need access to the Red Sea so they can trade with the Far East. The Egyptians have denied them access through the Suez Canal and the Straits of Tiran. Their southern port in Eilat is useless. If they were guaranteed free navigation through Straits of Tiran they would be satisfied."

"Their price for peace?"

"Their price for participating in a risky operation. France believes it is a just and reasonable request."

"Who would guarantee their access? Surely not Jordan."

"No. I imagine the U.N."

"They would trust the U.N.?"

"They don't have much choice if they want peace in the Middle East. They will be more likely to accept such a mission if it is their proposal to begin with. We can imagine that the Americans might propose something along those lines. Eisenhower believes in peacekeeping."

"Interesting. And the Israelis will retreat from Sinai when the time comes?"

"Yes."

"I assume you have already discussed this with the Israelis?"

"Yes. Preliminary discussions have gone well. They are onboard… so far."

"How do we know the Israelis won't sell us out and brag to the entire world that we are their secret allies?"

"We don't but it is not in their self-interest."

"…at the moment. But what about later?"

"We are not saying this strategy is without risk. But all three of our countries want Nasser marginalized."

"I don't want him marginalized. I want him destroyed."

"One never knows what can happen in a war."

There was a long silence as Eden considered. "Your thoughts?" said the French Ambassador.

"I would like to see more. The devil is in the details as they say," said Eden.

Challe pulled a set of maps from his briefcase and the conversation continued.

October 16, 1956 – New York, USA

At the request of the Secretary General of the United Nations and at Eisenhower's urging, Eden sent Lloyd to negotiate peace with Egypt at the U.N. Upon arriving in New York, Lloyd received a cable from Mahmoud Fawzi - Egypt's foreign secretary, saying he was looking forward to their discussions and was hopeful they could find a peaceful resolution. Lloyd was less enthusiastic.

To Lloyd's surprise, he found that discussions did go well and the two foreign secretaries made progress toward a workable solution for the security of the canal and appropriate compensation for investors in the Suez Canal Company.

When Lloyd called Eden to inform him of the progress, the response was not what Lloyd had expected. "Yes. Yes. Well done, Selwyn," said Eden. "Now, I want you to break off negotiations and fly back to London."

"What? Why?" said Lloyd.

"The why is not important right now. You will understand more once we meet. I don't wish to explain over the phone. One never knows who might be listening."

Eden hung up. Lloyd was crestfallen.

October 21, 1956 – Paris, France

Brigitte sat in her officer working on her Café Wars story when the phone rang. It was her contact at the airport. He told her that the Israeli Prime Minister's plane had just landed. Ben-Gurion, Perez and another man that he didn't recognize had exited the plane along with a large security detail. Brigitte slammed the phone down and raced out of the office.

She was on her way to the airport in a taxi when she saw a convoy around a limousine headed toward the center of the city. She told the driver to turn around and follow the convoy from a discreet distance. The driver questioned her motives until she showed him her press credentials. He shrugged and followed the convoy.

Brigitte was surprised when the convoy did not go to the government center in Paris but instead headed out of the city. She told the driver to continue following the convoy. He obeyed. It was going to be a good fare.

October 22, 1956 – Sèvres, France

No sooner had Lloyd arrived back in London than Eden sent him to Sèvres, France – a commune ten kilometers outside of Paris and away from the prying eyes of the press. His mission was to negotiate a secret Anglo-French-Israeli military pact with the principal aim of overthrowing Nasser and securing the Suez Canal.

When Eden explained his intentions, Lloyd understood why Eden did not want to go to the meeting himself. Deniability. Eden did not want to be seen collaborating with Israel in any way. For Eden, any sign of allying with the Israelis would be political suicide and greatly endanger Britain's relationship with the Arab nations. Britain needed to look like they were reluctantly dragged into the conflict and were only acting as peacekeepers. A noble knight coming to the rescue. Dean accompanied Lloyd to the meeting.

The French played matchmaker between the British and the Israelis. Bourgès-Maunoury, General Challe, and Minister of Foreign Affairs Christian Pineau represented France in the negotiations. The French were not as concerned with appearances because of their close relationship with Israel. They had a common enemy in the radical Muslims and Israel had been helpful in providing intelligence about arms sales to the Algerian rebels. France was Israel's western defender in the U.N. Some saw French support of Israel as an apology to the Jewish people for France's cooperation with the Nazis during the occupation.

Ben-Gurion attended the meeting along with Perez and Moshe Dayan - Chief of Staff for Israel's Defense Forces. There was a huge amount at stake for the Israelis. They would be committing almost their entire armed forces to the operation. Failure was not an option. Ben-Gurion did not trust the British. He remembered what it was like under British occupation and the way the British treated the Israelis. He had hoped to meet Eden so he could look him in the eye to judge his intent.

On arriving at the villa, Ben-Gurion soon realized that a meeting between the two leaders would never materialize. If the Israelis were to agree to the operation it would need to be on faith alone that the British and the French would not abandon them once they had committed their forces. It was a very risky proposition, but the potential rewards would be great.

Ben-Gurion resented that Israel was being used as a prostitute to provide services to the two western powers and he let the others know his mind. The perception could not be helped but it did not sit well with the Israeli Prime Minister. However, the French proposal could very well have been Israel's only opportunity to attack Egypt with the help of not one but two great western powers. It was a chance to destroy Nasser's military might and badly damage his reputation in the Arab world in one bold stroke. It was an opportunity that the Israelis could not pass up.

Eden had instructed Lloyd that the operation was to be expanded to include a bombing campaign targeting Cairo. Eden believed that if the Egyptian people were under direct threat, they would overthrow Nasser. The military leaders that took Nasser's place would sue for peace to prevent the rest of their army from being destroyed. Neither the French nor the Israelis liked the idea because of the potential for massive civilian casualties but they needed Britain to participate and agreed. Cairo would be bombed.

The discussions were held in a private villa and lasted three days. The outcome was the most famous and well-documented war plot in modern history. The Israelis codenamed their part of the plan Operation Kadesh, while the French had codenamed the French and British part of the plan as Operation Musketeer, and later after some alterations to the second phase, Operation Revise.

The document produced by the discussions came to be known as the Protocol of Sèvres. It was written in French and only three type-written copies were created, one for each country. At the end of the meeting, the Israelis insisted that the document be signed by all parties involved. They knew that if a signed document existed, even in secret, the French and the British would be less likely to betray them. The British especially would not want to risk exposure of the treaty. Ben-Gurion signed for Israel. Pineau signed for the French. Lloyd was hesitant. He handed a pen to his assistant Dean and said, "Congratulations, Sir Patrick. Your first treaty. You're now part of history."

Dean was also hesitant, but he knew he had little choice in the matter. He initialed each page, signed all three copies and placed one in his briefcase. The other two copies went to Pineau and Ben-Gurion. Each placed their copy into their individual briefcases.

October 24, 1956 – Sèvres, France

Lloyd and Dean left the villa together. Both men were exhausted after the long negotiations and Dean was particularly agitated that he had been required to sign the treaty. His signature was the only concrete evidence of British participation in the cabal. It was a shit sandwich that he did not enjoy eating.

As the British entered their limousine and left the estate, the French delegation exited the Villa. Pineau set down his briefcase on the ground to remove his overcoat. He climbed into the back of the French limousine, leaving the briefcase containing the signed copy of the treaty on the ground. The limousine drove off.

The villa's groundskeeper found the briefcase. He had been working at the villa for over thirty years and had seen the guests of the villa often leave things behind. *Rich people are so forgetful,* he thought. He placed the briefcase in a safe place inside the villa until the owner returned for it or send a messenger to retrieve it.

As the last limousine, trailed by its security detail in a sedan, left the estate, Brigitte slipped in through the closing gate. She knew she was on to something big when she had seen all the security vehicles and limousines coming and going over the last three days. She just didn't know what it was. She walked up the driveway. She still had on the same clothes she wore when she arrived three days earlier. She realized that she probably smelled bad and looked worse. She pulled some perfume from her purse and gave herself a spritz. She checked her hair in her compact mirror. She was right. It was worse but she did her best to fix it.

She didn't know what she would do once she reached the front door. Her best hope was to find someone, perhaps a butler or housekeeper, that knew the identity of the participants or overheard a revealing conversation. "Can I help you?" said the groundskeeper as Brigitte approached the house.

"Oh, I didn't see you there," said Brigitte, startled.

"I'm sorry. I wasn't lurking. Just trimming the rose bushes for winter," said the groundskeeper. "Are you here to pick up the briefcase?"

"Oh, ah…," said Brigitte wondering if the briefcase was inside the villa. "Yes. The briefcase. Is it inside?"

"Yes. Nice and safe," said the groundskeeper moving toward the villa.

"Quite a big meeting, yes?" said Brigitte following him.

"Oh, yes. Security guards made a mess of my flowerbeds. They should really have been more careful."

"I'll make sure to note it in my report."

"Very nice of you. You work for one of the ministers?"

"In a way, yes. I'm sort of a press secretary."

"I could never do that. Stay inside all day. Typing on a machine. I need the outdoors. I need to feel the dirt between my fingers. I don't use gloves. They're not natural."

"Is it hard work? Keeping the grounds?"

"At times. But very rewarding. Especially in the spring when the flowers bloom."

"I'm sure," said Brigitte. "You don't happen to remember the names of any of the guests, do you? I want to make sure I get their names correct for my report and I forgot my guest list back at the office."

"Oh, no. I am terrible with names."

"Too bad. Is there a housekeeper or butler I could talk with?"

"No. The security guards chased 'em all off before the meeting. I was the only one allowed to stay, and I wasn't allowed to enter. Someone had to lock up after they left."

The groundskeeper took off his muddy boots and left them on the front porch. Brigitte started to take off her shoes... "No. No. No need," said the groundskeeper. "Just my boots. Don't wanna be trampling mud on the floors. Your shoes look clean enough. Just give 'em a good scraping on the doormat before ya enter. It kicks off any pebbles that might scratch the wood floors."

Brigitte scraped her shoes on the door mat, and they entered the villa. Brigitte looked around the villa as the groundskeeper went off to retrieve the briefcase. The place was empty. There was nothing that gave her a clue as to who had been here, and why.

The groundskeeper returned and handed her the briefcase. "There you go. Might want to warn him to be more careful. One can never be sure that such a fine piece of luggage like that doesn't end up in the hands of a thief."

"You are absolutely right. I will warn him. Your country thanks you for your service," she said.

"Do you want me to call you a taxi?"

"That would be quite nice. Thank you."

The groundskeeper moved off to the study where the phone was located.

Brigitte exited the villa and walked back down the driveway, carrying the briefcase.

October 24, 1956 – Paris, France

Pineau arrived back at his office in his limousine. He reached for his briefcase, but it wasn't there. He looked under the seats and in the trunk. Nothing. He told the driver to wait and that he needed to make a call. He rushed inside the building.

He ran up the stairs to his office and had his secretary call the villa to inquire about his briefcase. She spoke with the groundskeeper who informed her about the nice woman that had already picked it up and was on her way to return it. The woman had not left her name. The secretary thanked him and hung up.

Pineau thought about the contents of the briefcase and began to panic. He told his secretary not to mention the briefcase to anyone. He needed to find that woman before she opened it, but had no idea where to look.

October 24, 1956 – Cairo, Egypt

Nasser sat at his desk staring out the window. He was not happy with the news that the British had broken off peace negotiations at the U.N. He would naturally turn the break in negotiations into a public relations win for Egypt by claiming that the British had no real intention of negotiating with the Egyptians. It was all a ploy to garner international attention. Egypt would look like the victim, not the aggressor. He would win support from other Arab leaders and more importantly... the people of Egypt.

But Nasser was concerned. He did not see the advantage the British might obtain by shutting down negotiations so quickly and without warning. Why not let the negotiations play out and then find some technical point to reject any agreement if that was the outcome they sought? It didn't make sense, and that bothered Nasser. He brought in his intelligence chiefs and asked what the British might be doing. They had no idea. They too could not see the logic in the British move.

The French were also being strangely quiet. They had stopped with their objections to Nasser helping the FLN in their struggle for independence. Was it possible that the French had decimated the FLN forces to the point they were no longer a threat to Algeria? He didn't know. The FLN leader, Ben Bella, had lived in Cairo as an exile, but had recently been kidnapped by the French while flying over international waters. Nasser decided to send some of his own agents into Algeria to check on the FLN.

The Israelis had been massing troops on the border, but that was not that unusual. Nasser did not like the reports that training of Israeli pilots in their new French jets was going well. The French were crazy to sell jets to the Israelis. It was a recipe for war to give Israel such advanced weaponry. The Israeli jets were a threat to his tanks and navy. His own pilots were also training in their new jets but the Soviets had sent instructors with no knowledge of Egyptian Arabic, so progress had been slower than he had hoped for. He knew he would have to respond to the Israeli threat soon, but the Israelis were so unpredictable, he could never figure out what they had in mind, and his intelligence efforts bore little fruit. Nasser was blind when it came to the Israelis, and it drove him crazy.

October 24, 1956 – Paris, France

Pineau's briefcase sat on Brigitte's bed. It was open. Brigitte had used a hairpin to pick the lock. Next to the briefcase sat the one-page document titled, "Protocol of Sèvres." It was written in French and she had read ever last word on the page in less than a minute. It was the longest minute of her life. She sat motionless just staring at the sheet of paper. She knew she was in deep trouble.

Upon reading the document she realized it would obviously be classified "Top Secret" if it had not been already. There was no getting around it, she had stolen a top-secret document. It didn't matter that she didn't know it was in the briefcase. Everything she had done in the last twenty-four hours gave the impression she was a spy. She had followed international officials to a secret location for a secret meeting. She had trespassed on to the secret location. She had lied about her identity to the groundskeeper. She had taken the briefcase when she knew it was not hers. And to top it all off she was living with Tom Coyle, a former CIA operative. America and France were allies but even allies spied on each other. Coyle might also be arrested and at the very least be deported from France, never to return. She gasped. She could lose Coyle because of what she had done.

She had stumbled on the biggest story of her career – an international scandal that would lead to war – and she couldn't tell a soul without risking arrest and imprisonment for treason. If she turned the document over to the French authorities, those involved in creation of the document would know that she had read it. They would lock her up at least until the war was well underway, and maybe for a lot longer than that. She had heard rumors that the intelligence community had a bad habit of disappearing unsavory characters rather than letting their secrets be revealed in a lengthy criminal trial. She shivered at the implication.

She stopped and reasoned with herself. *Brigitte, you're making a mountain out of mole hill,* she thought. *It can't be this bad. After all you didn't know what was inside the briefcase. If you had, you never would have taken it. The most you are guilty of is stupidity and petty theft… and maybe treason depending on the judge. There must be a way to turn this to your advantage. You just haven't thought of it yet.*

If she wrote about what she had found, they would know it was her that took the briefcase. If she turned over the document, it was like admitting she was guilty. If she kept quiet about it, they would eventually track her down. *If there is no way to win I might as well write my story,* she thought. *At least then I can claim protection under freedom of the press. Damien would surely come to my defense and hire a good lawyer to represent me. Then again… the government might shut down the magazine, citing national security.*

It was hopeless, or so she thought until a thought came to her. *There might be another way…*

October 25, 1956 – London, England

Eden stared at Patrick Dean's signature at the bottom of the Protocol of Sèvres document. "Were you out of your fucking mind?" said Eden to Lloyd seated across from his desk. "Why would you allow Dean to sign such a thing?"

"The Israelis insisted," said Lloyd. "We had little choice."

"Little choice? Do you realize that if this document ever becomes public it implicates all of us in a conspiracy to start a war?"

"Yes, sir."

"How many copies are there?"

"Three. This one, plus the Israelis and the French each have a signed copy."

"Get them back."

"How?" said Lloyd.

"I don't care. Just do it," said Eden.

October 25, 1956 – Paris, France

Brigitte stood in front of the Ministry of Foreign Affairs. In her hand was Pineau's briefcase, closed and locked tight. She took a deep breath and walked into the building.

Inside the reception area, she informed the guard that she had found the minister's briefcase and was here to return it in person. The guard offered to give it to the minister, she insisted on giving it to him herself. It didn't take long until she was escorted into Pineau's office.

Pineau did not say a word to Brigitte as she entered his office. They knew each other. His eyes focused on the briefcase. She handed it to him and said, "I assume this is yours?"

"Don't play games, Brigitte. You know it's mine," said

Pineau. "You opened it?"

"Of course. I needed to find the owner. I found your name on some of the documents inside and came here immediately. I knew you would be worried."

Pineau unlocked the briefcase and opened it. He looked through the documents inside. The Protocol of Sèvres was not inside. "Where is it?" said Pineau.

"Where is what?"

"The document."

"Which document?"

"You know to which document I am referring."

"I don't. What you see is all that I found inside."

"You are saying that the document is lost?"

"No. I'm saying it was never there."

"Did you destroy it?"

"No. How could I? It never existed."

Pineau considered for a long time before continuing and said, "How can I trust that the document does not surface at some point in the future?"

"If this document to which you refer was to suddenly appear, I could be accused of stealing it, could I not?"

"That or much worse."

"Why would I ever want that to happen?"

"I suppose you have a point. It is a very dangerous game you are playing."

"Look who's calling the kettle black."

"You realize that thousands of lives are at stake? French lives."

"I wouldn't know about that."

"And there is nothing you demand to ensure this non-existent document stays hidden?"

"No. I am a patriot. I will not play with the lives of French citizens… and soldiers."

Pineau's expression sharpened at the mention of soldiers. She obviously knew about the military plans. "Am I free to go?" said Brigitte.

"Of course. I have no reason to detain you," said

Pineau.

"You might say thank you? I did find your briefcase."

"Yes. You did. Thank you for returning it."

Brigitte got up and moved toward the door. She had pulled it off. She was still a free woman but something inside her couldn't just let the story go. It was too big. *A faint heart never filled a flush,* she thought. She decided in that moment to push a little farther. "You know... There is one little favor you could do for me," she said turning back to Pineau.

"And what might that be?"

"If there were any upcoming military activities, I would like to be given the chance to report on them as an embedded journalist. Like old times."

"You wish to jump with the French paras?"

"With the French? No. I had someone else in mind," said Brigitte with a smile.

October 26, 1956 – Jerusalem, Israel

Ariel Sharon sat in Dayan's office. He wasn't happy, despite being assigned the honor to spearhead the attack into Sinai. "Why doesn't she jump with her own troops? She's not even Jewish," said Sharon.

"She wants to report on the entire war. The French won't even arrive until your position in Sinai has been secured," said Dayan with a shrug. "I don't like it either, but the French are asking us to take her with us. They are our allies. Let's not piss them off before the war even starts."

"But after is okay?"

"Of course. They're naturally pissed off. They are French," said Dayan. "Ariel, it's one woman. How much trouble can she be?"

"I have a war to fight. I don't have time to play nursemaid, Moshe."

"And I'm not asking you to. She jumped with the French at Dien Bien Phu. I am sure she can take care of herself."

"I read her articles. At least she can write."

"Ben-Gurion thinks we could use the international press. She's an outsider. Her reports will be seen as unbiased."

"Unbiased. Great. Can we trust her?"

"The French say 'yes.' She has agreed not to report anything until after your initial operations have concluded."

"If she so much as looks sideways I will bind her and leave her for the scorpions."

"I think that's only fair," said Dayan.

October 26, 1956 – Paris, France

Coyle sat on the edge of the bed watching Brigitte getting ready to leave. "I don't understand. Why can't you tell me where you're going?"

"Tom, sweetheart, there are some times when I just can't tell you what I am doing. You're just going to need to trust me," said Brigitte as she moved into the closet.

She reached for her rucksack, jumpsuit, and jump boots. She opened a suitcase and placed them inside so Coyle would not see them.

"I do trust you. Is Bruno going?" said Coyle.

"No. I mean… I don't think so… Maybe… I don't know."

"How can you not know?"

"They didn't tell me."

"Who are they?"

"Tom, I love you, but I can't say anything more about where I am going or what I will be doing."

"When will you be back?"

"I don't know. But I will call you as soon as I can. It

may be a week or two."

"I am supposed to just wait around until you show up or call?"

"Yes. Now you know what most women feel like," said Brigitte giving him a kiss on the forehead.

FOUR

October 26, 1956 – London, England

Lloyd walked into Eden's office looking like an inmate on death row. Eden was reviewing operational plans.

"I'm here to report back on the signed documents you requested," said Lloyd.

"That had better mean you are happy to report that both copies are in your possession and are being locked away in the Tower of London," said Eden not bothering to look up.

"Unfortunately, that is not the case."

Eden looked up and said, "So, where the hell are they?"

"The Israelis refused to return their copy."

"Fucking Jews. I should have known better than to trust them. And the French?"

"They seemed to have misplaced their copy," said Lloyd knowing how stupid he sounded.

"They lost it?"

"Apparently."

"And you believed them?"

"They were very apologetic."

"Get out of my office."

Lloyd was only too happy to leave.

October 26, 1956 – Mediterranean Sea

Three squadrons of French aircraft flew over the Mediterranean Sea toward Israel. All the aircraft were marked with the black and yellow stripes that was to designate allied aircraft during the upcoming invasion. The first squadron was composed of French-built Dassault Mystère IVA jet fighters tasked with preventing air raids on Israeli cities. The second, equipped with American-built Republic F-84F Thunderstreaks, would provide ground support for Israeli, British and French forces once France entered the war. The third squadron was made up of French-built, twin-boom Nord Aviation Noratlas transports that would be used to parachute additional jeeps and other supplies to Israeli and French troops.

In addition to the aircraft, the French also sent three destroyers to protect the Israeli ports of Tel Aviv and Haifa from the Egyptian Navy or any other country that might enter the war against the allies. Discretion was essential. The French could not be seen to be helping the Israelis before they entered the war. Each aircraft and naval vessel had a plausible excuse for visiting Israel, such as refueling and resupply, repair, or training.

Last minute weapons and munitions shipments arrived by commercial freighter or were flown into the Israeli ports and airfields. The Israelis had never had so many new weapons and vehicles. Maintenance crews worked day and night to learn the procedures required to sustain the military's equipment in the field.

The buildup of new weapons and supplies put a strain on Israeli logistics. Jeeps, tanks and troop trucks had to be driven and shipped by rail to the various brigades stationed around the country. There wasn't enough time to transport everything that was delivered and needed. Some vehicles and supplies had to catch up with their designated units after they had already been deployed. Maintenance in the field was a logistical nightmare and spare parts for vehicles and weapons became a critical hindrance. The Israeli were known for their fighting abilities but they were always challenged by the logistics of keeping their armies adequately supplied in the field.

October 26, 1956 – Jerusalem, Israel

Harel knocked on Dayan's open office door. Dayan sat at his desk reviewing plans for the invasion.

"Do you have a few moments?" said Harel.

"Of course," said Dayan looking up from his paperwork.

"I've been thinking…" said Harel.

"Why does that worry me?" said Dayan.

"Not this time. We may have an opportunity."

"Go on."

"Are you aware that Field Marshal Amer and the Egyptian General Staff are in Syria to review plans for a potential invasion of Israel?"

"I read your intelligence report. That is not unusual."

"I agree. You are planning a general call up of our reserves before the invasion I assume?"

"Of course."

"What will Nasser do once he realizes that you are calling up our reserves?"

"He will call up his own."

"And who will he ask to do that?"

"The Field Marshal and his staff, of course."

"He will need to fly home, yes?"

"Yes," said Dayan trying to figure what Harel was driving at. And then it hit him… "On the eve of battle, we know when the Field Marshal of the Egyptian army will be returning to Cairo."

"Exactly," said Harel with a knowing smile.

"I want to kiss you," said Dayan.

"Please don't," said Harel.

October 26, 1956 – Israel

Over one hundred thousand Israeli reservists left their families and their jobs to report to their respective unit commanders. Public buses were commandeered by the army to convey the reservists to their units. A large number of the reservists were transported to the Jordanian border in hopes of convincing the Egyptians that it was

Jordan not Egypt that would receive the brunt of Israel's anger.

October 27, 1956 – Northern Syria

Field Marshal Abdel Hakim Amer and his staff were going over the plans of a proposed invasion of Israel with his Syrian counterpart and his staff, when Amer received a panicked call from Nasser ordering him back to Cairo immediately. After hanging up the phone, Amer turned to the Syrian General and said, "I'm sorry. The Israelis have sneezed and Nasser is convinced he has caught their cold once again. We must go."

"We understand," said the Syrian general. "It's too bad. We were so close to finishing. It would have saved you a trip back."

"Yes," said Amer considering, then turning to his chief Executive Officer. "Take the plane back with the rest of the staff. When you arrive, call up the reserves and prepare a status report on the current disposition of our troops."

"And if the president asks of your whereabouts?" said the Executive Officer.

"Tell him I was out inspecting the Syrian lines on the Israeli border and that I sent you back early so as not to waste any time carrying out his wishes. It will take me a few more hours to return."

"If we take the plane, how will you get back?"

"I'm sure the Syrian Air Force can accommodate me."

"Yes, Field Marshal," said the Executive Officer snapping to attention and saluting.

October 28th, 1956 – Mediterranean Sea

It was early morning when a lone Israeli pilot flew over the Mediterranean. He was flying a Gloster Meteor NF-13.

The Meteor was a first-generation British jet invented at the end of World War II and looked like Germany's Messerschmitt Me 262. It was well equipped to take on any prop-driven aircraft. Its wings were conventional straight wings while the newer NATO and Soviet jets used more aerodynamic swept-back wings.

The pilot was flying a long shot mission code named Operation Tarnegol. It was not unlike finding a needle in a haystack. He was told his target was an Egyptian Air Force Ilyushin Il-14, a Soviet-built twin engine cargo plane knick-named "Crate" by NATO. He was given the approximate route and flight schedule. He was to fly high using clouds as cover so as not to spook the intended target. It was a simple plan. Fly around in circles and hope the enemy aircraft shows up. After almost an hour and a half, he saw a cargo plane flying at five thousand feet appear from a cloud bank. He flew down to take a closer look.

The pilot and co-pilot in the Ilyushin cockpit did not see the Israeli jet as they passed below it. They knew they carried a valuable cargo of the Egyptian General Staff, but they were not expecting any trouble. The Egyptians and Israelis were at peace and they were flying over international waters. There was no reason for alarm.

The Meteor swept down behind the Ilyushin. The Israeli took his time lining up the plane's fuselage in his gunsights. His orders were to strafe the fuselage first in hopes of killing the Field Marshal then go after the aircraft's engines. The pilot squeezed the trigger and fired the aircraft's four 20-mm British Hispano MkV cannons mounted in its forward fuselage, just in front of the cockpit.

The burst of 20-mm shells ripped hundreds of holes into the Ilyushin's fuselage killing the entire Egyptian General Staff, three journalists and two crew members.

The Israeli pilot retargeted the engines one at a time and destroyed them. The burning plane crashed into the sea. There were no survivors. The Israeli pilot turned his aircraft toward shore and began thinking of what his wife was making for breakfast.

October 28th, 1956 – Jerusalem, Israel

Ben-Gurion and Dayan finished a dinner meeting during which they went over the final details of the operation. As Dayan prepared to depart, Ben-Gurion studied his countenance and said, "You seem worried, Moshe. That's not like you. You are usually so confident on the eve of battle."

"It's not the battle that concerns me," said Dayan. "It's the Americans. We have deceived them. Eisenhower is not a good friend to Israel but he is not an enemy either. I would hate to see that change."

"I doubt Eisenhower will do more than make a lot of noise. He hates war and he is facing a tough election. He cannot afford to lose the Jewish vote."

"Yes, but he is also a man of principle."

"Then he shall see our cause is just. Do not worry about the politics, Moshe. You have enough to worry about. Fight your battles well and let God handle the rest."

October 29, 1956 – Southern Israel

Brigitte rode a jeep into the camp bivouacking the 202nd Parachute Brigade just outside the port city of Eilat on the northern end of the Gulf of Aqaba. She thanked the driver and pulled her rucksack from the back of the jeep.

She saw Sharon talking with a group of officers. She had studied photos of him when he had fought in the Arab-Israeli War in 1948. He had gained weight along with greying hair. She approached and waited until he was finished before introducing herself, "Colonel Sharon, I am Brigitte Friang."

"I know who you are and what you will be… a pain in my backside," said Sharon.

"I assure you I will not."

"We shall see. You will be traveling with me in my jeep. I want to keep a close eye on you. Don't expect much sleep. We will be moving fast."

"We are not jumping?"

"No. If you'd like I can have you transferred to Major Eitan's 890th Para Battalion. They will be jumping."

"No. I would prefer to stay with you. I hear you are a man of action."

"Do not flatter me, Miss Friang. I do not have the time."

"Please call me Brigitte."

"Fine. Brigitte, get some sleep. You're going to need it. We move out at 0150," said Sharon moving off. "And don't forget to pee. We don't stop for potty-breaks."

October 29, 1956 – Sinai, Egypt

It was just past noon. The Sinai was still and desolate. The ground was hard, the clay soil baked by the sun and lack of water. It was a hard life for those that lived here. Few did. Most chose to live in the mountains where there were springs and some vegetation for their goats. But even in the mountains, little grew. Rocks of all sizes and shapes covered most of the land. It was a farmer's nightmare.

Telephone poles broke the barren landscape. Their wires hummed in the wind. The harmony was broken by the thrum of aircraft engines approaching from the northeast. A group of four P-51 Mustangs appeared over the horizon. They had a blue Star of David against a white circle painted on their wings and mid-fuselage. The P-51 World War II fighter was tough and dependable but could not compete with the new jets in air-to-air combat. It still had a role to play in air-to-ground support. There were still some missions better suited for slower aircraft. The formation broke, and the individual fighters peeled off in different directions.

One of the aircraft swooped down close to the desert floor. The pilot kept his speed as he flew directly toward the line of telephone poles spread out across the desert. At the last moment, he twisted his aircraft sideways pulling up slightly so the end of his left wing did not plow into the ground. The wing hit the telephone wires stretched between two poles and snapped them in two. The ends of the wires fell to the earth.

Communications were cut, severely crippling the Egyptian army's command and control, leaving the thirty thousand troops in the Egyptian 3rd Infantry and 8th Palestinian Divisions completely in the dark and without instructions. The pilot flew on, keeping low to the ground and away from any villages where he might be spotted. There were more telephone wires to be cut deep in the Sinai.

October 29, 1956 – Central Sinai

Late in the afternoon, sixteen Douglas C-47 Dakotas – escorted by Meteors, Ouragans, and Mystère fighter jets – carried the Israeli 890th Paratrooper Battalion across the Israeli border into Egypt. They flew one hundred and thirty miles behind enemy lines to the eastern side of the Mitla Pass just thirty miles east of the Suez Canal. It was the threat of hostilities so close to the vital shipping lanes that would give the British and French a pretext to intervene.

Major Rafael Eitan jumped with the first group of paratroopers and landed safely. He designated a rally point and ensured that any wounded were attended to by his medics. Two of his paratroopers had broken their legs. That kind of loss was to be expected with a jump this size.

He would arrange for their evacuation as soon as possible but at the moment he needed to gather his men back into a fighting unit with defensive positions.

The ground before the pass was flat and ideal for landing paratroopers. It was not ideal for defending the lightly armored paratroopers and offered no cover. It was not a hard jump in the sense that he could see all of his men and where they were landing. *But so can the Egyptians*, he thought as he looked toward the mountain pass three miles in the distance. *They could already be waiting.*

His mission was simple. Hold the mouth of the pass until Sharon arrived with the rest of the brigade. He didn't like the plan and thought his battalion should at the very least move into the mountains where there was good cover. He had three hundred and ninety-four men mostly armed with Uzi submachine guns and a few light machine guns. They would be of little use against the Egyptian jets and tanks. In folds of the mountain they would stand a chance. They could hide. But those were not his orders and he obeyed orders.

He and his men moved up to within a mile of the mouth of the canyon. They used their portable shovels to dig foxholes and trenches. It was hard work in the desert heat. The first few inches of soil were clay baked hard by the sun. After that it got a little easier. There was no natural cover, so the holes had to be deep. He and his men knew what was coming. It was going to be a hard fight. He sent out reconnaissance units in all directions. He wanted to know what was coming before it arrived. He needed time to prepare.

After sunset, transport aircraft parachuted eight jeeps, four 116-mm recoilless guns, two 120-mm mortars, extra ammunition and food to Eitan and his men.

October 29, 1956 – Algiers, Algeria

Coyle walked into the reception area of the transportation wing commander's office. "You may go right in, Monsieur Coyle. The Colonel is expecting you," said the receptionist.

Coyle entered the office to find Colonel Rodolphe Cerf sitting behind his desk. "Monsieur Coyle, please have a seat," said Cerf.

"Why the urgency? I was scheduled to fly this morning," said Coyle as he sat across from the Cerf.

"Yes, well…I am afraid I have some bad news. We have decided to terminate your contract, effective immediately."

"What? Why? Did I do something wrong?"

"On the contrary, you are an excellent pilot."

"Then why the cold shoulder?"

"Cold shoulder?"

"Why are you firing me?"

"Ah. Political necessity has required the French Air Force to loan out your C-119 for a short amount of time. We will not need your services until it is returned."

"Okay. A little notice would have been nice."

"I just found out myself an hour ago. The good news is that the Spanish transportation company that will be borrowing the C-119 would like to hire you as the pilot."

"And my crew?"

"Unfortunately, they are French and cannot be allowed to go with you. The Spanish will be supplying you with a new crew. I have been assured they are familiar with the operation of twin-engine, heavy-lift aircraft. The Spanish will ask you to deliver two jeeps and a shipment of spare vehicle parts by parachute to an undisclosed location in the Sinai desert."

"The Sinai?"

"Yes. There is an Israeli military convoy in badly need of the replacement jeeps and spare parts to repair their vehicles. Vehicles sold them by the French government. France, of course, cannot be seen to help the Israelis since they have invaded Egypt. We are selling the parts to a company in Spain. What the Spanish company chooses to do with the parts once in their possession is completely up to them."

"A political switch-a-roo."

"Switch-a-roo?"

"A shell game."

"Shell game?"

"Never mind. Please go on."

"When you have completed your mission with the Spaniards and your plane is returned, we would like to rehire you with an appropriate signing bonus, of course."

"And if I refuse?"

"Why would you refuse?"

"Because I don't like being played the fool."

"I see," said Cerf. "Perhaps you would see the mission in a better light if you knew that Brigitte Friang is with the Israeli convoy."

"Brigitte is in the Sinai?" said Coyle.

"From what I have been told... yes."

Coyle took a moment to consider and said, "Alright, Colonel. You've got yourself a deal."

October 29, 1956 – Southern Israel.

Sharon's jeep was at the head of a mixed column of jeeps, trucks, half-tracks, armored cars and French-made MX-13 light tanks. The trucks were pulling artillery guns. Brigitte sat in the backseat of the jeep trying to get comfortable. Sharon's radio operator sat across from her. There was little room because of the two extra tires, jugs of water, four rucksacks and multiple radios. She finally decided to sit on her own rucksack which gave a little more room at her feet. She wore her khaki jumpsuit, a floppy-brimmed bush hat buttoned on one side the way the Australians like to wear them, and a pair of sunglasses. She thought about putting on some suntan lotion but knew it would just cake

73

up from the dust once the jeep started moving. She elected to burn.

A squadron of twenty-two P-51 Mustangs flew overhead and out into the desert mountains. Their mission was to strafe and bomb anything and anyone in the path of the convoy.

Sharon gave the signal to move out. The convoy drove up the highway along the Israeli border. Their mission was to reach Major Eitan's para battalion at the mouth of the Mitla pass within thirty-six hours. It was a very tight schedule.

October 29, 1956 – Cairo, Egypt

Nasser loved spending time with his family. It was the only time he could relax, and his aides had strict orders not to disturb him unless it was a life and death emergency. He was watching his son blow out the candles on his birthday cake when he received word from one of his aides that the Israelis had crossed the border into Egypt. He considered staying with his family until his boy had opened his presents. After all, there had been so many reports of Israeli incursions. Most were just simple raids to avenge an attack on one of their villages by the Fedayeen. But this report seemed different somehow and he decided to excuse himself, much to his family's disappointment.

He walked to his office inside the presidential palace and listened as his intelligence officers made their reports. Four different sightings of Israeli forces crossing the border and all of them reported to be brigade strength. There was also a sighting of paratroopers dropping in the valley near the Mitla Pass. He didn't like it. "Tell General Amer I would like to speak with him as soon as possible," said Nasser to one of his aides.

Amer walked down the hall and entered Nasser's office. Allah had saved Field Marshal Amer from the Israeli jet and he had offered prayers of thanks on his flight back to Egypt later that day. He was emotionally drained after receiving word that his entire staff was missing and presumed dead. Nasser was demanding reports on the Israeli troop movements every hour.

Amer told Nasser he believed Jordan was the Israelis' intended target. The troops that were called up were transported to the Jordanian border and a good share of their armor and artillery had been transported to Eilat. The Israelis had often complained about their lack of access to the Gulf of Aqaba. Amer guessed that they were going to attack the Jordanian port just across their northern border. By seizing the Jordanian port, Nasser would be forced to allow cargo ships to freely navigate the bay. If not, the Jordanians would be cut off and their economy crippled. While Nasser had no great love for Jordan and its king, he had promised to be the leader of all the Arab people, and that included the Jordanians. "We should be prepared to help the Jordanians and take back the port of Aqaba," said Amer to Nasser. "Their king will owe us, and the Jordanian people will see you as their savior."

"Yes. Yes. But what about the reports of Israeli paratroopers dropping into the Sinai?" said Nasser

"Raiding parties. Nothing we have not seen before. The local police units are well armed and will handle them."

"I see. And the Israeli troop movement away from the Jordanian border?" said Nasser.

"A ruse. The Israelis playing games, trying to confuse the Jordanians. Their moves are so transparent."

"And your intelligence staff agrees with you?"

"Unfortunately, most of my staff was lost in the attack over the Mediterranean. God rest their souls."

"I am sorry for your loss. They were great patriots and will be missed."

"But if they were still here, I believe they would agree with me."

"I see."

"As a precaution, I suggest we send our destroyer *Ibrahim el Awal* to Haifa. If the Israelis try anything we can bombard the port and destroy their coastal oil installations."

"Yes. Very good. Keep me updated."

"Yes, your excellency."

Nasser left Amer's office and walked back to his own. Nasser trusted Amer. They had known each other for many years and Amer had always been loyal. That is why Nasser gave him the position of head of the Egyptian Armed Forces even though Amer had little practical combat experience. Nasser needed the military's support to stay in power.

Most of the Egyptian military officers were appointed through family or political connections. Promotions were based on perceived loyalty, not on merit. The officers did not associate with the non-commissioned soldiers who they saw as beneath them. This general attitude created morale problems. While the Egyptian soldiers felt a duty to fight for their country, they did not believe their officers had their best interests at heart and were often reluctant to obey orders that would put them in harm's way. It was a military culture where obedience was based on threats and fear rather than pride and honor.

The Egyptian forces were substantial and had been built up since Nasser became Egypt's leader. The air force was particularly impressive with its new Soviet-built MiG-15 jet fighters and I1-28 jet bombers. The arms deal had replaced an abundance of the military's obsolete equipment.

The Egyptian army under General Amer's command had a mobilized strength of one hundred thousand soldiers. It was grouped into two main bodies. The first had the mission to protect the Sinai and the Gaza Strip from Israeli invasion. The second was tasked with protecting the canal zone from possible Western actions.

The Sinai forces included the 3rd Infantry Division, the Palestinian Division and the 2nd Motorized Border Battalion. The canal zone was guarded by the 2nd Infantry Division and the 1st Armored Brigade. In all there were eighteen brigades that the Egyptians could deploy against any invading force. The infantry soldiers were equipped with Soviet-built 7.62-mm carbines.

Each infantry brigade was supported by an artillery battery of Soviet 122-mm or British 25-pounder guns. They also had an anti-tank company using 17-pounder or 57-mm guns. There were also four heavy mortar regiments each with three batteries of 120-mm mortars.

The three armored brigades had a variety of trucks, armored personnel carriers and Soviet-built BTR-152 scout cars. They were also equipped with Soviet T-34s and JS-3s tanks and British Centurion MK-3s tanks. A few units even hand American-made Sherman tanks. This mixing of British, Soviet and American vehicles made maintenance of the armored brigades a logistical nightmare. Spare parts had to be carried for all types of vehicles and were not interchangeable. Even fueling was a problem. The Soviet-built vehicles used diesel while the British and American-built vehicles used petrol. This meant that each refueling unit had to carry large quantities of both types of fuel.

The anti-aircraft brigades were probably the best trained of all the Egyptian units. They had high morale and were diligent with their training efforts. They were equipped with Czech-built long barrel 20-mm cannons, 30-mm Hispano and 40-mm Bofors light anti-aircraft guns. The anti-aircraft units were deployed at strategic points on every airfield, along the Canal Zone, and at Port Said.

Technically, the Egyptian army could match any military force in the Middle East or North Africa except for Algeria, which was French. However, leadership, training and esprit de corps were questionable.

The regular army was backed up by National Guard units manned by one hundred thousand volunteers and a strong police force. Their training was poor compared to the military and their weapons, early models of British Lee Enfield .303 rifles, were antiquated. Even with the inferior weapons the National Guard and the police force were still useful while guarding strategic buildings and positions. Most of the volunteers were brave and would hold their ground during a fight. Their role was defensive rather than offensive.

The Egyptian Navy had four destroyers, seven escort vessels, two corvettes and eight wooden mine ships. The biggest threat came from the smallest vessels in the Egyptian Navy - fourteen motor torpedo boats. A well-placed torpedo could sink even the mightiest of warships. Even with the threat of torpedoes, the war planners in London, Paris and Jerusalem didn't feel the Egyptian Navy was much of a threat and paid it little heed.

They were more concerned about the Egyptian civilians that would need to be properly managed after Nasser surrendered. Without doubt there would be some Egyptians that would go on fighting as guerillas or terrorists. France already had its hands full fighting the Algerians and was not anxious to occupy another country with a large and unruly civilian population. It was conceivable that the fighting could go on well after the Egyptians surrendered.

October 29, 1956 – Quntilla, Egypt

Quntilla was in the northeastern desert of Sinai just a few kilometers past the Israeli-Egyptian border. It was more of an Egyptian outpost than a town. Its soul function seemed to be as a warning beacon to the rest of the Egyptian forces on the Sinai. It had also been a staging area for cross-border Fedayeen raids on the Israeli towns near the border. Sharon wanted his pound of flesh and decided the detour was worth it, even though he and his men had an incredibly tight schedule to meet.

It was late in the afternoon when the 202nd arrived. Sharon sent two companies of paratroopers around the back of the town. The sun was behind the Israeli forces and would give them a distinct advantage if they could attack before nightfall.

Only seven of the French-made AMX light tanks were available for the first incursion into Egypt. The other six tanks were still in transit. Sharon could not afford any more time and decided to use what was available. He sent his reconnaissance units to scout the town while his artillery and mortar teams set up and his paratroopers moved into position.

The recon units reported back that there was only one company of Egyptian soldiers in the town. *Hardly worth the effort,* thought Sharon. *Still, it will be good to blood the men with a quick victory.*

He gave the order to fire. A barrage of 75-mm shells from the tanks and artillery slammed into the town and the Egyptians ran for cover. Israeli 120-mm mortars followed up the artillery and tank barrage, tearing up the few buildings in the town and showering the Egyptians with rocks and chunks of hardened clay.

Seventy thousand feet above, Powers was flying his U2 on yet another reconnaissance mission. This was his third mission in less than a week and he was sure to be grounded by the flight doctors after this one. It was unusual to see much activity on the ground below. The plane flew so high that everything looked like specks of dirt and sand unless it was very large, like a ship or a bridge. Powers was surprised when he saw small flashes of light followed by black puffs of smoke. He couldn't tell who was firing on whom, but he was fairly sure people were dying, judging by the number of tiny explosions. *So that is what war looks like,* he thought.

He pressed the record button on the camera remote several times and shot a series of high-resolution photographs of the activity below. Although few would be allowed to ever see the photographs, he was capturing the first images of the Sinai War. He was an observer of a critical moment in history and he could tell no one. Such was the life of a CIA reconnaissance pilot.

On the desert below, Sharon saw an opportunity for a quick victory during the Egyptians' initial confusion. He sent mounted paratroopers into the front of the outpost in the hopes of overrunning the Egyptian positions before they could organize their defenses. As the vehicles approached two of his halftracks and one of his jeeps exploded from a well-hidden minefield. The frontal attack was stalled as the Israelis moved to rescue the wounded soldiers from the demolished vehicles.

The paratroopers in the rear of the town attacked and easily overran the Egyptian positions. The battle was over in less than fifteen minutes. The Israelis had first blood.

There was no time to celebrate. Sharon ordered the seventy-two prisoners escorted back across the border into Israel where they could be interrogated. Only one of Sharon's men had been killed and a few others had light wounds. The brigade remounted their vehicles and moved on into the hills as the sun disappeared into the west.

October 29, 1956 – Washington D.C., USA

Eisenhower was just sitting down to breakfast on the patio of the White House. Allen Dulles approached with the reconnaissance photos shot by Powers in a folder tucked under his arm and said, "They've done it. The Israelis have crossed the border in strength. Four brigades at least. There is also word of paratroopers near the Suez Canal. Eisenhower set down his grapefruit knife. He had lost his appetite. He hated war. After World War II, he had had his fill and prayed never to see another. He stared out at the falling leaves on the trees that surround the White House grounds. "I always loved the fall colors," he said. "Why do the Israelis have to fuck up a nice autumn morning?"

"What are we going to do?" said Allen Dulles. "I mean, it's the Israelis. If we try to stop them, you'll lose the Jewish vote."

"If you think I give two shits about the election right now, you don't know me, Allen."

"I'm sorry, Mr. President. You're right. What do you want me to do?"

"Easy. Come up with a miracle." said Eisenhower.

"Yes, sir. I'll work on it."

"In the meantime, find your brother and tell him we need to draft a letter to the U.N."

"Yes, sir. Right away," said Allen Dulles moving off and leaving Eisenhower with his thoughts. Very dark thoughts. He knew what war meant more than most and he feared for the mothers and fathers of the sons that would fight.

FIVE

October 29, 1956 - Kafr Qasim, Israel

At 4:30 pm, a troop transport carried a platoon of border police into the Israeli village of Kafr Qasim on the Jordanian border. The village was mostly populated by Arab Muslims sympathetic to the Egyptian cause. The Israeli leaders were concerned that if Jordan entered the war, the Arabs in the border towns would riot and commit acts of terrorism. It was decided to declare and enforce a 5pm to 6am curfew in all Arab border towns, starting on the night of the Israeli invasion.

Lieutenant Gabriel Dahan, the unit commander, stepped from his jeep and was approached by a sergeant already in the town. "I told the mayor about the curfew. He is concerned that we didn't give the people enough warning."

"Of course, he is," said Dahan. "They needed time to plan their resistance and we didn't give it to him."

"He says there are about four hundred villagers working the nearby farms and they don't usually come back into town until after sundown."

"That is unfortunate for them."

"Surely you do not want us to shoot civilians?"

"That is what happens when people don't respect authority."

"But those farm workers don't— "

"Enough, Sergeant. We are on the verge of war with these people. This is no time for sentiment." said Dahan interrupting. "You have your orders."

"Yes, sir," said the sergeant snapping to attention and saluting before moving off.

Roadblocks were established on the main roads leading in and out of the village. At six o'clock in the evening, a flatbed truck with wooden siderails pulled to a stop at one of the roadblocks. The twenty-eight farm workers riding in the back of the truck took out their identification papers and offered them to the soldiers. To their surprise, the soldiers were not interested in their papers and waved them off. The sergeant in charge of the roadblock said, "Cut them down."

The soldiers obeyed and opened fire with their Uzi machineguns. The defenseless passengers were trapped in the back of the truck. Many were children between the ages of eight and seventeen. The Muslims fell like cut timber in a forest, one on top of another, until there was nobody standing in the back of the truck.

Clashes with angry family members and friends of the fallen continued throughout the night. By morning, forty-nine civilians had been killed and thirteen severely wounded. No Israeli police were killed during the operation.

When Ben-Gurion heard the news of the Kafr Qasim Massacre he was furious and ordered a full investigation. He also ordered a two-month news blackout on the matter so as not to enflame the Muslims living in Israel any further.

October 29, 1956 – London, England

It was early evening. U.S. Ambassador to Britain, Winthrop Aldrich, had opera tickets. He loved the opera, especially at Covent Garden – the Royal Opera House. It was a magnificent venue. He loved dressing up in a tuxedo for the event. He knew it was pageantry but he didn't care. He looked good in his tux. He was already standing by the front door when he heard the doorbell ring. He took a quick glance at his watch as he went to open the door.

He was perturbed when a messenger from the Foreign Office appeared on his doorstep and informed him that the British Foreign Secretary would like to see him as soon as possible. He knew that last minute calls by the Foreign Secretary went with the job, but why did they always need to happen when he had such good seats. Resigned, he grabbed his formal coat and top hat and headed out.

Aldrich was escorted into the Foreign Secretary's office where Lloyd was waiting. "Thank you for coming," said Lloyd.

"Of course, Mister Secretary," said Aldrich.

"I hope you weren't heading out somewhere special for the evening," said Lloyd referring to Aldrich's formal wear.

"No. No. Just another embassy party. How may I assist you?" said Aldrich hoping to move things along and catch the second act.

"I understand Lodge will be speaking at the U.N. tomorrow and that he plans to label Israel the aggressor in their spat with the Egyptians."

"Spat? They invaded with four brigades."

"Nonetheless, if they are labeled an aggressor it could activate the Tripartite Declaration of 1950 and we could be forced to defend Egypt against the Israelis."

"And what is wrong with that? The Israelis should cease and desist immediately."

"Yes, but we do not want to encourage Nasser. He brought this upon himself by refusing to recognize the Israelis and colluding with the other Arab nations to attack Israel."

"The Egyptians have been doing that for years. They are hollow threats."

"Not anymore. They are well-armed with Soviet weapons and they intend to use them."

"If you have some intelligence about an impending Egyptian attack that you would like to share, I am all ears."

"It's common knowledge that the Egyptians, and especially Nasser, hate the Israelis and want them wiped off the map. Nasser is giving the Fedayeen free rein to attack the Israeli settlements along the border. The Israelis have a right to defend themselves."

"Again, old news. Besides, the Israelis have dropped paratroopers at the Mitla Pass. That's an awful long way from the border."

"Britain cannot side with Nasser. It would destroy our relationship with Iraq, Jordan and Syria. Please tell Eisenhower to refrain from labeling the Israelis an aggressor."

"First of all, I don't tell President Eisenhower anything. I inform him when he asks my opinion. Second, my opinion is that you are barking up the wrong tree. I believe the Israelis are an aggressor and should be labeled as such."

"Alright. Then ask him to hold for one day. France and Britain are working on a solution that we think might be equitable to all parties involved."

"Really? What might that be?"

"I don't have time to go into the details. But Prime Minister Mollet and his Foreign Minister Pineau are on their way to 10 Downing Street as we speak. I would ask that America take pause for the sake of the alliance."

Aldrich held his tongue. Lloyd was playing the good ole' boy card and America was just supposed to follow along like an ox pulling a cart. He didn't like it one bit. "I will speak with the President but I cannot be sure what he will say."

"Thank, Mr. Ambassador. That is all I ask."

"I expect you will keep us well informed?"

"Of course. I hope you have a pleasant evening. My aide will show you out," said Lloyd, dismissing Aldrich in typical British fashion.

October 29, 1956 - Alexandria, Egypt

The crew of the *ENS Ibrahim el-Awal*, an Egyptian hunt-class destroyer, loaded supplies and ammunition from the dock. There wasn't much time before they were due to sail. Many of the young crew members had never been in battle and were noticeably nervous. The officers did their best to keep them busy and focused on the task at hand.

The *Ibrahim* was originally named the *HMS Mendip*. It was a British Royal Navy vessel that had been decommissioned after World War II because the ship's hull was considered unstable in the open ocean. The British sold it to China Nationalists but reneged on the deal when it became clear that the Maoists were overrunning the mainland and the civil war in China would soon draw to an end with the communists winning. The British saw no value in turning over a destroyer to the Chinese Communists which they one day may need to fight. They canceled the deal while the destroyer was en route up the Yangtze river and sent another destroyer to reclaim it. The Chinese objected but they didn't want to start a war with the British over a well-used naval vessel… at least not yet.

The destroyer was on its way back to London when the Egyptians offered to purchase it. The British were only too happy to rid themselves of the obsolete vessel and gave the Egyptians a good price based on the ship's scrap-value. When the destroyer traveled through the Suez Canal, the British captain docked the vessel as it approached the northern end. He and his crew stepped off the ship. The Egyptian captain and his crew stepped on and the deal was done. The British even left the Egyptians two months of rations in the ship's galley.

The Egyptians had one hundred and forty-six officers and enlisted men manning the vessel. The British Navy had taken good care of the *Ibrahim* as they did with all their vessels. It was a point of pride for the world-class British navy. However, the ship was lightly armored and its weapons were smaller than most of the newer ships in its class. The *Ibrahim's* main armament consisted of two twin 4-inch gun turrets operated remotely. The main guns fired thirty-five pound shells accurately up to seven miles. Its radar was based on older technology and was only capable of spotting surface vessels six to eight miles out and aircraft twelve miles out. In an age of warfare where jets traveled at almost six hundred miles per hour that gave the ship's defenses too little warning before they were attacked. It was an obsolete hand-me-down but the Egyptians made the most of it.

On the bridge of the *Ibrahim*, Major Rushdie Tamsyn stood across the navigational table from Lieutenant Ali Ganim. Tamsyn was twenty-seven years old, young for a commander of one of Egypt's most powerful warships. A nautical map was spread out and held down with a coffee cup and several lengths of lead weights to keep it from rolling up. The map showed the northern coastline of Egypt and western Israel along with the shipping lanes of the Mediterranean Sea. "We make our way along the coast. We stay out of the shipping lanes and avoid any patrol boats. Hopefully, no one will spot us. We should reach Haifa tomorrow morning. With luck, the Israelis won't know we are coming."

"And if we are discovered?" said Ganim.

"Maybe we fight. It doesn't matter. Once we start bombarding the oil refineries and the harbor, the Israelis will send their destroyers to stop us."

"How many do you expect?"

"I don't know. The Israeli ships tend to be kept in groups and attack as a pack."

"Like wolves?"

"Yes. Like wolves. Once we have inflicted damage to their facilities and destroyed their ships, we break off the engagement and head for Lebanon."

"Why Lebanon?"

"It's neutral. The Israeli's won't attack us once we reach their harbor in Beirut."

"So, when do we go back to Egypt?"

"When it's over. President Nasser doesn't want to lose our vessel. We strike and then run for safety. Those are our orders and we will carry them out."

"Yes, Captain."

"We sail in one hour. Make sure the ship and men are ready," said Tamsyn as he moved off. He was confident and surprisingly serious for such a young man. He loved the navy and his country. He was proud of his crew and drilled them to sharpen their skills in battle whenever possible. The Egyptian navy was notoriously stingy about expending ammunition during training. They believed the expensive shells were better used killing Israelis.

October 29, 1956 – London, England

It was late in the evening when Mollet and Pineau met with Eden at 10 Downing Street. There was very little to discuss. Everything had already been decided. The meeting was a façade for the Americans and the U.N. The French and British needed to look like they were working feverously to come up with a solution to the Israeli invasion. Instead, they drank scotch. "I am concerned that we are lying to the Americans. If Eisenhower finds out what we are doing—" said Mollet.

"He won't find out as long as we stick to the plan and keep our heads cool," said Eden.

"And if he does?"

"So, what if he does? What is he going to do? Side with Egypt against his greatest allies? Trust me, Eisenhower is far more concerned about the Soviets then he is about the Egyptians or the Israelis. He needs Britain and France to help check Soviet aggression. Besides, it is in America's interests to have the Suez Canal secured and functioning properly. They need oil too. If we hand him a done deal, Eisenhower will do nothing," said Eden followed by a long sip of his scotch.

October 29, 1956 – Eilat, Israel

The Israeli 9th Infantry Brigade waited until the last of Sharon's convoy had left Eilat so as not to confuse the different units. The commander of the 9th, Colonel Abraham Yoffe, had learnt the hard way to avoid confusion when it came to the men under his command. He was a serious man.

Once clear, the convoy of jeeps and trucks of the 9th headed south on the coastal highway paralleling the Gulf of Aqaba and crossed the Egyptian border. They were a ragtag group of soldiers mostly made up of home guard and other reservists. They were supplied by the leftovers from the other brigades in the Israeli Defense Forces. Their weapons were obsolete and many needed repair. Some of the older weapons only had a few rounds of ammunition and were intended to be discarded when the last round was fired. The 9th didn't have any tanks. It had its own artillery but most of the rifling inside the barrels had been ground smooth from too much use. There was some question as to their accuracy but nobody wanted to test them because they had so few shells. The artillery specialists were sure that the weapons would make a lot of noise during a firefight and could be used to discourage the enemy. Besides… they could get lucky and hit something important.

The Israeli generals liked to use the 9th as a diversionary force and to hold installations already captured. It was felt they would be nothing more than cannon fodder in a real battle. They may not have been the best soldiers and their uniforms didn't match, but they were brave and they had families and employers back home that depended on them.

Their mission was to capture Ras al-Naqb, a coastal town on the shores of the Straits of Tiran. It would be used as a staging area for an assault on Sharm el-Sheikh - a key strategic port and Egyptian naval base on the Red Sea. It was the ships from the Sharm el-Sheikh naval base and the 6-inch guns at nearby Ras Nasrani that enforced the blockade that kept Israeli ships from passing through the Straits of Tiran.

Yoffe and Major Heman Rocker, his Executive Officer, rode in the lead vehicle as the column approached a low rise in the mostly flat terrain. Lieutenant Lemuel Bloom, a recon platoon commander, stood at the base of the rise and waved with both his arms. Yoffe ordered the convoy to stop, climbed out of the vehicle and approached Bloom. "How does it look, Lieutenant?" said Yoffe.

"Not good. You can see for yourself. It's just over that rise," said Bloom.

With Bloom in the lead, Yoffe, and Rocker climbed a small rise that shielded the convoy from view. They laid flat on their bellies and crawled to the top. One mile in the distance was Ras al-Naqb. They took out their binoculars to study the town's layout and defenses. "As you can see, the northern edge of the town is defended with artillery and heavy machineguns. The Egyptians are well dug in," said Bloom.

"You'd think they were expecting us," said Rocker.

"A frontal assault would be suicidal. They would rip us to shreds. Is there another way?" said Yoffe.

"The eastern side is flanked by the Gulf of Aqaba. There are several patrol boats armed with 50-cals that patrol the coast."

"That's not a concern. I wasn't planning on getting wet anyway," said Yoffe.

"Right," said Bloom. "The western side is flat and gives their guns a clear field of fire. The southern side of the town is the least protected and is surrounded by low hills. They keep it well patrolled but there are only a few machinegun emplacements and no artillery."

"I like that. Let's do that," said Rocker.

"So how do we get there without being detected?" said Yoffe.

"I found a wadi."

"A wadi?" said Rocker.

"Yeah. You know… a dried-up riverbed," said Bloom.

"I know what a wadi is. I just don't know why it helps us," said Rocker.

"I was getting to that part," said Bloom showing them the wadi's path on a small map he retrieved from his pocket. "It leads right into the hills behind the town. We can use the hills to the west to cover our approach then duck down into the wadi."

"Can our vehicles traverse it?" said Yoffe.

"I doubt it. The ground is very uneven. Besides the engine noise might tip them off."

"So, we go on foot and hope to god they don't discover us?"

"That's what I would suggest," said Bloom.

"Well done, Lieutenant," said Yoffe.

"Yeah, ya sneaky bastard," said Rocker playfully slugging Bloom in the shoulder.

It was approaching midnight when Bloom took the lead with Yoffe right behind him. They were followed by six hundred riflemen as they made their way through the hills to the west of the town. Yoffe had decided to lead the raid himself. He was a veteran fighter. He knew how to keep a level head and not panic no matter how bad things seemed at the time. If anything went wrong, he was the battalion's best chance of survival.

Bloom asked Yoffe to keep the battalion hidden in the hills while he alone went in to the wadi to ensure they were indeed alone. He disappeared into the darkness and slipped into the dry riverbed.

He moved quietly for about three hundred yards before he heard something up ahead in the darkness. He slowed and chambered a round into his Uzi submachinegun. He didn't dare use his flashlight. He moved forward, his eyes trying to catch a glimpse of whoever was in front of him before they got a glimpse of him. He heard something moving through the scrub brush to his left. He whipped the barrel of his gun around. Whatever was out there was moving closer. He slipped his finger into the trigger-guard and onto the trigger. He lined up his shot to where he thought the intruder would appear. And then he saw... a goat walking toward him. He relaxed and had the sudden urge to pee. The goat was followed by several more. It was a small herd. The goat's herder must have been using the wadi to keep the goats from wandering too far off during the night. But where was the herder? Had he seen Bloom and gone back to the town to warn the Egyptian soldiers stationed there?

Bloom heard another noise. This time he was sure it was human. It was voices whispering in Arabic. The voices were young, like that of teenagers. He moved toward a small rise where several bushes were growing. He used the barrel of his Uzi to push back the branches of one of the bushes. A teenage boy and girl were in the throes of passion, lying on a blanket. They didn't notice him standing above them until he said in Arabic, "Either of you lose a goat?"

They both snapped around, startled. The girl grabbed for her blouse and covered herself. The boy just stared at the gun barrel wide-eyed. Bloom shushed them with a finger to his lips.

Bloom returned to retrieve his commander and the battalion. They slipped into the wadi and moved along the riverbed. They came up to the goats and moved through the herd. Bloom explained about the young goat herder and his girlfriend. They were both from the town. Bloom had tied them up. He didn't have a gag, so he told them he would shoot them if they made any noise. They believed him and stayed as quiet as synagogue mice.

Yoffe signaled for his men to stop near the end of the wadi. He and Bloom moved to the edge of the riverbed and peered over the embankment.

They were about fifty feet from the closest hill behind the town. There was a patrol of six Egyptian soldiers keeping an eye on the hills. "Shit," said Yoffe quietly.

"They weren't here a few hours ago," said Bloom.

"They must've gotten the news that we crossed into the Sinai and they aren't taking any chances."

"There are only six of them. Maybe we can overpower them before they can warn the others."

"We'd have to be pretty lucky to get all six without one shouting out and I'm not feeling very lucky at the moment," said Yoffe considering. "Wait a minute… I've got an idea."

Twelve Israeli soldiers lifted the goat herd up the embankment. Bloom grabbed a bush branch and used it to herd the goats toward the Egyptian patrol. He moved up as far as he dared to ensure the goats were heading in the right direction. Then he ducked down and crawled back into the wadi on his belly.

The goats could not find anything to eat on the barren desert floor and wandered toward the hills. The Egyptians heard and then saw them coming. "Where's their owner?" said one of the soldiers.

"Maybe they're lost," said another.

"Anybody up for some roast goat?" said a third.

"I could eat," said the corporal leading the patrol.

The patrol moved toward the goats into the darkness of the desert and away from the back of the town.

Yoffe and his men slipped over the embankment and into the cover of the hills behind the town without being seen. They laid down an ambush for the patrol in case they returned.

The battalion formed a skirmish line along the hillside. On Yoffe's signal, the battalion moved in unison toward the town. Yoffe had no real idea what he and his men would find in the town, but he knew they needed to move fast if they were going to keep the element of surprise. It worked.

The Israelis moved through the streets and alleys of the town like a virus invading a body. Most of the Egyptian soldiers were asleep and easily overpowered. The fortified outposts at the front of the town were caught completely by surprise and never got their guns turned in the right direction before they were overrun.

Yoffe and the 9th Brigade had accomplished the impossible. They had captured a well-fortified position around a key strategic point and captured over six hundred enemy soldiers without firing one shot and without the loss of life on either side; Israeli or Egyptian. And the best trophy of all was the capture of the Egyptian artillery that they would use to replace their own. His men celebrated. Yoffe couldn't help but smile a little.

October 29, 1956 – Cairo, Egypt

The British embassy in Cairo was a beehive of activity. Eight trashcan incinerators had been set up on the lawn and one staffer was given the job of stirring the ashes as they were created, allowing oxygen to reach the fire. There was no time to separate the top-secret cables and documents from everyday paperwork. Everything within the embassy was burned. It was a long night.

October 30, 1956 - Al-Qusaymah, Egypt

It was still dark when the Israeli 4th Infantry brigade, under the command of Colonel Josef Harpaz, approached the town of al-Qusaymah in northern Sinai. Al-Qusaymah was important to the Israelis for three reasons. First, it was the geographical center for any military force entering the Sinai from the north, and therefore strategically important. Second, the Israelis planned on using the town as a jumping off point for their attack on Abu Ageila. Third, Al-Qusaymah protected Sharon's 202nd Airborne Brigade's northern flank as it advanced toward the Mitla Pass.

It was three in the morning when Harpaz stopped his column and went forward to investigate with his binoculars. His infantry had ridden in trucks and commandeered buses as far as they could before the sand of the desert became too much for the wheels. When a vehicle lost traction in the sand, the men riding in back would dismount and another vehicle with a tow cable would pull it free. It was a time-consuming process and their advance slowed to a crawl. When more vehicles were stuck than moving, Harpaz gave the order to abandon the vehicles and continue on foot. His men groaned. Many of the soldiers in his command were reservists and not accustomed to hard marching, especially in sand and rocky terrain.

The soldiers had marched all through the night to reach this point. Harpaz figured a half hour of rest and some food would do a lot toward boosting their morale and give them the strength they would need for the coming battle.

Hiding within a patch of boulders, Harpaz could see Al-Qusaymah was protected by an Egyptian National Guard Brigade. The Egyptians were well dug in facing the northeast toward the Israeli border. Harpaz realized that a frontal assault would be costly. His brigade had a battery of heavy mortars that they had carried with them but no armor elements. The Egyptian heavy machineguns and recoilless rifles would rip his men to shreds as they advanced across the flat desert in front of the enemy lines.

The Israeli armored brigades had been ordered not to

engage before the morning of the October 31st so that the Egyptians could not determine the seriousness of the Israeli invasion and would not commit more troops to fighting in the Sinai. If Egyptian armor showed up and attacked the Israelis, Harpaz and his men would need to face the armor with light weapons. The Israeli infantry had been taught how to defeat armor with bazookas and portable anti-tank guns but Harpaz knew it would be costly. There just weren't that many places to hide.

He returned to his brigade and pulled his battalion commanders together for a strategy session. He used a stick to draw in the sand and lay out the assault scenario. He elected to split his force in two and assault the town from both sides in a pincher movement. The Israeli mortars would bombard the Egyptian positions, pinning them down as the Israeli infantry units moved into position and attacked. Speed and surprise were key. They would attack in twenty minutes which left little time for preparations. The Israelis had been trained for quick actions. Everyone knew their job.

Harpaz was concerned that over half his force was made up of reservists. Three days earlier, they were baking bread, working in construction and reading their children bedtime stories. It was jarring going from a civilian life straight into a war. Even though he knew they were well trained from dozens of weekend training sessions and practice maneuvers, he was unsure how they would perform. He hated the idea that some would just become cannon-fodder and die in the desert. He mixed the reservists in with the veteran soldiers. He knew this would make many of his units less effective but it would save lives. Before crossing the border, Harpaz had gathered his unit commanders and NCOs and instructed them to watch out for the reservists as much as possible. The lives of the reservists were in their hands. "This will not be the only war we will fight against the Arabs. We need to conserve every Israeli life we can to ensure our nation's survival. All the weapons in the world will not save our people if we have no one behind the trigger," he reminded them.

The lack of cover meant the split-off Israeli element needed to stay out of range of the Egyptian guns as they moved into position at the rear of the town. They marched in a wide arc across the desert and used the remaining darkness to hide their move from the Egyptians.

Once the Israelis were in position, the assault started with a volley of 120-mm mortar shells. Dozens of explosions sent metal shards of shrapnel across the enemy positions wounding several Egyptians in the initial volley. The Egyptians took cover and kept their heads down. A second mortar volley included smoke shells to limit the Egyptians' view of the approaching Israelis and create confusion. The National Guardsmen fought their best in a defensive position with a trench or sandbags to protect them from the enemy's mortars and bullets. They watched the front, expecting Israeli tanks but saw none through the smoke screen. They fought fiercely as the Israelis advanced on foot.

Harpaz was surprised when he heard heavy engines and cannon fire coming from behind. His first thought was that the Egyptians had brought up an armored battalion without being spotted by his reconnaissance patrols and were attacking his position from the rear. He was surprised again when the tank shells exploded on the Egyptian positions and not his. He turned and saw the tanks of Colonel Uri Ben-Ari's 7th Armored Brigade firing their cannons and machineguns as they approached the Egyptians from both sides as he had done. A lieutenant wearing a tanker's headgear approached and identified himself as Ben-Ari's aide. "Colonel Ben-Ari sends his regards and wonders if you need anything?" said the lieutenant.

"Yeah. A little warning would be nice," said Harpaz. "Tell your Colonel thank you for the support but to be careful where he shells. I have men attacking from the rear of the enemy positions. I would hate to have them massacred by our own tanks. We'll send a signal to cease fire when our troops reach the enemy trenches."

"Yes, sir," said the lieutenant. He saluted and moved off to rejoin his commander.

When he saw the tanks supporting the Israeli infantry's advance, the Egyptian commander knew the battle was hopeless. His trenches would soon be overrun no matter how bravely his men fought. His duty was to save as many men and weapons as possible. A report that Israeli troops were approaching the rear of the town made him realize that his window of escape was limited. There was still time to flee if his men moved quickly and spiked their heavy equipment so the Israelis could not use it against them in the future. He ordered his men to retreat and make their way to the Egyptian defensive positions farther west.

The entire battle lasted less than two hours and causalities were light on both sides. A small number of the Egyptian soldiers and their officers were rounded up and taken prisoner. They were sent back across the border where they could be held and watched without difficulty. The Israelis celebrated the victory with a quick meal, giving the men a chance to exchange stories of individual heroics of the battle. Harpaz was proud of them. Even the reservists had performed well. He knew that Abu Ageila would be a different story and not so easily taken.

October 30, 1956 - Mitla Pass, Egypt

Just before sunrise, Major Eitan woke from a short nap. He was curled up at the bottom of the foxhole he had dug the night before like the other men in his outfit. In the distance, he could hear the high-pitched howl of jet engines approaching. He didn't know if they were Israeli jets sent to give his men air cover as the sun rose or Egyptian jets sent to attack. He pulled out his binoculars and scanned the horizon to the northeast where Israeli jets were most likely to appear. The sky was empty. He turned toward the west in the direction of the mountains between his men and the Egyptian airfields bordering the Suez Canal. Again, he saw nothing in the sky but he could hear the jet engines coming closer. He kept watch. A few seconds later, two British-built Gloster Meteor fighter-bombers appeared over the mountains. Eitan was hopeful. Both the Israelis and the Egyptians had Gloster Meteors in their air forces. They were still too distant to make out the insignia. They could have been Israeli jets returning from a mission against the Egyptian airfields and passing over on their way back to an Israeli airbase. His hopes were dashed when four Soviet-built MiG-15s flying escort also appeared. He didn't need to see the insignia. He knew they were Egyptian. "Air raid," he yelled to his men, many still asleep.

There was little the Israeli paratroopers could do except hunker down in their foxholes and hope Israeli jets showed up. Eitan ordered his radio operator to request air support but he knew it would probably be over by the time any help could arrive.

The Meteors swooped low hugging the desert floor while the MiG-15s flew high to watch for the Israeli jets Eitan was hoping to see. Each Meteor launched sixteen three-inch rockets. The rockets plowed into the Israeli positions. Three jeeps exploded and flew into the air. The Israeli paratroopers kept their heads buried below the tops of their foxholes. Firing their weapons at the fast-moving jets was a waste of ammunition that would be needed for any ground attack that came their way. The paratroopers resisted the temptation to fight back. They were well trained and disciplined. One of the rockets hit a foxhole and exploded killing the two men inside. The meteors finished their run, then banked hard and came in for another pass. The Egyptian pilots unleashed the four Hispano 20-mm cannons located in the nose of each aircraft strafing the Israeli foxholes. Another Israeli was hit and torn to shreds by the large caliber projectile. It was a quick death.

With their munitions expended and not wanting to press their luck against the possible arrival of the Israeli Air Force the Egyptian jets broke off their attack and headed back the base.

The Israelis buried their dead and said prayers for their lost friends. Eitan knew this was just the beginning. The Egyptian military could not allow any Israeli force to remain on Egyptian soil, especially this close to the Suez Canal. The Egyptian Air Force did not worry Eitan. He would lose men to their air raids but they could not destroy his battalion outright without tangling with the Israeli Air Force at some point. Tanks, armored cars and halftracks, on the other hand, could roll right over his positions and kill ever last one of the paratroopers. It was armor that Eitan feared most. He knew the Egyptian armor would be coming in force sooner rather than later. His battalion's survival would depend on Sharon and the rest of the brigade arriving before the Egyptians attacked in force. Sharon continued to radio reports of the brigade's progress. It was not going well.

October 30, 1956 – Sinai, Egypt

In the Sinai, Sharon and the 202nd needed to cross over the Negev Desert to reach the Themed Oasis where they could intersect with Highway 55 before they hit the mountains. The Negev was a roadless wasteland of low hills. Sharon's vehicles were forced to navigate off-road during the night to keep on schedule. The scouts did their best to find a path over the hills but sometimes their path was more fit for goats than vehicles.

By the time the sun had risen, the convoy had lost sixty vehicles and many of the six-wheeled trucks had at least one of their wheels riding on a rim. Seventeen out of eighteen of Sharon's precious artillery guns had fallen into sand dunes and had to be abandoned until the recovery platoon he left behind could dig them out. Four of his tanks were also lost to the desert. It had been a very hard first night. The drivers were exhausted and falling asleep at the wheel. The Negev had swallowed them whole and spit them out far worse for wear than when they had started the night before. The cavalry riding to the rescue was having a tougher time of it than the men they were trying to save.

There was no stopping now. They were behind schedule. Those left behind would have to catch up. Everyone complained, but nobody gave up. The hills disappeared and were replaced by featureless flatlands surrounded by treeless mountains. It was all rock and sand as far as the eye could see. *Perhaps I should let them rest for a few minutes once we reach the oasis,* thought Sharon. *But there is a battle that must be fought first.*

SIX

October 30, 1956 – New York, USA

America's U.N. Ambassador, Henry Cabot Lodge, was an eloquent speaker and a strong debater. Although a diplomat and a politician, he didn't mix words and that was why Eisenhower liked him. He was also the former senator for Massachusetts and had been a key player in the movement to draft Eisenhower into running for president. It worked, and Eisenhower was grateful.

Lodge had arrived early in the morning to the U.N. in hopes of presenting his resolution before the Russian Ambassador arrived. The Soviets had a nasty habit of vetoing anything proposed by the United States just because they could. However, the Russian Ambassador was a heavy drinker and a late sleeper. He usually didn't arrive at the U.N. until mid-morning. This made the opening of the daily session the best time to present controversial resolutions and hopefully vote on them before the Soviet delegation arrived.

Lodge stood in the United Nations assembly hall and presented the resolution that he and Eisenhower had drafted, naming Israel as the aggressor in the Sinai Invasion. The resolution demanded Israeli forces stop immediately and retreat from the Sinai or the Israeli government would face the harshest of consequences. Lodge knew he would have wide support for the resolution. The Israelis were not well liked because they always seemed to act in their own self-interests and didn't seem to give a diddly-squat about the rest of the world. While it was somewhat understandable for a nation surrounded by enemies and always on the verge of war to constantly protect its own self-interests, national self-interest was not a founding principle of the U.N.

When it came time to vote, Lodge was stunned to see

both the British and the French Ambassadors use their veto to quash the American resolution. When asked why America's greatest allies would do such a thing, the British Ambassador explained that Britain and France were working on their own joint proposal and would submit it to the assembly shortly. Lodge was not happy and gave them both a piece of his mind. This was an embarrassment to both the U.S. and the NATO Alliance.

October 30, 1956 – Washington D.C., USA

Eisenhower was again livid when he was informed of the veto and spent most of the morning spitting out expletives for the British and French Prime Ministers as he paced in the oval office. Eisenhower felt trapped. He needed Britain and France to defend against Soviet aggression, but they were acting in their own interests instead of common European and global interests. He was also trying to placate the new independent Arab nations to keep them away from Soviet influence. Siding with the two largest colonial powers in the Middle East, Britain and France, did not help that effort.

Eisenhower didn't understand how the British and the French could possibly see this conflict in the Sinai as more important than the alliance they had formed with America to deal with the Soviets. And yet here they were stabbing America in the back at the U.N. *It was insane,* he thought. *Completely insane. What value is there in having allies that we cannot trust? Why don't they see that? Do they honestly think that because of our special relationship America will do nothing?* Eisenhower considered for a few moments and realized that was exactly what the French and the British thought… and for the moment they were right.

October 30, 1956 - Sinai, Egypt

The 202nd convoy pulled to a stop on a mountain road. Another vehicle had a snapped an axle in a deep pothole. "Oh, thank god," said Brigitte jumping out. "I need to pee so bad my back teeth are floating."

"Why would your back teeth be floating?" said the driver.

"I don't know. It's something the Americans say," she said.

Brigitte looked around the treeless and flat landscape. There was no place for privacy. She moved up beside a truck, pushed the driver's rearview mirror so it faced inward, unbuttoned her jumpsuit and squatted near the back wheel well. Several nearby soldiers whistled and howled. She flipped them off and continued to relieve herself. "Oh, my god, that's better than sex," she said.

Sharon climbed from his jeep and said, "This road is ridiculous. Damn Arabs should know better."

He walked back to inspect the damaged vehicle and said, "How do they expect us to keep on schedule without giving us the proper spare parts."

"The French shipped the vehicles without spare parts to expedite their delivery before the invasion," said Sharon's transportation officer.

"Can you fix it?" said Sharon, referring to the broken axle.

"I am afraid not. We'll have to abandon it. We will need to transfer the troops and supplies to another vehicle."

"How are we supposed to do that? We are already bursting at the seams."

"I was hoping we could load a few more troops onto your jeep."

"Yes. Yes. Of course. The more the merrier."

"Colonel, if we lose another truck the men will be forced to walk."

"Then let's not lose one."

"If we slowed down that might be..."

"We have a schedule. We are not slowing down," said Sharon, angry at the thought. "Tell your driver to be more careful."

Sharon looked out at the distant horizon. It was Dayan that had come up with this crazy plan, but it was his duty to see it executed successfully. Eitan's paratroopers were depending on him and he felt the weight of the responsibility. It made him more short-tempered and unusually snappish when mistakes were made. Failure was not an option he could accept.

October 30, 1956 – Abu Ageila, Egypt

Abu Ageila was a village in northern Sinai located sixteen miles from the Israeli-Egyptian border. It was a strategic center for the entire northern Sinai with three main road crossings and a large reservoir built by the British that provided water to the local residents and the nomadic Bedouins. The village of Abu Ageila had no natural or man-made defenses beyond sandbags and trenches. On its own it could be easily taken by the Israelis and retaken by the Egyptians. To the east of the village were a series of ridges and plateaus that formed a natural defensive position paralleling the main road leading from the Israeli border. This series of ridges and plateaus overlooked Abu Ageila and allowed Egyptian artillery and anti-tank guns to rain fire down on any forces attacking the village. The Israelis nicknamed it the "Hedgehog."

To the north of the Hedgehog were a series of sand dunes that made the approach difficult for infantry and almost impossible for wheeled and tracked vehicles. To the south were Jebel Halal, Jebel Dalfa and Jebel Wugicr – rocky promontories that dominated the lowlands around them. The road from Al-Qusaymah passed between the southern promontories and below the hedgehog. The natural cliffs and hills that formed the Hedgehog created defensive positions that could only be assaulted from either the Umm Qataf Ridge or the Ruafa Ridge. The Hedgehog was a natural stronghold that was easily defended.

Protecting the crossroads and the village were three thousand Egyptian soldiers of the 17th and 18th battalions of the 3rd Infantry Division commanded by Colonel Sami Yassa. The soldiers held a series of fortified trenches and bunkers on the Hedgehog. Artillery allowed for mutual fire support of the Egyptian defensive positions. Israeli forces advancing on the Hedgehog and village outnumbered Egyptian forces four to one. The Egyptians had no armor but had ten Archer anti-tank guns, seven 57-mm guns, six 25-pounder artillery pieces, two 30-mm cannons and a mix of 40-mm Bofors and Czech 57-mm guns. The Egyptian guns and artillery were well-placed inside their defensive positions on the Hedgehog and the surrounding area.

Both the Israeli and Egyptian Air Forces were a very real threat to the forces on the ground and to each other. Although both sides possessed jet fighters based on the latest technology, the Egyptian Air Force outnumbered the Israeli Air Force by a significant margin. The Israeli Air Force had two significant advantages over the Egyptian Air Force. First, Israeli pilots were better trained and more aggressive than their Egyptian counterparts. Second, the Israeli ground crews were trained to turn around the aircraft that had landed in a minimum amount of time. Fast-turn-around created a force multiplier by keeping more Israeli jets in the air longer than the Egyptians.

The Israelis could not go around the Hedgehog without risking encirclement or having their supply lines cut. By taking the Hedgehog from the Egyptians the tables would be turned, and any Egyptian counter-attack on Israeli forces in the Sinai would face the same risks. It was the key to the northern Sinai and the Israeli border. It was worth fighting for. It was worth dying for.

The Israeli southern command was under Major General Assaf Simhoni. Experience told him that even with all his firepower and manpower the assault on the Hedgehog would be costly in both lives and equipment. But there was no getting around it. It had to be taken.

Colonel Yehuda Wallach was in command of the 38th Division which included the 4th Infantry Brigade commanded by Colonel Harpaz, the 10th Infantry Brigade commanded by Colonel Shmuel Golinda and the 7th Armored Brigade commanded by Colonel Uri Ben-Ari. In all, twelve thousand soldiers and the majority of Israeli armor were under Wallach's command. His mission was critical to Israel's war plan. Failure to take the Hedgehog could put Israel in danger of a massive Egyptian counter-attack and even threaten the young country's existence.

October 30, 1956 - Abu Ageila, Egypt

Major Izhak Ben-Ari was ordered to probe the Egyptian defenses at Umm Qataf, one of the two possible avenues of approach to the Hedgehog. He was under orders to avoid combat with the enemy during daylight while the Egyptian Air Force was still a threat. The Israeli plan was to wait until the Egyptian Air Force was neutralized before attacking the Hedgehog. That way they could use their own aircraft to occupy the Egyptians while the Israelis assaulted the stronghold. That wouldn't happen until November 1st at the earliest, based on the Operation Kadesh timetable. But Simhoni and Wallach needed to understand what they were facing to form an effective battle plan. It was Ben-Ari's job to reconnoiter the Hedgehog and return with the intelligence.

Ben-Ari's reconnaissance force was mostly made up of jeeps and halftracks. They were like a worm that dangles in front of a fish. They would watch how the fish strikes and, in doing so, determine the size and power of the forces they would face during the actual assault. They could also make note of the current positions of the Egyptian guns, information that could be relayed to the Israeli fighter-bombers once they arrived and to Israeli artillery batteries. But Ben-Ari and his men were not prepared for the ferocity of the Egyptian defense.

As his vehicles climbed the slopes, the Egyptians opened fire with their anti-tank guns, heavy machineguns and artillery. Several of Ben-Ari's vehicles were hit and immobilized. A half-dozen of the drivers and passengers were badly wounded or killed. The Egyptians poured on the fire and inflicted even more damage to the Israelis trying to rescue and recover their men. Ben-Ari's reconnaissance mission turned into a full-on attack as the commander of the 7th Armored Brigade ordered more units up the slope to protect the Israeli retreat. Some of the tank commanders pressed forward and for a moment it looked like the Israelis could take the position.

The Egyptians also suffered greatly as the Israeli tanks, heavy mortars and artillery opened fire, pounding their positions. Reinforcements arrived and bolstered Egyptian defenses, pouring even more fire down on the Israelis. The Egyptian commander Colonel Yassa was badly wounded by mortar shrapnel and was evacuated from the battlefield. Yassa was replaced by Colonel Saadedden Mutawally who was unfamiliar with the Egyptian defensive positions and the layout of the Hedgehog.

As the fighting intensified, Ben-Ari ordered the Israeli front to spread out so their tanks and artillery could bring more firepower on to the Egyptian positions. Unknowingly, the Israeli new offensive positions had expanded into the range of the artillery and anti-tank guns in the village of Abu Ageila. The Egyptians opened fire from their second defensive position with devastating effect. The Israelis lost several of their tanks in just the first minutes of the bombardment.

Wallach ordered an end to the unplanned attack. The

Israelis gathered their wounded and dead and retreated from the hillside, leaving many of their vehicles punctured with anti-tank shell holes and burning. It was the beginning of what promised to be a series of bloody battles for the Hedgehog. For the first time in the war the Israelis had lost a battle and were bogged down. Their confidence was far from shattered, but their noses were bloodied. The Egyptians cheered. They had held their ground and kept their honor.

October 30, 1956 - Abu Ageila, Egypt

Wallach sat in a jeep eating his MRE dinner. Colonel Ben-Ari, the commander of the 7th Armored Brigade approached. "Well that was a disaster," he said.

"You eat yet?" said Wallach.

"I don't feel much like eating."

"You gotta keep your strength up and your mind sharp… for your men's sake."

"I'll eat after I check on the wounded."

"Oh, that should build your appetite."

"I'm sensing sarcasm."

"You would be correct," said Wallach finishing his meal. "Uri, we've got to find another way up the Hedgehog. I'm not sending any more tanks up the Umm Qataf unless we are attacking on two fronts minimum. Three would be even better. It's too much of a meat grinder when they are able to consolidate their forces."

"We've looked. There is no other way except for Ruafa Ridge on the west side of the Hedgehog. But we can't get to Ruafa Ridge without taking heavy losses because of mine fields and passing under Egyptian artillery."

"Send your scouts out again. There has to be something, somewhere."

"Alright. Will do, Boss," said Ben-Ari moving off.

"And don't forget to eat," Wallach called after him.

October 30, 1956 - Abu Ageila, Egypt

Ben-Ari assigned an armored reconnaissance team to once again scout the Hedgehog for an unseen path through the plateau. He wondered about the wisdom of sending more men in harm's way to search for a path that he already knew didn't exit, but he had his orders.

Lieutenant David Frischman rode in the lead halftrack as his team moved along the bottom of the Hedgehog. He was going over terrain that he had previously scouted and it didn't sit well with him. It felt like his commander was questioning his competence as a leader. If there was some way through the Hedgehog he and his men would have found it the first time.

Frischman was surprised when one of his men pointed out what looked like a ravine in the side of the mountain. He radioed his team to stop and take up defensive positions. He stepped from his halftrack and moved toward the ravine.

As he moved closer he saw that the ravine was well hidden because the hillside was made of rock, dirt and sand. The colors on the inside walls of the ravine matched the outside walls perfectly and the walls were close enough together that they didn't cast shadows from the sun except at noon. He understood why he and his men missed it the first time, but he didn't relish the idea of explaining the mistake to his commander. The area was called Al-Dayyiqa on the map but showed no markings of a path.

He ordered half of his men to follow him into the gorge while the other half kept watch outside. The first thing that he noticed was that the width of the walls was about twelve feet, barely enough to fit a tank. The ground was uneven but passable. There were a few large boulders that had fallen from above blocking the path, but he knew his men could remove the obstacles with cables and chains if needed. He and his team moved about thirty yards through the ravine before it opened up into a small canyon with high cliffs. Before him was a bridge and beyond that was a gap that looked like it led all the way through the Hedgehog as if the plateau had been cleaved in two. He felt both stupid and lucky. He and his men exchanged giddy glances until machinegun fire racked the walls around them. They hit the deck.

Frischman's recon team had surprised the Egyptian soldiers guarding the canyon and the hidden gap. He couldn't see where the shots were coming from. There were plenty of places a light machinegun team could hide. His first inclination was to retreat back to his vehicles and report to his commander. This was big news. He decided he needed to know the size of the Egyptian force protecting the canyon before he reported. He ordered one of his men, a young corporal, to cross the bridge and get a better look at what they were facing.

His men gave the corporal covering fire as he made a run for the bridge. Bullets pelleted the ground around him. He dove behind a boulder to catch his breath before crossing the bridge. Frischman waved him forward. He gave Frischman a thumbs up and took off running.

The corporal hit the bridge at a dead run. He was almost half way across when the bridge exploded in the middle cutting it in half and sending half the bridge into the air like a hinged catapult. The corporal had instinctively hit the deck when the explosion occurred. He was launched through the air and landed near Frischman. He was lucky and only suffered a broken arm plus a nasty splinter of metal from the bridge. "Sorry, sir," he said to Frischman. "I didn't get all the way across like you wanted."

Frischman shook his head in disbelief and said, "You did just fine, corporal. We found out what we needed to know." The team medic tended to the corporal. The Egyptian machinegun stopped firing. Frischman had his men cease fire to conserve ammunition. The canyon was quiet. "Shall I have the men move up, Lieutenant?" said a sergeant.

"No. We stay put. I don't think they're done."

Frischman was right. A series of explosion inside the gap brought down the high walls and kicked up a thick cloud of dust.

When the dust settled, Frischman and his men moved forward with caution. The Egyptian soldiers were gone, believing they had blocked the gap and that there was nothing left to guard.

Upon closer inspection, Frischman found that the actual damage was superficial. The boulders that dropped from the walls had shattered into pieces when they hit the ground and could be easily cleared. Those that were still intact could be moved to the side. Even the demolished bridge was not a problem because there was no water in the riverbed and the banks were shallow slopes that could be traversed with tracked vehicles.

Frischman and his men moved through the gap. Twenty minutes later they came out on the western side of the Hedgehog. They stayed hidden so as not to reveal their discovery to the Egyptians. The gap through the Hedgehog was still viable.

Frischman and his men went back through the gap to the eastern side. He left his platoon to guard the canyon in case the Egyptians returned. Then he took one of the halftracks and went to report his findings to his commander. He couldn't stop smiling. He felt like a fox that had just discovered a hole into the hen house.

October 30, 1956 – London, England

Eden, Lloyd, Mollet and Pineau sat in Eden's office at 10 Downing Street. Eden's secretary served champagne. On a nod from Eden, his secretary departed the office. Eden raised his glass and said, "To a victorious intervention and the end of Nasser."

They drank and congratulated each other with hearty handshakes.

At his desk in the reception area, the secretary opened a drawer and retrieved two letters already signed by Eden and Mollet. The letters were addressed to Nasser and Ben-Gurion. Each letter demanded that the armies of their respective nations cease hostilities and retreat to positions a minimum of ten miles from the shores of the Suez Canal within the next twelve hours, or Britain and France in unison would be forced to take the necessary action to separate the two warring parties and protect the canal. The letters were simple in wording and could only be construed as ultimatums. The secretary handed each letter to couriers that would deliver them to the Egyptian and Israeli Embassies. Even though the letters carried the date of October 30, 1956, they had been written and signed two days previously.

Fifteen minutes after releasing the ultimatum letters to Egypt and Israel, Eden stood before Parliament and lied. He told the backbenchers and ministers that Britain and France had acted in the name of peace to protect the canal. Parliament was shocked. As far as any of the members knew, Britain and Egypt were negotiating an agreement to protect the canal and pay fair compensation to the canal's investors. Britain was supposed to be disengaging from Egypt and washing her hands of the whole affair. Now, Britain was offering ultimatums and threatening military action. All of this was at a time when NATO had its hands full with Russian aggression. At the end of Eden's short speech, one of the members said, "There is nothing in the United Nations charter that allows a nation to declare itself the World's police force. Are the Americans supporting us? Are they giving us their full backing or are we doing this off our own bat?"

"We have been in close talks with both the Americans and the U.N. Security Counsel," said Eden. "We will continue to advise both as to our progress."

"If either Egypt or Israel refuse to comply with your ultimatum, will Britain send in ground troops?" said another member.

"Britain will do whatever is necessary to protect its interests and reputation. We do not ask for war, but we will not turn our backs if war is offered," said Eden.

There was a growing murmur in the chamber as Eden left Parliament without further comment.

October 30, 1956 – Washington D.C., USA

Eisenhower was in a meeting with his cabinet when he received word of the ultimatums. He was furious and cursed openly. "That back-stabbing weasel," he said. "The son-of-a-bitch is backing me into a corner. If he thinks I don't have the gumption to respond, he's dead wrong."

"Is it a threat or do they actually plan on using military force?" said Emmet Hughes, one of the cabinet members.

"It's not just a threat. They're throwing down the gauntlet and daring Nasser to pick it up. The poor bastard has no choice but to defy the Western powers or lose all his standing with the Arab community," said Eisenhower. "Eden's gambling that America will choose NATO over Egypt. It's a bad bet on his part."

The normally out-spoken cabinet was sheepish at seeing the president's anger. "Will the United States join Egypt against our Western allies?" asked Hughes.

"The Soviets are not going to stand still for this," said another cabinet member. "They've already backed Egypt with weapons and loans. They could back them with their military. Are we willing to risk World War III over Egypt for God's sake?"

"The British and French are playing right into the Soviet's hands," said Eisenhower. "It's like they're handing the Soviet's the Middle East on a silver platter."

Eisenhower excused himself from the meeting and walked out on to the patio where he could chain-smoke three cigarettes and think more clearly. He could not understand why the British and French would put their most powerful ally in such a precarious position. He was sure they understood that if the United States was seen to be siding with Israel it would end America's influence with the Arabs and clear the way for the Soviets. The Middle East and its oil would be lost. He was also sure that Eden and Mollet both knew that Nasser would have no choice but to reject the ultimatum. Nasser could not back down while Israeli troops were on Egyptian soil. His own people and military would not stand for it, not to mention how such weakness would be seen by the other Arab nations.

Eisenhower realized that Britain and France had every intention of going to war with Egypt. He didn't know what role Israel would play in all of this and he didn't care. They could end the conflict at any time by simply withdrawing their forces. But of course, the Israelis wouldn't do that without winning some sort of concession. The Israelis always demanded treasure for their blood. The British and French were purposely allowing Israel to stay on the battlefield, a condition that Nasser could not accept. Nasser would fall into their trap. Britain and France would attack Egypt. If the Israelis were smart, they would accept the ultimatum and let Britain and France deal with Egypt. They would be in a much stronger position to negotiate their withdrawal once Egypt's armed forces were mauled by the Western powers. *Britain and France get the canal and Israel gets whatever it wants,* thought Eisenhower. *It's like they planned it all along.*

October 30, 1956 – Cairo, Egypt

Standing by the radiofax machine, Nasser read the ultimatum letter that had been forwarded to him by his embassy in London. At first, he thought it must be some sort of mistake. After giving it further thought, he realized it was deadly serious. *This is insane,* he thought. *They know I cannot possibly accept this. Why would they risk angering Jordan, Iraq and the Saudis by siding with the Israelis?* He considered for a few moments more, then came to that conclusion that they must be bluffing. They have no intention of going to war. It was the only thing that made sense.

SEVEN

October 30, 1956 – Mitla Pass, Egypt

It was just past noon when Major Eitan received a radio call informing him that a French reconnaissance plane had spotted an Egyptian armored column heading for the Mitla Pass. There was little they could do except reposition their two cannons to face the pass. Even that wouldn't really matter. The Egyptian tanks would run right over the Israeli positions once they arrived. It was far too early to expect Sharon and his tanks to arrive in time. The Israeli paratroopers would fight furiously because that is what they did best, but if there was ever a lost cause, this was it. He informed his men and they made their last-minute preparations.

October 30, 1956 – Mitla Pass, Egypt

The Egyptian armored column approached the eastern mouth of the Mitla Pass. The Egyptians were looking forward to giving the paratroopers a good whopping. They remembered the Arab-Israeli war when the Israeli armor and air force destroyed many of their tanks. Now, it was their turn. The Israeli paratroopers were lightly armed and would be no match for the Egyptian armor. They would make them bleed.

They were less than a mile from the road leading into the mountains. The tank commanders riding in their open hatches could hear nothing above the sound of their tanks' engines. Each kept an eye out for any approaching enemy vehicles or aircraft. It was the commander in the lead tank that first saw the strange sight on the horizon. It was difficult to tell what it was.

At first, he thought it was a camel caravan because of

how it stretched across the desert horizon. As the sight drew closer he realized it wasn't camels at all. It was a squadron of twenty propeller-driven P-51 Mustang fighters flying just fifteen feet off the ground and heading straight for the armored column.

The commander radioed the other vehicles in the column and they turned to face the oncoming threat. He requested air support which he knew would arrive too late if it arrived at all.

The Mustangs stayed low, making it difficult for the columns mobile anti-aircraft guns to get a good angle. The Mustangs were offering their front profile as a target. There wasn't much to hit. The Egyptians unleashed their anti-aircraft guns and the machine guns on their tanks and armored cars. For a few seconds, it looked like the Israeli pilots were planning on ramming the tanks at high speed. At the last moment, the Mustangs pulled up and released the five-hundred pound bombs that each carried under its belly. The pilots focused their attacks on the tanks and several achieved direct hits. The bombs obliterated the tanks, sending several of their turrets tumbling through the air. The Mustangs swung around and unloaded with a mix of Hispano 20-mm cannons and 50-cal machine guns strafing the Egyptian column. Once the Israeli pilots had fired all but a few rounds in their guns, they headed for home back the way they came.

The Egyptian armored column was a shamble with a dozen vehicles burning. Dead and wounded Egyptian soldiers lay scattered on the ground. Their commander no longer considered his brigade fit to fight. He collected the wounded and dead, then turned his surviving vehicles away from the mountain pass and headed back across the Suez where it was safe. The Israeli paratroopers on the other side of the pass had been saved and they didn't even know it.

October 30, 1956 – Cairo, Egypt

Britain's Ambassador to Egypt, Sir Humphrey Trevelyan, was shown into the office of the President and was greeted by Nasser. They sat. Trevelyan was fidgety. "Are you okay, Sir Humphrey?" said Nasser.

"Yes. Yes, of course. It's just all this canal business," said Trevelyan. "I don't sleep well."

"Would you care for some tea?"

"No, thank you. I am quite alright. How may I help you Mr. President?"

"Are you aware of the letter your government sent to our embassy in London concerning the current Israeli invasion of our sovereign state?"

"Yes, of course. I want to assure you, I have nothing to do with it."

"Of course not, Sir Humphrey. I recognize it as the work of Prime Minister Eden. And you may inform your Prime Minister that we respectfully decline."

"Decline?"

"Yes. Decline."

"That is a grave mistake, Mr. President. Prime Minister Eden is not a man to be trifled with."

"And I do not care to trifle with him. But Egypt cannot accept a cessation of hostilities until the Israelis depart from our land. It is not possible."

"I see. And you understand the consequences of such an action?"

"I am not taking any action. I am simply refusing to comply with Britain and France's request."

"Request?"

"Yes. I find it incredible that Britain or France would demand anything from Egypt after the way we have been treated. Therefore, it must be a request. One which I respectfully decline."

"I see. Is there anything else you wish for me to convey to my government?"

"Beyond my warmest regards… no. You may leave."
Trevelyan rose and left Nasser's office, dumbfounded.

October 30, 1956 – London, England

Eden stood in his office and dictated a letter to Eisenhower. His secretary struggled to keep up. "Egypt has brought this upon herself by endangering an international waterway, by colluding with other Arab nations to attack Israel and by continually defying the U.N.'s mandates," said Eden. "Britain wanted to bring the letter of ultimatum up to a vote in the United Nations until we realized that the U.N. could not act quickly enough to protect the canal. Britain and France had to act to protect our vital military and commercial interests. We pray you understand that we truly had no choice in the matter."

"Do you believe Eisenhower will accept your explanation?" said the secretary.

"Don't be dense. Of course he will accept it. What choice does he have? He's not going to go to war over Egypt, especially not against his two most important allies in Europe… not if he wants NATO to survive," said Eden. "Eisenhower is focused on Soviet aggression. He needs Britain and France to remain strong so they can help him defend Europe against the communists. He will stomp up and down and make a lot of noise to impress the other national leaders with his concern, but in the end the Americans will play ball and do nothing. It's somewhat ironic… Eisenhower hates war. That's really his biggest weakness. He's afraid to use the big stick."

October 30, 1956 – Washington D.C., USA

Eisenhower sat in the oval office, Eden's letter on the desk next to him as he wrote a response. He needed to be careful. He was only six days from an election and the American public was watching with great interest. If Eisenhower helped Egypt he would lose the Jewish vote in New York, New Jersey and Florida, resulting in the loss of the presidency. He had already made the decision to sacrifice his second term as president if it meant peace. Eisenhower had decided long ago to navigate his life on a moral course no matter the consequences.

Eden was right about Eisenhower needing Britain and France as a check against Soviet aggression. But Britain and France had far more to lose than America if a Soviet invasion did occur. Eden was right about one other thing... Eisenhower hated war. He had seen enough death and destruction for a lifetime. He would do anything to avoid it... almost. He had led the allies to victory against the axis forces in World War II. He knew how to use the big stick better than most.

The letter he wrote to Eden in response was diplomatic and not overreactive. Yes, he was mad. Really mad. But he was also the leader of a Superpower. He knew it and he knew Eden knew it. He needed to be the adult in the room. The letter started by reminding Eden of Britain's obligation under a Tripartite Agreement to defend Egypt against any aggressor. By crossing into the Sinai, Israel was clearly the aggressor in the current conflict. Britain was therefore obligated to defend Egypt against Israel. Eisenhower knew there was little chance of Britain accepting its obligation, especially given Eden's personal hatred of Nasser. Eisenhower was simply pointing out that Britain was on shaky ground legally. He also assuring Eden that America would keep its word and support the agreement as promised.

Eisenhower went on to point out that it was the United Nations, of which both Britain and France were member countries, that was tasked with the responsibility of settling disputes, not the individual member countries. Britain and France should both support the U.N. ceasefire declaration when it was finalized and abandon their own.

He went on to explain that his biggest concern was that the Soviets would use this conflict to drive a wedge between Western and Middle Eastern nations. The Soviets were patiently waiting in the wings to offer the Arabs assistance when they were willing to accept it. Britain and France were playing into the Soviet's strategy and the Soviets were only too willing to exploit current events to their advantage. He was concerned that Britain and France's actions could bring about World War III if the Soviet's entered the fight. He appealed to Eden to recognize the higher cause and keep the peace.

Eisenhower knew that the letter would fall on deaf ears. Britain and France were committed to see this through and he was determined to stop them. He just didn't know how at this point. Britain and France had both shot themselves in their respective feet but failed to recognize it. Britain and France were dependent on Middle Eastern oil to drive their economies and their militaries. Any interruption in the shipping lanes through the Suez Canal could have a disastrous effect on both countries. They were playing with fire.

Experience had taught Eisenhower that it was better to wait for a workable solution then to act half-heartedly. He would let events unfold and look for an opportunity that he hoped would materialize before it was too late and the world spiraled out of control. He was a man struggling to keep his balance on a very thin wire.

October 30, 1956 – Sinai Highway 50, Egypt

Coyle sat in the cockpit of his C-119 along with his Spanish flight crew. His new copilot spoke some English which Coyle saw as an improvement over his French crew. He could see the two Meteor jet escorts out his side window flying beside his larger aircraft like guardian angels. The Israeli Air Force had sent their jets to the Egyptian border as a precaution. Coyle wondered if he wouldn't be safer without them. His plane was not considered hostile to the Egyptians since the French Air Force symbols had been painted over with company decals on the wings and a Spanish flag on the fuselage.

The navigator checked his calculations and spoke to the co-pilot in Spanish. "He says we should be approaching the drop location," said the copilot to Coyle.

"Good. Find me a nice flat place to set her down," said Coyle.

"Why? Our instructions were to parachute the jeeps and supplies."

"If we parachute them they are likely to get damaged in the landing. From what I hear, this convoy has enough problems. Two more broken jeeps aren't gonna help much."

"You are the pilot," said the copilot with a shrug.

"Yes. I am," said Coyle with a smile.

The C-119 and the two Israeli jets flew over Sharon's convoy twisting its way through a mountain pass. "That would be our supply drop," said Sharon looking up.

Brigitte recognized the twin-tailed aircraft that roared over her head and said to herself, "Coyle?"

Coyle spotted a level valley a few miles ahead of the vehicles. He did a quick pass to ensure there were no large rocks or hidden gullies. Except for the road carved through the middle of the valley, the ground featureless and smooth. "Flat as a pancake," said Coyle.

He banked the aircraft and brought it in line with the longest part of the valley. "Why don't we use the road?" said the copilot.

"Potholes," said Coyle. "We're safer landing off-road.

The soil looks like clay. It's probably hard and level. Just be ready to throttle up if we see something nasty and have to abort."

"Si, Señor," said the copilot.

The wheels of the C-119 touched down on the hard-packed valley floor. The propellers pitch reversed, slowing the aircraft down and kicking up a dust storm. At the end of the valley the plane turned around and headed for the road that ran through the center of the valley floor. It pulled to a stop as the first of the convoy's vehicles exited the mouth of the mountain pass.

The two Israeli jet escorts were ordered to return to their airbases in Israel. The pilots had other priorities and could not wait for the C-119 to unload, reload and takeoff. Their mission was to see that the vehicles and supplies were delivered to the 202nd. They had accomplished their objective and were anxious to get back into the fight. They peeled off and headed northeast. The C-119 would return alone. It was not an Israeli plane with Israeli markings. There was little risk the Egyptians would attack it. In addition, the Israelis were quickly gaining air superiority over the northeast Sinai which they had already overrun. The Egyptians were more focused on defending their ground forces from the advancing Israeli task forces than destroying cargo aircraft.

With a rucksack over his shoulder, Coyle stepped out of the side door in the aircraft's fuselage along with the rest of the flight crew. "Let's get her unloaded as fast as possible," he said to the crew.

The flight crew went to work, opening the back doors on the cargo hold and lowering the steel ramps. The first jeep pulled up and Brigitte jumped out with a big smile on her face. "Hello, Darling," said Coyle.

"Tom, what are you doing here?" said Brigitte wrapping her arms around his neck and kissing his face a dozen times.

"The French... I mean the Spanish sent me on an errand," he said.

Sharon approached. He didn't look happy. "I don't know who you think you are, but you took a big risk landing here," said Sharon.

"I'm the guy that just brought you two working jeeps and a cargo hold full of spare parts. You can just say thank you," said Coyle.

"You gave away our position."

"That could be, but I figured it would be worth it not to damage your jeeps in a drop."

"That is true. We need the jeeps and the parts," said Sharon, swallowing his pride. "Thank you."

"Don't mention it."

"Can you take our wounded back with you?" said Sharon.

"Of course. My flight crew could use some help unloading. I'd like to take off as soon as possible."

"I will see to it," said Sharon moving off and barking out orders in Hebrew to his men.

Coyle turned back to Brigitte and unslung the rucksack. "Are you staying?" said Brigitte.

"No. Just thought you could use a few things."

"You brought me presents?"

"I did. I'm a really thoughtful boyfriend."

"Yes. You are," said Brigitte grabbing the rucksack from his hands, setting it on the ground and opening it. Inside was two bottles of her favorite wine, a large block of hard cheese, two boxes of crackers, three large baguettes, two dried salamis, three cans of sardines, and a bar of soap. "A bar of soap, really?" she said holding it up.

"I figured you could use it."

"I can if I can ever find enough water to take a quick bath," she sniffed herself. "Do I smell bad? I can't tell anymore."

"Darling, you smell like fine roses to me," he said

giving her a big hug and a kiss.

"You Americans. You are such romantics."

"Damn right."

Brigitte tore a piece of bread from one of the baguettes and opened a can of sardines. "I'm starving. I haven't eaten since breakfast," she said.

"So, what are you doing with the Israelis? I thought France was angry with them," said Coyle.

"Things are not always as they seem," she said. "I suppose I do owe you an explanation."

"It'd be nice. Seeing how I came all this way."

"I wanted to report this war from the beginning."

"How did you even know there was going to be a war?"

"I have my contacts."

"In the Israeli army?"

"Yes. Well… I've met a lot of people over the years."

"I'm gonna have to call bullshit."

"Don't. Just trust me. If I could tell you, I would."

"Alright. Any idea when you'll be home?"

"Not really. When it's over I suppose."

"Okay. I'll be waiting."

"I know you will. That's why I love you," said Brigitte taking another bite of bread. "Do you want some of this?"

"No. I've got a sandwich in the cockpit."

"A sandwich? What kind of sandwich?"

"Meatloaf and ketchup. The kind you don't like."

"Ah. Very smart."

"No. Just crafty."

They laughed and enjoyed their few minutes together as the Israelis unpacked the last of the supplies from the aircraft and rolled out the two jeeps. The Israelis loaded up their wounded soldiers, twenty-two in all. It was time for Coyle to go. "We'll, darling. I'd better let you get back to your war," said Coyle. "I'd try and talk you into coming with me, but that wouldn't be right. You are who you are and that's why I love you."

"I love you too, Coyle. We'll be together again soon. I promise," said Brigitte.

"When you get back maybe I'll take you to that bistro you like. Get ya some more of those snails you're so found of."

"You mean the one where we took Bruno?"

"Yeah, that one."

"Maybe we could invite him. We had such a nice time."

"I suppose."

Brigitte could see Coyle was put off by the suggestion of Bruno. "What is it with you and Bruno? I know you're friends."

"I suppose we are. But when it comes to you... he's still your ex-lover."

"Coyle, if I wanted to be with Bruno, I would be with Bruno. It's you I love. You have nothing to worry about. He's just a friend."

"... that you once shared a bed with."

"Do you really want to discuss this now?" she said wrapping her arms around his neck.

"No. You're right. I'll see you back in Paris."

"Bye, Coyle."

"Goodbye, Brigitte."

They kissed deeply. Coyle boarded the plane. The plane revved its engines and took off across the desert floor. As it approached the end of the valley, it lifted into the air. It flew over the convoy and Coyle waved its wings as if to say good-bye one last time. The plane banked in a gentle circle and headed northeast toward the Israeli border. After a moment, it disappeared over a mountain. Brigitte felt strangely sad, almost remorseful. She didn't like the feeling. It scared her.

October 30, 1956 – Sinai Desert, Egypt

Israeli Lieutenant Alon Hirschfeld was flying his Gloster

Meteor jet fighter at eight thousand feet when he first spotted the cargo aircraft below. He was alone. His wingman had engine trouble early on their mission and had to turn back to Israel. Hirschfeld elected to continue the mission rather than turn back. It was important. A small convoy of Egyptian troops had been spotted along the canal just outside the city of Tor. It was his mission to destroy the convoy before it crossed the Suez Canal. The Israelis knew that any troops that escaped their initial assault would need to be faced at a later time, possibly during an invasion of Israel itself.

Hirschfeld's sister had married a farmer and moved to a small town near the Israeli-Egypt border. She and her two-year old son were killed during a Fedayeen attack. To him, this mission was an opportunity for revenge.

He had found the Egyptian troops traveling along a road paralleling the canal just a few miles from the chain ferry that would take them across to the safety of the western side with its anti-aircraft guns. He swooped down and fired all sixteen of his 60lb rockets with armor-piercing warheads. It was overkill. The vehicles were trucks and jeeps with only one armored car. He destroyed the lead and the rear vehicles on his first pass, killing the occupants and blocking in the other vehicles in the convoy. The next pass was straight up the center of the convoy. He flew low to improve his aim. He hadn't seen any anti-aircraft weapons in the convoy and even if he had, he was sure he would destroy them in the next thirty seconds. He annihilated six more vehicles with his remaining rockets. The explosions from the TNT-packed warheads were powerful and send shrapnel flying in all directions killing the drivers and passengers. The third pass was a strafing run meant to kill as many troops as possible. He fired half of the shells in his four 20-mm Hispano cannons mounted in the nose of his aircraft before he realized he had run out of targets. Nothing was moving below and all the vehicles were burning. He was sure there would be some Egyptian soldiers playing dead until the air assault was over but he didn't care. He had killed enough to satisfy the loss of his sister and nephew. He headed back to Israel. He had waited a long time for a war... for revenge.

It was on the return flight that he saw Coyle's Boxcar flying below him. It was headed northeast. He flew down behind it to take a closer look.

He flew directly behind the aircraft so as not to spook the pilot or crew. He had never seen a C-119 before and was sure that there was no such aircraft in the Israeli Air Force. He wasn't as sure about the wing and tail markings. He knew they weren't Israeli but they didn't look Egyptian either. He also eliminated French and British aircraft. It was possible that it was an Egyptian ally plane or a commercial aircraft drafted into service by the Egyptians. It was a big cargo plane capable of carrying several platoons of Egyptian troops. He wasn't sure if the Egyptian forces had paratroopers but he wasn't going to take any chances. The unknown aircraft was heading toward Israel and that made it a threat. His rockets were gone but he still had half of his 20-mm ammunition. That would be enough for the slow flying propeller-driven plane.

Coyle was relaxed now that he knew Brigitte was safe. He knew she could take care of herself but she was in a war zone and just seeing her made him feel better about life. He loved her. It wouldn't be long before he would pop the question and ask her to marry him. He just needed the right opportunity. The Spanish crew was chit-chatting among themselves when the co-pilot saw the first tracer rounds streak past his side window. He turned to warn Coyle when several rounds pierced the cockpit tearing him to shreds. Blood splattered across the windshield.

Coyle reacted, banking the plane hard in the opposite direction and increasing the engine throttles to their maximum position. There was nothing he could do for his co-pilot, who was now headless. His heart was pounding, adrenaline pumping through his body. As the aircraft turned he looked out the side window and caught a glimpse of the fighter jet pursing him. He could tell by the insignia that it was Israeli. "Son of a bitch. It's Israeli," said Coyle turning to his engineer. "Get on the radio. Find his frequency and call him off."

"Que?" said the engineer.

"R-A-D-I-O, damn it. Use the radio," said Coyle making hand signals.

The engineer finally understood and used the radio. He twisted the dials in increments trying to find the frequency of the Israeli pilot. He was speaking Spanish into the headset but was sure the pilot would understand that the aircraft was not Egyptian if he could only find the frequency.

The Israeli jet dove down for another attack. This time he sighted the cargo hold of the aircraft where he thought the paratroopers were located. He fired again.

Inside the cargo hold, the wounded Israeli soldiers watched in horror as 20-mm shells punched golf ball sized holes in the fuselage. Five of the wounded soldiers were torn to pieces. There was no surviving the large caliber bullets when they hit flesh and bone. The wounds were massive. There was nothing the medic could do but hang on and pray.

Coyle took his aircraft as low as possible, hugging the desert. He saw a small mountain range and headed straight for it. More rounds punched into the cockpit and killed the engineer on the radio. Only Coyle and the navigator were left. The navigator was strapped in his seat and crossing himself while reciting Hail Mary's. Coyle heard an explosion on the right side of the aircraft. He couldn't see the engine from where he was sitting. Instead he looked down at his oil pressure gauges. The right gauge spun to zero. He turned to the navigator. "Look out the window.

The right engine," said Coyle, motioning with his hands.

The navigator nodded that he understood, unstrapped and moved toward the right window. He used the sleeve of his flight jacket to wipe away the blood splatter and looked out. The right engine was on fire. He turned back to Coyle and made a cut-throat sign. "Shit," said Coyle pulling the right throttle back to starve the fire of fuel.

Two more shells shattered the front windshield, barely missing Coyle's head. Coyle knew that the navigator didn't understand what he was saying but he felt like he should tell someone what he planned on doing just in case they wanted to object. "We are sitting ducks up here. A few more passes and he'll kill us for sure. I gotta put her down," said Coyle to the navigator busy strapping himself back in.

Coyle studied the terrain below. The aircraft was approaching the mountain range. There was a mouth to what he assumed was a canyon. *If I can wedge her inside that canyon we might stand a chance,* he thought.

The navigator saw what Coyle was doing. "Tren de aterrizaje. Tren de aterrizaje," said the navigator signaling the landing gear with his hands.

"No. The ground is uneven. If our landing gear hits a boulder or rut, we'll cartwheel. The cargo hold will tear off. Everyone in back dies. We land on her belly. It's safer," said Coyle making hand motions.

"No. No. Tren de aterrizaje."

"Trust me. I have a lot of experience at crashing," said Coyle waving off the navigator.

The navigator cursed in Spanish, abandoning his argument, and went back to his prayers. Coyle guided the nose of the aircraft into the center of the canyon mouth. At the last second, he pulled the nose up and let the twin tails of the aircraft touch down first. The fuselage was forced down and slapped the ground. The plane was still moving at over one hundred miles an hour when the two wings hit the sides of the canyon walls and ripped off. The wing fuel tanks exploded sending balls of flame into the sky followed by dense black smoke. The fuselage was protected against the explosion and flames by the rock walls as it continued to slide on its belly deeper into the canyon. The fuselage came to a stop as it ran out of room and wedged itself between the two canyon walls.

The Israeli pilot saw the explosion as the aircraft entered the canyon. He wasn't satisfied. He banked his jet and went in for a closer look.

Coyle sat in his pilot's chair. He was bleeding from a cut on his forehead and he felt like he may have a couple of broken ribs from the safety straps that held him in place during crash. He was alive. He would see Brigitte again. He shook off his malaise and slipped off his safety harness. "You okay?" he said to the navigator.

"Estoy bien," said the navigator unbuckling himself from his seat.

"We gotta get out of here," said Coyle moving toward the doorway into the cargo hold. The navigator followed him. The doorway was jammed closed when the airframe bent inward as the fuselage wedge itself into the canyon. Coyle kicked the door open. What he saw shocked him.

Most of the wounded soldiers were dead either from the enemy aircraft barrages or from being pummeled to death in their beds when the fuselage walls had crushed inward on impact. The Spanish cargo boss was still strapped in his seat with his leg blown off at the hip. He had bled to death. His assistant, an eighteen-year-old Spaniard, knelt by him and was crying as he tried to stop the bleeding. The navigator gently pulled the boy away and pushed him toward the back of the plane. The Israeli medic was still alive and attempting to treat the survivors. "We've got to get the survivors out. Now," said Coyle.

"I can't move these men. They'll die. Take anyone that can still move and get them out. I'll stay with the others," said the medic.

Coyle nodded. There wasn't time to argue. He ran to

the back of the fuselage and opened the cargo hold doors on the back of the aircraft. They too were jammed shut. He kicked at them, but they didn't budge. The navigator joined him kicking at the doors. Coyle turned to the survivors that could still move. "You wanna live?" said Coyle.

They joined him kicking and pushing. One of the doors moved a little and created an opening. Sunlight poured through into the cargo hold. Coyle grabbed a torn piece of tubing from one of the crushed beds and used it as a pry bar to force the door open. It opened enough that the men could slip out. Coyle went out first so he could help the others.

Above, the Israeli pilot saw through the black smoke that the fuselage was wedged into the canyon and was still intact. He figured he had enough ammunition for one last strafing run to finish off any survivors. He lined up his jet and opened fire.

The bullets pelted the ground in back of the aircraft and marched forward toward the fuselage. Coyle turned and watched as the stream of bullets moved straight toward him. There was no time to move. "Brigitte," said Coyle as he closed his eyes and prepared to die.

The jet's cannon ceased firing. The aircraft had run out of ammunition. The Israeli pilot cursed. He turned his aircraft toward home.

Coyle heard the bullets stop hitting the ground. He opened his eyes. It was still. He heard the jet passing overhead, the sound of its engine fading in the distance. He was fairly sure he was still alive but not certain until the cargo hold door swung open and hit him in the back of the head. The first wounded Israeli squeezed through the opening. Coyle snapped out of it and helped the man. He wasn't sure what had happened but there was no time to think. Right now, people were in danger and it was his job as the pilot to figure out how to get them to safety.

EIGHT

October 30, 1956 - Mediterranean Sea

Major Tamsyn stood on the bridge and watched the horizon as the *Ibrahim* made its way along the Egyptian coast. The destroyer's anti-aircraft guns were kept pointed in the direction of Israel. It was the Israeli jets the crew feared most. It was unlikely the Israeli warships would risk an attack while the *Ibrahim* was so close to the Egyptian coastline and still under the protection of the artillery batteries on shore.

The Israeli Air Force was much more brazen and the pilots would risk all if they thought they could sink one of the few destroyers in the Egyptian navy. It was the Egyptian destroyers that were the biggest threat to Israeli commercial shipping and often boarded ships to inspect for weapons and harass the crews. If caught in the open ocean the *Ibrahim* would be seen as a target of opportunity and get strafed by the Israeli fighters. It was unlikely that one or two fighters could sink her, but the jets' machine guns and unguided air-to-surface missiles could inflict terrible damage on the crew of the lightly-armed vessel.

It wasn't long before the ship's lookout spotted multiple vessels on the northwestern horizon. They were out of radar range and the Egyptian destroyer was headed in the opposite direction. The approaching ships were too far off to visually identify from which country they hailed. Tamsyn ordered his radio operator to report the sighting to naval command on shore in Alexandria

Unknown to Tamsyn, it was the first sighting of the British-French invasion fleet approaching Port Said. These ships were in addition to the French and British vessels already stationed in the eastern Mediterranean. The Egyptian navy was vastly outnumbered and outgunned. The Egyptian crews were no match for the well-trained

French and British crews.

As the *Ibrahim* approached the Israeli coastline, it changed course and made its way farther out to sea to avoid being spotted by Israeli lookout posts on shore. Israeli patrol boats were also less likely to venture too far from the shore and the protection of the Israeli artillery batteries.

As per the agreement with the French and British, the Israeli warships in the area had been ordered to steer clear of the approaching fleet. Neither of the three conspiring nations wanted to risk a confrontation with the uninformed ship captains. As far as the captains of the vessels were concerned, they were on a war footing and would see any approaching vessel as a potential threat. Until the ultimatum expired, the best policy was to keep the two sides well apart from each other.

The three Israeli ships in the area were also decommissioned WWII hand-me-downs from Western navies - the *INS Yaffo*, a Z-class British destroyer, her sister ship *INS Eilat*, and a Canadian River class frigate, *INS Miznak*. The two Z-class destroyers were the most capable warships in the Israeli fleet. At four and a half inches, both ships' main guns were larger that the guns on the *Ibrahim* and their gunnery radar was more advanced. It was a small miracle that the *Ibrahim* was not spotted by the Israeli vessels as they moved away from the British-French fleet.

October 30, 1956 – Rafah, Gaza and Rafah, Egypt

The city of Rafah was important to both the Egyptians and the Israelis. Rafah was a border city split into two parts. Half of Rafah was located on the southern end of the Gaza Strip, a Palestinian territory. The other half of the city was in the northern Sinai and therefore part of Egypt.

It was a strategic supply route for the Fedayeen as they carried out their cross-border raids on Israeli settlements. Being allies of the Palestinians, the Egyptians naturally stationed troops in the Gaza Strip. The Egyptian forces located at Rafah discouraged Israeli forces from retaliatory strikes against the Fedayeen hideouts. It was a powder keg to war.

The Israelis saw their assault into the Sinai as an opportunity to cut off the Gaza Strip from Egyptian forces and destroy the Fedayeen encampments.

In addition to cutting off the Gaza Strip, Rafah was also the eastern anchor to the northern highway that paralleled the Mediterranean coastline. Any attack from northern Egyptian forces would need to go through Rafah to reach Israel. Rafah was a natural blocking point to any Egyptian or Israeli invasion.

Recognizing the importance of the city, Dayan assigned two brigades the task of capturing Rafah - Israeli 1st Infantry Brigade commanded by Colonel Benjamin Givli and 27th Armored Brigade commanded by Colonel Haim Barlev.

The Egyptians also saw Rafah as the key to the Gaza Strip and to their plans to attack Israel at some point in the near future. The Gaza Strip elongated the border between Egypt and Israel. The Egyptians could station military units inside the Gaza Strip during peace that could quickly strike deep into Israeli territory during a war. It made any Egyptian assault much more effective and made the Israelis think twice before starting any conflict. The Egyptian reinforced 5th Infantry Brigade was stationed at Rafah and commanded by Brigadier General Jaafar al-Abd. The 87th Palestinian Infantry Brigade was used as a reserve. The Egyptians were well armed with artillery and anti-tank batteries. They also had a squadron of Sherman tanks that gave them a small but mobile armor punch that could counterattack if required.

Al-Abd deployed most of his forces five miles to the

south of Rafah. The geography of the area transformed the desert into a defensible salient with few avenues of attack. Dunes protected the southern flank of the salient. The Egyptians placed minefields on both sides of the dunes to protect their southern flank for several miles. In the center of the salient were eighteen small hills that provided a series of high points and concealment for his troops. The Egyptians had built a series of trenches and bunkers on each hill and surrounded them with barbed wire and well-positioned minefields. Artillery and anti-tank guns overlapped their firing zones so that all points within the defensive zone could be defended from multiple angles.

The Israelis started their assault as the sun set. The assault consisted of three spearheads. Speed was the key. The battle plan was to overrun the Egyptian positions with a blitzkrieg-style assault and mop up later with follow on forces. Dayan knew that if the Israeli forces could get the Egyptians to break and abandon their positions there was little chance of them forming any viable counterattack. He didn't worry about chasing after them and reducing their forces. That would come later.

To the south of the Egyptian salient outside of Rafah, an Israeli engineering company was charged with clearing a path through the minefields paralleling the dunes. Once cleared, two infantry battalions would make their way through the minefield and over the dunes to attack the Egyptians in the Rafah salient from their southern flank. An Israeli battery of 120-mm mortars and 12 anti-tank guns firing from the top of the dunes would support their attack.

A battalion of Sherman tanks from the 27th Armored Brigade would attack the salient from the north. Colonel Barlev's biggest fear for his men was the Egyptian Archer anti-tank guns. They were deadly accurate in the hands of a well-trained fire team and capable of penetrating the armor on all the Israeli tanks and half-tracks. Barlev was depending heavily on the Egyptians' lack of training and poor leadership to prevent the annihilation of his battalion during the assault.

Two more infantry battalions would attack the center of the salient from the east. By hitting the Egyptians from three sides simultaneously, the Egyptian commander would be obliged to divide his forces. If any of the three spearheads achieved a breakthrough it could be exploited with a mechanized battalion of riflemen in half-tracks held in reserve.

The engineers were the first to approach the Egyptian positions using the cover of darkness. They used American-made WWII mine sweepers to identify the positions of the minefields. They marked the borders of the minefield with small flags. Their goal was to find the access path in one of the minefields created by the Egyptians. The access path was a highly-held secret that gave Egyptian units approaching from the south safe passage through the minefields and into the Egyptian defensive positions inside the salient. The other option was to clear a path by finding and removing the mines. The Israelis needed a path wide enough for their tanks and half-tracks. The Israeli engineers discovered that the Egyptians had laid out their minefields three deep. The engineers used the access paths they found in two of the minefields and removed the mines in a third minefield to make their own path.

The engineers worked all night undetected. When the sun rose, the pathways were marked. The pathways wound like snakes through all three minefields. They were tricky to navigate in the dark, and even trickier under fire. A squad of engineers kept guard to ensure the Egyptians didn't move the marker stakes. The Engineers drew maps of the paths by hand for each platoon leader. It wasn't enough. One wrong step would not only result in the death of several soldiers from an exploding mine, it would give away the Israeli positions, inviting Egyptian artillery strikes. Colonel Givli ordered that two engineers, one in the front and one in the rear, would accompany each Israeli platoon through the minefields during the assault.

October 30, 1956 – Sinai Desert, Egypt

Coyle stared at the black smoke rising into the sky at the mouth of the canyon. He didn't like the look of it. It would attract attention and they were in a war zone. There was no way to put the fire from the ruptured wing tanks out until the fuel was exhausted. It was bad enough he was shot down by an Israeli, now he had to worry about Egyptian patrols. He wasn't sure what would happen if the Egyptians found him and his Spanish crew members. Technically, America and Spain were not at war with Egypt but if they were captured with the Israelis they might be seen as spies or sympathizers. Somehow, he thought that might be worse than being an actual Israeli soldier in uniform. He didn't want to find out.

The medic tended to the wound on his forehead. "How much water do we have?" said the medic.

"Three liters, I figure. We lost most of the water in our emergency tank to a couple of bullet holes," said Coyle.

"That won't last long. The wounded men need more than the rest of us. Their bodies need fluids to rebuild their blood supply. Dehydration will kill them as sure as a bullet."

"Alright. But I am going to need some water if I'm going to cross that desert and get help."

"You're going out there?"

"We don't have much choice. If we stay here we're likely to die of thirst or get picked up by an Egyptian patrol. I'm not sure how kindly they're going to treat you Israelis."

"At least we won't die of thirst and the men will get the medical treatment they need."

"You sure about that? I bet they're pretty pissed off

right about now. You know… the Israelis invading their country and all."

"The Fedayeen invade our country almost daily. At some point you have to fight back."

"Is that what all this is about? Showing the Arabs the Israelis can't be pushed around?"

"Part of it, I suppose. It's worked in the past. They attack us. We bloody their nose. They go off and pout until they attack us again. It's a vicious circle. But it's the only way we can survive."

"Hell of a way to live."

"I agree. We all hope to live in peace one day."

"Good luck with that."

"I could happen. It's got to happen. We can't keep hating each other forever."

"I suppose. Well, I better get going. I'll send help as soon as I get picked up."

"What about them?" said the medic motioning to the Spaniards.

"I don't know," said Coyle. "I'll ask 'em."

Coyle walked over to the Spaniards and said, "I'm heading out. Do you wanna go with me or stay here?"

The Spaniards looked confused. Coyle walked through the whole thing again but with hand motions. The Spaniards discussed it between themselves and then the navigator motioned that he and the cargo assistant would go with Coyle. "Alright. You're with me I guess."

Coyle grabbed a map and the survival kit from the cockpit. There were no firearms on board, but he took the flare gun with three flares and placed them in his rucksack. The knife in the survival kit had matches hidden in a compartment in the handle and a compass at the end of the hilt. He used the compass to determine their current location and marked it on the map. He studied the surrounding area on the map and determined the safest and quickest path was to head for the Egyptian city of Arish along the coast. While he was sure there would be

Egyptian soldiers in the city, he was also sure there would be some civilians who might be willing to offer assistance. It was a chance he had to take. He needed to get help back to the surviving Israelis as soon as possible. Coyle also figured the coast would be safer than heading back toward the border. The Israelis were advancing and the Egyptians were retreating. Both sides were trigger-happy and Coyle wanted no part of it. His options were limited. Arish seemed like the best bet.

Coyle and the Spaniards set out across the desert and headed north toward the coast. The only visible life was the occasional bird flying over, agama lizards and yellow scorpions, nicknamed the Deathstalker by the Arabs. Coyle knew there were also snakes in the Sinai but he hadn't seen one. He was not a big fan of any kind of snake. They were fast and liked to slither up the dark hole formed between a man's leg and his trousers while the victim was sleeping. It gave him the shivers just thinking about it.

The terrain was rough, covered with rocks and uneven. The air was dry. It was the end of October so the temperature was more bearable than the summer but still hot by Coyle's standards. It didn't take long before he took off his flight jacket and slung it over his shoulder. The map didn't show any wells or natural springs along the path they were taking. They would need to stretch their meager water supply as long as possible if they were going to survive. It was big if.

October 30, 1956 – Themed, Egypt

Sharon laid on his belly on a small hill and surveyed the area with his binoculars. Themed was a well-guarded oasis in the center of the Sinai. It was the only water in hundreds of square miles of barren desert. It was also a crossroads for a major road through the Sinai. The Egyptians saw it as a key strategic point. The Israelis agreed. The entire oasis was surrounded by barbed wire and minefields. Five machinegun positions guarded the road and the entry to the oasis. The Egyptians were in no mood to share.

The convoy was running low on vehicles and tanks. Sharon did not want to risk an attack through the minefields. They would attack the main gate and enter the oasis on the road which they knew would be safe. He elected not to use his artillery but had his mortar teams set up their weapons. With luck, they might be able to take out one or two of the machinegun positions. At the very least, they would force the Egyptians to keep their heads down while the Israelis advanced.

Sharon insisted that Brigitte stay back from the fighting. When she protested, he gave her a pair of binoculars so she could watch and threatened to leave her behind when the convoy moved out if she didn't obey his orders. After only one day of traveling with the Israeli colonel, Brigitte had learnt that Sharon was not a man to be taken lightly. She settled on the binoculars.

It was still early in the morning and the sun was once again at the Israelis' backs. There was a slight breeze out of the west making the smoke mortar rounds that usually covered any advancing troops little more than useless. Three AMX light tanks and ten halftracks would lead the attack into the oasis. The rest of the battalion would follow on foot.

It was a narrow road giving the Egyptians an ideal killing zone if the Israelis chose to stay away from the barbed wire and minefields. Captain Dane Salomon, a company commander, rode in the lead halftrack following the three tanks.

The attack opened with an Israeli mortar barrage on the Egyptian machinegun positions. As Sharon had hoped, a mortar round exploded inside one of the sandbagged positions killing the machine gun crew. As the tanks came within range of the machineguns, the Egyptians opened fire. The machine gunners concentrated their fire on the driver and gunner portholes. It was a long shot but occasionally a bullet would find its way through one of the small openings ricocheting inside the vehicle with deadly effect. The tanks fired back against the well-fortified machinegun positions. To fire accurately, the tanks stopped on the road bringing the entire battalion to a halt.

One of the Egyptian machine gunners switched his target to the Israeli troops on foot. The raking machinegun barrage was devastating against the unprotected foot soldiers. There was no place for them to hide. They could only lie as flat as possible on the road and hope a stream of bullets did not find them and that the tanks or halftracks didn't back up and run over them.

The driver of the lead halftrack pulled off the road to go around the tanks and continue the attack. "No. Stay on the road," said Salomon but it was too late.

The halftrack only made it ten feet off the road before it hit a mine. The explosion knocked the halftrack on its side, killing the driver and the machine gunner. Salomon was badly wounded in the leg. He could see the blood pumping out through the gash created by the mine's shrapnel. He knew he didn't have much time before he fell unconscious from loss of blood. "God, give me a fair wind for three minutes," he prayed.

To his amazement, God listened and the breeze calmed. The air was still. Salomon grabbed a rucksack filled with smoke grenades. He was protected from the machinegun fire from the belly of the tipped over halftrack. He climbed to his feet. The pain in his leg was intense. He needed to be standing to give his throw any distance. He pulled the pin on the first grenade and threw it over the side of the halftrack towards the Egyptian machinegun positions.

The grenade landed short and started spewing out smoke. The breeze kicked up again but this time out of the east and it carried the smoke right over the Egyptian positions. The machine gunners were blinded by the smoke and could only see a few feet in front of their positions.

Salomon looked to the sky and said, "Thank you."

He threw more grenade in different directions until there was a cloud of thick smoke around the oasis.

The Israeli commanders saw their chance. They ordered their tanks to cease fire and ordered their men on foot forward. The soldiers ran down the road toward the main gate.

The Egyptians continued to fire blindly in the direction of the road but with little effect. Israelis jumped over the sandbags and overran the Egyptian positions. They fought hand to hand using their knives and pistols.

As the smoke cleared, the Egyptian positions were silent and the Israelis were streaming into the oasis through the main gate.

Captain Salomon smiled and fainted, collapsing to the ground. Fortunately, a soldier saw him fall and called for a medic. His war was over, but he survived.

Sharon counted the dead and wounded. Four Israelis lost their lives and six were seriously wounded. Over fifty Egyptians lay dead on the battlefield. The rest had run off through a secret path through the minefield at the back of the oasis.

Seeing that the battle was over, Brigitte emerged from her hidden observation position and approached the oasis. She asked the names of the dead and wounded. She made notations in her notebook and took photos of the aftermath of battle.

Sharon let his men rest for thirty minutes while three DC-3s dropped fuel and ammunition onto the desert floor. The DC-3s turned and flew back toward the border. The platoon in charge of the motor pool refueled the Israeli vehicles.

Halfway through the refueling process a squadron of Egyptian MIG-15s and Il-28 twin-engine bombers jets flew over the mountains and into the valley.

The Israelis ran for cover. There wasn't much. The MIG-15s swooped down and strafed the defenseless Israeli soldiers with their 23-mm autocannons while the bombers went after the convoy of vehicles stretched out along the desert floor. The Israelis were lucky. The Soviet jets were new and the Egyptian crews had only a minimum amount of training in them before the invasion had started. Even with their lousy aim, the Egyptian jet crews were able to kill four more Israelis soldiers and destroy six more vehicles including one of the tanks. Satisfied with the damage they had done to the convoy and out of ammunition, the Soviet-made jets flew off.

The time the Israelis could have used to rest and relax was used instead to tend to the wounded and transfer supplies from the damaged vehicles. Sharon knew it would take time to get the convoy organized after the aerial attack. It was time he didn't have. There were a number of vehicles that had been refueled before the attack and were ready to leave.

Sharon pulled Major Mordechai "Motta" Gur aside and ordered him to take whatever was available and attack Qalaat el-Nakhl, the last village the convoy would encounter before reaching Eitan's battalion of paratroopers at the mouth of the Mitla Pass. Sharon knew Motta was smart and aggressive. He trusted him to take the objectives assigned to him. Motta listened carefully to Sharon's instructions and went to work. Twenty minutes later, Motta and his battalion were on the road heading west. He took Sharon's only remaining artillery gun plus another that had been rescued and caught up with the convoy just after the aerial attack. He left the tanks behind because they were too slow but took all the halftracks that had enough fuel to reach Nakhl.

October 30, 1956 – Qalaat el-Nakhl, Egypt

Qalaat el-Nakhl was nicknamed Fortress of the Palms which was curious because the entire area lacked any visible vegetation. It was a valley in the middle of a mountain range and the crossroads between two major highways. Whoever controlled Nakhl controlled the western Sinai.

It was home to the Egyptian 2nd Motorized Border Battalion. The ranks were made up of both Egyptian and Sudanese troops. Two companies from the battalion had been destroyed by the Israelis at Themed and the remaining companies knew the Israelis were heading their way.

Just before the mouth of the mountain pass, Motta ordered his column to stop. He and his commanders crept over a hilltop and spied on the garrison below.

The Egyptian garrison at Nakhl was well prepared to receive them with both artillery and heavy machineguns dug in deep and surrounded by sandbags. "Shit," said Motta. "Anybody got any bright ideas?"

"We could pull back and use the mountains for cover to reposition our forces. That would allow us to approach more from the side or back of the garrison," said one of the commanders.

"There is no time to reposition our forces. Besides, the longer we wait the more chance of being attacked by their air force. We attack from this point. We attack now," said Motta.

His commanders kept quiet.

"Great. It's settled then," said Motta. "We go straight at them. Once we exit the mountain pass, we'll spread our vehicles out in a line. On my order… we charge. Speed will be the deciding factor. We need to overrun their positions before they tear us to shreds."

"And if there is a minefield?" said one of the

commanders.

"Simple. We're fucked," said Motta. "I want our two artillery pieces placed on this hilltop. It should give them a clear shot at the Egyptian positions. They should target the artillery first and keep firing until our forces overrun the Egyptian positions. Our mortars will lay down smoke in front of the Egyptian machineguns then hit them with anti-personnel rounds until our forces intermingle. Lastly, have our four heavy machine guns take up position on both sides of the line. When the attack begins, they should target the enemy machineguns and lock down their guns so that they can keep firing accurately on the enemy positions even after the smoke obscures their vision. They are to break off their firing once our troops reach the enemy positions. At that point, our mortars, artillery and heavy machineguns are to target any Egyptian reinforcements. If everything goes to shit, our mortars, artillery and heavy machineguns will cover our retreat. Any questions?"

There were none. "May God be with you. Move out," said Motta and the commanders made their way back to their units.

What Motta and his men did not know was that an Egyptian lieutenant had escaped from the Israeli troops at the oasis and fled on a motorcycle to the battalion HQ at Nakhl. He had arrived one hour before Motta and his convoy.

When questioned by the battalion commander as to why he left his post, the lieutenant explained that he felt it was his duty to warn the rest of the battalion of the ferocity of the Jews and the makeup of their forces. To cover his own cowardice, the lieutenant exaggerated the Israeli numbers and their skill. He made it seem as if it were impossible to defeat them and that the Israelis would show no mercy when the Egyptian forces were overrun.

The lieutenant's description was not lost on the major that commanded the battalion. He knew that the lieutenant was probably making up much of what he was saying to save his own skin. But he also knew there was probably some truth to what he was saying. After all, many veterans of previous encounters with the Israelis had told similar stories of the Israelis' no mercy mindset. The major had been told he must hold the crossroads at all costs and that surrender was never to be an option for the commander of the garrison at Nakhl. It was a condition on being assigned the command. He was confident in the layout of his defenses. He had had plenty of time to prepare and had been warned of a possible attack just before the communication lines to Cairo had been cut. His artillery and machineguns would lay waste the attacking Israelis, then he would lead his own merciless counterattack and destroy them before they could retreat. This was his opportunity to show his superiors what he was made of and finally receive the promotion he desired. It was a solid plan.

As Motta's vehicles drove out of the mouth of the mountain pass and lined up across the valley floor, the artillery, mortars and machineguns opened fire. Motta had ordered the troop trucks to line up behind the jeeps and halftracks. The trucks were taller than the other vehicles and, even though they didn't have any weapons, they gave the impression that the mobile fighting force was much larger than it was in reality.

The Israeli mortars and heavy machine guns were having a murderous effect on the Egyptian lines. The Israelis were well-trained and their aim was accurate. The Egyptians were the opposite. Their commanders did not have much combat experience and preferred not to waste expensive ammunition on training. They would conserve their ammunition for real battle with the Israelis.

To everyone's surprise, one of the Israeli artillery shells made a direct hit on an Egyptian artillery gun destroying it completely and killing the gun crew. It was a very lucky shot. The effect was amplified as a stack of artillery shells stored too close to the gun exploded in rapid succession creating a huge ball of flame like a mini-Armageddon. The well-placed shot and the resulting devastation struck fear into the Egyptian troops and their commanders.

The Egyptian major looked at the Israeli forces lined up and ready to attack. He informed his next in command, a young captain, that he was in charge of the garrison's defenses while the major went to inspect the outposts and ensure there was no surprise attack from behind. The Egyptian troops and unit commanders watched as their battalion commander drove away in his jeep. Morale plummeted.

Motta gave the order to advance. The line of Israeli vehicles raced toward the Egyptian positions at full speed. The drivers prayed that there were no mines in the path between their vehicles and the Egyptians. Fortunately for the Israelis, the battalion commander had elected not to place mines in front of his positions so that this troops would not be hindered when they counterattacked. The vehicle-mounted machineguns opened fire, raking the Egyptian lines. The Israeli mortars fired their smoke rounds just as the Egyptian guns opened fire.

The battlefield was shrouded in smoke. The Egyptians knew the Israelis were coming but they could not see them and that made the situation even more frightening. A few decided to follow their commander's example and left. Troops watched as their comrades ran from their posts. It was contagious. The Egyptian lines rolled up as more and more fled.

When the Israeli vehicles overran the Egyptian positions, they found them silent and empty. The smoke cleared. Only the dead and severely wounded remained. The rest of the Egyptian soldiers and their commanders had fled across the valley and disappeared into the hills. An entire Egyptian battalion had disappeared without a trace.

The vehicle commanders reported back to Motta watching from the hillside. He couldn't believe it. The Israelis forces had taken the garrison at Nakhl without the loss of one Israeli soldier or even a vehicle. With the taking of the crossroads came the control of the area. All remaining Egyptian forces in the north of the Sinai were cut off from reinforcements and resupply.

The Israelis found six Russian-made armored troop carriers inside the garrison with the keys in the ignitions. They were commandeered and filled with ammunition for their machineguns, spare parts, and Israeli troops.

Within one hour Motta had his convoy on the move again except for a small contingent of paratroopers left to watch over the garrison and the wounded Egyptian soldiers until Sharon and the rest of the brigade arrived. They were behind schedule but now had a clear path to Eitan's paratroop battalion at the Mitla Pass.

October 30, 1956 – Sinai Desert, Egypt

The sun was setting in the western horizon as Coyle and the two Spaniards walked through a flat desert valley. The ground was solid, the sun having baked the soil to a hard shell. There were few rocks, which Coyle found strange. *Why no rocks?* he thought. *Maybe they were swallowed by the clay whenever it rained.* That explanation seemed logical and he decided he must be correct, since there was nobody that spoke English to discuss his hypothesis.

In the distance, he saw another low mountain range like the one they had emerged from over an hour earlier. Everything seemed the same. He worried that they might be going in circles. He pulled out his compass on the end of the survival knife and checked their direction. They were still heading north as he had planned. He looked up at the mountains and noticed dark clouds sweeping in over the desert. "Maybe we'll get some rain," he said to the navigator.

The navigator looked confused again. He pointed to the dark clouds and motioned rain with his hands. The navigator nodded that he now understood and said, "Lluvia. Bien."

"Yeah. Lluvia. Bien," said Coyle.

The cargo assistant lagged behind. He was depressed because of his boss's death. "Tell your buddy he has to keep up. We have a long way to go," said Coyle using his hands to motion.

The navigator yelled back in Spanish to the boy. The boy picked up his pace. A flash of lightning from the approaching storm caught Coyle's attention. There was another flash that followed within a few seconds. The air cracked from the thunder. The wind was kicking up. The dark clouds were moving fast, directly toward them. Coyle looked down at the hair on his forearm. It rose like a balloon had been rubbed against it, creating static electricity.

"Oh, shit," said Coyle as it dawned on him that they were the tallest and wettest objects on the desert floor. Their bodies would act as conductors to the lighting. Coyle looked around. There was a small grouping of boulders on a rise about a half mile off. It was better than nothing. "Come on," he said motioning to the others and breaking into a run for the rock formation.

"Vamanos," said the navigator to the boy. They broke into a run and followed Coyle toward the rocks.

The storm moved toward them like an angry beast with more violent lightning strikes and loud claps of thunder. Coyle hoped it would start raining. Rain would make everything around them wet and they would no longer be the only conductors. A bolt of lightning hit the desert floor and the crash of thunder followed immediately. The storm was almost on them. Coyle was the first to reach the boulders. He turned and waved the others on like a coach cheering them on. "Move your asses," he said.

The navigator made it to the boulders and turned to cheer on the boy. More lightning strikes. Coyle and the navigator knelt beside the boulders and watched in horror as two more lightning strikes hit the earth with bright flashes. A third strike hit the boy. His momentum carried him forward and he tumbled to the ground in a mix of dust and smoke. The navigator moved to help him. Coyle pulled him back. "No. You can't help him," said Coyle. "He's gone."

Coyle was right. The boy had died the moment the lightning entered his head and exited his shoe forming a long-charred tunnel through his body and organs. There was no blood. The wound was instantly cauterized. He laid motionless on the desert floor. Smoke rose from the hole in the top of the boy's head and out a hole in his shoe.

Coyle and the navigator waited until the storm passed before emerging from behind the boulders. It still hadn't rained. Coyle used his knife to crack hardened clay and dig a hole in the desert floor. They buried the boy to keep the critters away until they could return and retrieve his body. Coyle and the navigator stood over the grave. "What was his name?" said Coyle.

"Nombre?" said the navigator.

"Yeah. Nombre."

"Fue Louis," said the navigator.

Coyle grunted. He thought about asking the navigator's name but decided against it. He had been told the man's name when they first met, but he had forgotten it. Instead he said, "You like meatloaf?"

The navigator looked confused. Coyle reached into his rucksack and pulled out the meatloaf sandwich he had retrieved from the cockpit. He tore it in two and gave half to the navigator. "Gracias," said the navigator.

"You're welcome," said Coyle.

They ate staring down at the boy's grave. For some reason, it seemed appropriate to eat. Like a wake.

October 30, 1956 – Mitla Pass, Egypt

It was night by the time Motta's column reached the eastern end of the Mitla Pass. Lightning from a distant storm in the north silhouetted the vehicles as they approached. Eitan's paratroopers were relieved and cheered. They were slightly alarmed when they saw the six Soviet armored troop transports at the head of the column but relaxed when they saw the heads of Israeli drivers popping out of the hatches.

When they pulled to a stop, Motta's paratroopers hopped out of their vehicles and embraced Eitan's paratroopers like long lost cousins. Both groups of Israelis were happy to see each other. Tears welled in some of their eyes. Others laughed and made jokes. They had linked up and accomplished their mission. Motta's troops had been traveling and fighting for two days straight and were on the verge of exhaustion. Before they could sleep they would need to set their vehicles up in defensive positions, set up their weapons and dig foxholes where necessary. Eitan's paratroopers kept watch on the pass and surrounding terrain.

Sharon and the rest of the brigade were not far behind. Near midnight, they pulled into the defensive perimeter. Like Motta's men, they dug their foxholes, set up their weapons and parked their vehicles. With Eitan's paratroopers keeping watch, the rest of brigade ate their first hot meal and slept. The cavalry had saved the day but needed a nap before they would be ready to fight again. Even the bravest of men can only go so long without sleep.

October 30, 1956 – Sinai Desert, Egypt

The night was cold. The desert had given up its heat within the first two hours after sunset. Coyle and the Spaniard were exhausted from walking most of the day and tomorrow didn't look like it was going to be any easier, especially since they were running low on water.

They found shelter in a rock outcropping. The Spaniard had gathered kindling from dried up bushes and a tree that had long since died. Coyle warned him that the fire needed to be kept small so it would not be spotted. They did not want to be taken prisoner by the Egyptians. They ate two packages of stale crackers from the survival kit. They would save the one can of spam until the morning when they needed the added energy it would give them.

They were lucky. They both still had their flight jackets that provided welcome warmth. Coyle thought about trading off guard duty while the other slept, but he realized that they were both so exhausted either of them could easily fall asleep during their watch. He abandoned the idea. They would risk it. They both slept. Coyle dreamed of snakes and scorpions.

October 31, 1956 - Mediterranean Sea

It was three in the morning when the *Ibrahim* swung out in an arc and approached the port of Haifa from the west. Once in range, Tamsyn ordered his main guns to open fire. The bombardment rained down two hundred shells in just a few minutes.

On shore, the two security guards watching over the Israelis' precious oil supply ran for cover. They both served in the Israeli navy as reservists and knew the power of a destroyer's guns. A shell scored a direct hit on one of the oil bunkers and ignited the petroleum fumes at the top of the tank. The explosion lit up the night sky and the nearby port.

On board the *Ibrahim* the crew cheered on seeing the explosion. As the light from the explosion faded, one of the lookouts on board the *Ibrahim* spotted the outline of a large vessel docked in the port. He informed the gunnery commander, suggesting that it might be one of the Israelis' destroyers. The gunnery commander ordered the gun crews to change their target to the port in hopes of hitting the ship while it was boxed in in the harbor and an easy target. Unbeknownst to the gun commander the ship tied to the dock was not Israeli. It was French.

The French captain and his officers were reviewing the status of the Egyptian fleet with Israeli intelligence officers and going over last-minute details of the planned assault on Port Said when the first explosions occurred. They instinctively ran for their ship.

The attack of the Egyptian destroyer on Haifa presented a difficult political problem for the French. They were not technically at war with the Egyptians until 4:30 a.m. which was still several hours away. If the French were found to be colluding with the Israelis hours before their invasion it could cause an international crisis.

The French captain had strict orders not to engage the Egyptian ships until the ultimatum expired. He was however allowed to defend his ship should it come under fire from any aggressor. The first shell landed in the harbor as the French officers reached the gangplank of the *Kersaint* – a cold-war era destroyer with three twin five-inch gun turrets controlled by the world's latest gunnery radar system.

Boarding his vessel, the French captain was in no mood for niceties, and ordered his gun crews to return fire. The *Kersaint's* guns swung around and fired in unison.

On board the *Ibrahim*, Captain Tamsyn knew he was outgunned when six five-inch sells landed around his ship. Fortunately for the Egyptian crew, the French missed with their first volley. Tamsyn was not going to wait around for a second volley. He ordered his helmsman to take the destroyer out to sea at full speed. Tamsyn knew that the *Ibrahim* stood a much better chance of surviving a gun battle with a modern warship in open sea. Even with modern radar-guided weapons, hitting a moving target while taking into account currents and the rocking motion of the waves was not an easy task for any gunnery commander. Most of the time it was doggedness or sheer luck that allowed either side to hit the other. The *Ibrahim* was lightly armored for a destroyer and it would not take much to sink her if the enemy gunners found their mark.

Tamsyn ordered his guns to continue to fire on the destroyer in hopes they would cast off their lines and become more inaccurate in their firing as their ship moved. It worked and the *Kersaint* gave chase.

The *Ibrahim* had a substantial lead by the time the *Kersaint* was up to speed, but the French vessel was faster by almost three knots. Tamsyn ordered a change of course and steered toward Lebanon. The *Ibrahim's* best hope was to reach Syrian waters and the safety of the Syrian shore batteries. The Israelis were not yet at war with Syria, but the Syrians were unpredictable and might fire on an Israeli warship chasing an Egyptian destroyer.

Tamsyn and his crew were pleasantly surprised when the *Kersaint* broke off her pursuit. The Egyptian crew cheered. Tamsyn was more pensive about the unexpected move. *Why did they break off their attack?* he thought.

The answer came in the form of two Israeli destroyers and a frigate, an Israeli task force commanded by Captain Shmuel Yanai.

The French captain on the *Kersaint* knew that his argument for defending his ship was weak at best once the Egyptian destroyer headed out to sea. He did not want to tip France's hand in the upcoming war. He radioed the Israeli navy to inform them of the *Ibrahim's* course and returned to the fleet sailing near Port Said.

The Israelis sent a Douglas Skytrain C-47 transport plane to search for the *Ibrahim*. The Israelis often used their aircraft for different types of missions. They had to make do with what they had on hand and not worry about the plane's intended use. It didn't take long before the C-47, nicknamed Dakota, spotted and identified the Egyptian destroyer. The pilot radioed the ship's position to the Israeli task force sailing along the southern coast.

The Egyptian crew spotted the slow-moving transport plane shadowing them. The Dakota's pilot was cautious and kept out of range of the *Ibrahim's* anti-aircraft guns. Tamsyn radioed the Egyptian Air Force and requested aircraft reinforcements in case the Israelis sent their jets. His request was denied. The Egyptian Air Force commanders did not want to send any of their planes that far into Israeli territory when they were needed to protect the homeland.

The Israeli frigate *INS Miznak* took up the pursuit of the *Ibrahim*. The *Ibrahim* was still performing evasive maneuvers in the open waters just in case the *Kersaint's* captain changed his mind or was staging some sort of ruse to fool the Egyptians. The *Miznak* headed northeast straight towards the *Ibrahim's* position at maximum speed and made good time. The *Miznak* was no match for the larger Egyptian ship. Her purpose was not to fight but rather to prevent the *Ibrahim* from doubling back and drive the Egyptian destroyer toward Beirut. If the *Ibrahim* engaged the *Miznak*, the captain of the *Miznak* had orders to run. The Israelis had so few ships they could not afford to lose even one.

As the *Miznak* pursued the *Ibrahim*, the two Israeli destroyers *INS Yaffo* and *INS Eilat* turned northwest and sailed at full speed to cut off the Egyptian ship's escape into Lebanon. At five in the morning the *Eilat's* radar acquired the *Ibrahim* and the two Israeli destroyers pushed to intercept it as it made its final turn toward the port in Beirut.

A few minutes later, the radar operator picked up a second set of contacts - four surface vessels approaching from the west. Yanai realized that his task force may have fallen into a trap. The four approaching vessels could be Syrian. His two destroyers could be caught in a pincer-type maneuver between Egyptian and Syrian forces. There was a good chance that the frigate *Miznak* could escape the trap if it was warned in time. The two Israeli destroyers would stand a better if they too broke off the pursuit of the *Ibrahim* and headed out to open sea. The Egyptian warship would escape unharmed.

Yanai decided to break silence and identify his ships. He sent a Morse code signal using the ship's search lights in the direction of the four approaching ships. He waited for a reply that could very well determine the fate of his ships and crew. One of the four ships signaled back identifying themselves as neutral American vessels from the U.S. Navy 6th Fleet. Yanai and his men on the bridge were relieved. The Israelis continued their pursuit of the *Ibrahim*. The American ships turned 180 degrees about to avoid getting caught in the crossfire from the battle that was about to unfold.

The Israeli destroyers closed to within six miles of the Egyptian destroyer and used their radar to calculate the position of their target. Their guns turned toward the *Ibrahim* and at nine thousand yards they opened fire.

With two Israeli destroyers bearing down on the bow of his vessel and an Israeli frigate approaching astern, Tamsyn knew he and his crew were in trouble. He radioed for help from the Syrians and the Lebanese. He received no reply. He had little choice but to fight against the odds. The *Ibrahim* returned fire.

The Israelis kept their shelling hot and heavy. One of the lookouts reported an explosion followed by black smoke on the extreme bow of the *Ibrahim*. The Israeli shell had pierced the forward deck, passed through the ship and exited through the starboard hull. The dark holes in the hull and deck looked a lot more serious than they were in reality. The shell had passed through the anchor's chain compartment and did no real damage to the ship. The Egyptians were lucky. A depth charge rack was nearby and would have created a massive explosion, if hit.

The Israelis didn't let up. They didn't know how much time they had before other vessels or aircraft joined the fight. They wanted to sink the *Ibrahim* before others could come to her rescue. Another lookout reported a second hit on the stern of the *Ibrahim*.

A round had hit underneath the *Ibrahim's* aft gun mount and damaged the magazine hoist, dramatically slowing the gun's rate of fire. The shell had pierced the deck and detonated inside the ship. One piece of the shell destroyed one of the boilers, and another piece damaged some machinery. A third piece of the shell destroyed one of the turbogenerators which fed the electrical system.

A third shell slammed into the forward deck underneath the main gun turret, damaging its operating mechanism. With several of his crew killed and badly wounded, Tamsyn gave the order to turn about and head due north back out to sea. He wasn't sure where they would go but anywhere was better than the deadly triangle the Israeli ships had formed. The safety of Lebanon would have to wait.

As the *Ibrahim's* crew prepared to flee the battle, one of the Israeli shells penetrated the upper deck over the engine compartment and badly wounded several of the engineers. The *Ibrahim* was slow with a speed of only seventeen knots. It wouldn't take the Israelis long to close in. The counterfire from his guns was slow and sporadic. The gunnery crews were tired and their aim was abysmal.

Two Israeli Ouragan jets appeared on the horizon and flew toward the *Ibrahim*. The Egyptians opened fire with their anti-aircraft guns with little effect against the fast flying jets. The jets fired thirty-two unguided air-to-surface missiles scoring only one hit. The armor-piercing warhead penetrated the weather deck, went through the wardroom, and exploded in a machinery space, further crippling the *Ibrahim*. With their missiles expended, the Israeli pilots strafed the decks of the *Ibrahim* with their Hispano 20-mm guns. Several more of the *Ibrahim's* crew members went down wounded or dead.

Tamsyn knew it was just a matter of time until the Israelis caught up with his vessel. The only question was how many of his crew would die before the battle was over. Tamsyn was not afraid of dying himself. He had come to grips with the possibility long ago. He knew that he could be court-martialed if he did not continue fighting until the last man or he ran out of ammunition, but he didn't care at that point in the battle. He wanted to save his crew. He considered scuttling his ship before abandoning her but knew that it would be difficult to penetrate the ship's hull without a massive explosion that would kill many more of his men. His men had fought the Israelis bravely. They had done their duty. It was time to let go. Tamsyn ordered a flag of surrender to be hoisted above the bridge.

Colonel Menachem Cohen, the captain of INS *Eilat*, was surprised when his lookouts reported that the *Ibrahim* had hoisted a flag of surrender. At first, he thought it a trick. No captain of a modern warship had ever hoisted a flag of surrender. He ordered a message sent in Morse code by searchlight asking the captain of the *Ibrahim* to declare his intentions. The message that came back said that the Egyptian captain was indeed surrendering his ship. Cohen sent another message requesting that the *Ibrahim* cut its engines and come to a full stop. The *Ibrahim* stopped. The *Eilat* pulled alongside the *Ibrahim* and trained its guns on the hull of the ship should it restart its engines or open fire. Cohen ordered an armed boarding party to sail over to the Egyptian destroyer and take its crew captive.

The surrender went off without incident and the battle was over. Israeli intelligence officers scoured the ship for intelligence that might reveal the Egyptians' war plans. They found little information of use. The Egyptians didn't have a plan, except to react.

Tamsyn was transferred to the *Eilat* where he met Cohen and officially surrendered his ship, as was naval tradition. Tamsyn asked that his wounded crew members be evacuated and for additional men to help fight the fires above and below deck. Cohen agreed but said that his men would fight any fires.

The Egyptian prisoners left their ship under guard and the Israelis took over. The Israeli chief engineer inspected the Egyptian ship and reported that the damage was relatively superficial and the *Ibrahim* was in no danger of sinking. Cohen was miffed. Warships were rarely taken in modern warfare, but he was happy to oblige.

The *Ibrahim* was towed back to Haifa and the damage repaired. Months later, the destroyer was recommissioned into the Israeli navy as the *INS Haifa*.

NINE

October 31, 1956 – Mitla Pass, Egypt

When Sharon awoke the next morning after reuniting his forces, he saw the obvious problem facing his brigade. The mountains overlooked the Israeli positions. He wondered why the Egyptians had not already attacked. They would have a clear advantage using the mountain ridges for protection.

He received his answer when the first Israeli jets arrived overhead and scouted the mountains – There were no Egyptian forces in the Mitla Pass.

Sharon and the other commanders were puzzled on hearing the news. Why would the Egyptians not protect such a strategic point? The Mitla Pass was the gateway to the middle of the Suez Canal Zone. It was easily defensible and didn't require a large force.

The Egyptians were more concerned with protecting the Suez Canal than any of the passes leading to it. They had placed the majority of their armed forces in the Sinai near the shores of the canal and not in the mountains bordering it.

It was clear to Sharon and the others that this was a strategic mistake. The 202nd Brigade needed to occupy the pass or face the consequences of an Egyptian force gaining a well-covered position that could rain down artillery and mortar shells on the Israeli forces with impunity. The Israelis would have no choice but to withdraw, which could endanger Operation Musketeer and Operation Revise. With the threat of the Israelis gone the British and French military would lack a legitimate reason to invade Egypt and protect the canal.

Israeli intelligence reported that an Egyptian armored brigade was forty miles to the northeast at Bir Gifgafa and had changed direction to advance on the Israeli positions.

It was almost like the Egyptians had been listening in on the Israelis and realized their blunder. The Egyptian redeployment would quickly develop into a race to see who could occupy the pass and the surrounding mountain slopes first. Sharon's brigade was weak. His men were exhausted and he had left a battalion at the Nakhl crossroads and a company at Themed Oasis to protect his communication lines. With only three tanks and a few artillery pieces, his brigade looked more like a battalion. He needed to put his men in a defensible position before the Egyptians counterattacked.

Sharon radioed Dayan at Army HQ in Jerusalem, informed him of the Egyptian armored movements and asking for permission to occupy the empty pass. To his amazement, he was denied. Dayan and the Israeli leaders were concerned that the pass was too close to the canal and, because it was a key strategic point, could be considered within the restricted zone that British and French had declared. Sharon argued that it would be better to take and hold the pass until the British and French forces arrived. His troops could simply withdraw at the first sign of Western soldiers. The British and French could then occupy the pass without having to fight for it with the Egyptians. Dayan was concerned that things could quickly get out of hand if the Israelis were found to occupy the pass. Sharon persuaded Dayan to at least allow him to scout the pass but on the condition that Sharon's reconnaissance units were to pull back the moment they encountered a large force of Egyptians.

Sharon selected Motta to lead the reconnaissance mission. Motta and his men were to attempt to take the entire twenty miles of the pass before stopping. He gave Motta specific instructions to break off any engagement with the enemy that threatened to become a large-scale battle. Motta agreed.

Motta took two companies of paratroopers in the six Russian armored troop carriers, plus several halftracks and the three remaining tanks into the pass. They would move fast, hoping to catch any Egyptian forces by surprise.

The reconnaissance force rounded a bend less than a mile into the pass and came under heavy fire. The Egyptians had hidden behind the ridges of the mountain and nearby caves hoping to ambush the unsuspecting Israelis. The Israeli jets were flying too fast to spot them. They had placed a truck in the middle of the road to block the Israelis from advancing.

The first two Israeli halftracks were hit with Soviet-made recoilless rifle rounds and exploded, killing the drivers, gunners and several of the troops inside. Motta ordered a third halftrack to push the Egyptian truck out of the way while the first Israeli tank moved up and provided covering fire. The halftrack succeeded in pushing the truck off the road but ended up crashing into a wadi when the driver was blinded by a ricocheting bullet through the halftrack's viewing porthole. Lieutenant Arieh Crespi, one of the company commanders, was also killed.

A few moments later, the light tank was hit with a recoilless rifle round killing the gunner. The tank could still move but the main gun was useless. Within the first five minutes of battle, twelve Israelis had died and the rest of the convoy was under heavy fire from the surrounding ridgetops.

Motta refused to retreat despite his orders. He had been taught by Sharon never to leave his men, dead or wounded, behind. This allowed the paratroopers to fight without reservation. They knew if they were wounded their comrades would come and get them. If dead, their bodies would be returned to their families. It gave them courage. Motta was not about to betray that trust. He and his men fought on.

They were fortunate to have the Russian troop carriers which were enclosed in armor and allowed the soldiers inside to shoot out through gun portholes. The armor on the Soviet vehicles was heavy enough to resist heavy machinegun fire but could not deflect a direct hit from a recoilless rifle. The paratroopers kept a sharp-eye out for any signs of a recoilless rifle team setting up their weapon and would pour fire on their position until the enemy was killed or retreated.

Once the convoy had entered the pass, Sharon had lost radio contact with Motta and his men. He could hear the distant explosions and gunfire but had no idea as to the ferocity of the ambush.

To make matters worse, an Egyptian squadron of British-made Vampire jets flew into the valley and strafed the paratrooper position outside the pass. The twin-tailed Vampires had four 20-mm cannons and had been purchased by Egypt from the Italian Air Force using Syria as an intermediary. Their maneuverability at high speeds made them ideal for air-to-ground attack. The Israeli lost five more vehicles and three paratroopers were killed with several more severely wounded. The Israelis were being torn apart and were taking heavy losses.

October 31, 1956 – Cairo, Egypt

Once word reached the Egyptian commander that the Israelis had attempted to take the pass, he ordered several battalions to redeploy across the Suez. A chain ferry was used to transport the troops and their light vehicles across the canal. Tanks and halftracks were too heavy for the ferry and had to be left behind. The battalions were still well-armed with fourteen medium machineguns and twelve anti-tank guns. Many of the battalion officers found excuses not to cross with their men and left them leaderless. The NCOs carried out the redeployment. In some respects, this worked to the Egyptians' advantage. The men respected the NCOs and loathed the officers. They fought more valiantly when only led by their platoon commanders.

When the majority of the Egyptian force had crossed Suez, they set out for the Mitla Pass. They took up positions on the Heitan defile just past a bend in the road near the top of the pass. As more troops made it across the Suez they joined their comrades in the pass and waited for the Israelis.

October 31, 1956 – Mitla Pass, Egypt

The Egyptian companies that had been battling with the Israeli units most of the day, pulled back so that the larger force could confront the enemy. The Israelis, once again, did not know what they were facing as they advanced through the pass.

Below the mountain pass, Sharon redeployed his men to form a defensive position facing outward from the mouth of the pass. His concern was that the Egyptian armored column might use another pass to cross over to the eastern side of the mountains and attack the Israelis from the rear.

Sharon received his first reports of the ambush when Motta send back a soldier to give Sharon the message in person. Sharon was running low on troops and vehicles, but he did his best to shore up the beleaguered assault force. He sent Eitan with several companies of paratroopers to reinforce Motta and his men.

When Eitan and his reinforcements arrived, Motta ordered the halftracks to push the damaged vehicles out of their path and clear the road. The Israelis again pushed forward deeper into the pass, carefully watching the ridges above them.

No sooner did the first battle end than the second one started. The Israeli vehicles rounded a bend in the mountain road and encountered the larger Egyptian force waiting in ambush. The Egyptian anti-tank guns were well placed to cover the road and several Israeli vehicles were immediately destroyed, killing several drivers and passengers. The Israelis were in trouble again but they didn't retreat. Instead, Motta send a company up the side of the mountain ridge in hopes of flanking the Egyptian anti-tank gun positions. Black smoke rising up from the burning vehicles hid the Israeli flanking maneuver and kept the anti-tank guns from destroying more vehicles. The Israelis were forced to scale a large cliff to avoid Egyptian fire as they climbed to the top of the ridge.

When the Israelis reached the top of the ridge they came under heavy fire from well-positioned Egyptian machineguns placed on the ridgetops on both sides of the road. The Israelis were pinned down and taking more losses. With the Egyptians having two angles of attack, the Israelis were unable to get at the anti-tank guns. Realizing the situation was hopeless, the Israeli company commander ordered his men to gather their wounded and retreat down to the road and the safety of the armored vehicles.

Hour after hour the two sides chipped away at each other taking a shot when the opportunity arose through the dust and smoke. It was a stalemate, which meant that the Israelis were unable to take their objective, and therefore losing.

Motta and Eitan were determined to break through and secure the pass. They decided to try again to clear the enemy position on the ridgetops. This time they would send men up both sides of the road and attack simultaneously denying the Egyptians the ability to concentrate their fire. At the same time, they would send a halftrack and the two remaining tanks up the road to engage the Egyptian units at the bottom of the ridgeline. It was an all-or-nothing push to overrun the Egyptian positions and take the pass. The Israelis had three advantages: aggressiveness, training, and leadership. Bravery aside, the Israelis were far better fighters than the Egyptians. The Israeli soldiers were led well by their officers unlike the Egyptians who believed their blood and lives were often being wasted.

The eastern ridge was even more rugged than the western ridge making it difficult to maneuver. But the ruggedness offered the Israelis more covered positions behind rocks and gullies. The Israelis were able to close in on the Egyptians. Once they were within throwing distance, the Israelis attacked with a new ferocity, hurling grenades over the top of the ridge into the Egyptian positions. The Israelis were experienced at timing their grenade detonations so they exploded as they landed rather than rolling farther down the ridgeline.

One by one, the Israelis on the eastern ridgeline rolled up the Egyptian machinegun positions and drove the supporting troops into retreat until they controlled the top of the ridge. Then they turned their weapons on the western ridgeline just as the Egyptians had done to them. With two angles of attack the Egyptians soon realized their positions were untenable and retreated, spiking their anti-tank guns and leaving them behind.

After two hours of fierce combat, some of which was hand-to-hand, the Israelis were in control of the ridges on both sides of the road. They turned their guns on the Egyptians still fighting below on the road. It was a slaughter. The Egyptians broke and ran. The Israelis were too exhausted to chase after them. It was enough that they had taken the pass and now had a clear path to the roadways paralleling the eastern banks of the Suez Canal.

Sharon entered the pass with the rest of his brigade which took up defensive positions. He was shocked by what he saw. Thirty-eight Israelis were dead and one hundred and twenty were wounded. Two hundred and sixty Egyptians lay dead alongside the road. The battle for Mitla Pass had been the bloodiest and most costly for both sides up to that point of the war.

October 31, 1956 – Suez Canal Zone, Egypt

An Israeli scout plane spotted the Egyptian armored battalion as it turned west toward the Suez Canal. He radioed back to headquarters to report his discovery.

When the Egyptian commander realized that the Israelis now held the high ground in the pass, he broke off his advance. An attack against the Israeli positions would be too costly, and his tanks were needed to protect the canal. The generals in Cairo would need to come up with another plan to root the Israelis out of the mountain pass.

October 31, 1956 – Mitla Pass

Once again, the Israeli paratroopers could rest peacefully, knowing they had accomplished their objective and were in a strong defensive position. Nobody felt like celebrating. The cost was very high and most of the soldiers that fought that day lost close friends that would be missed in the days to come. Instead, prayers were said for the dead, and the wounded were cared for by the medics.

The Israeli engineers cleared an area on the flatland at the mouth of the pass and created a makeshift landing strip. DC-3s landed, dropping off supplies and picking up the wounded. The paratroopers had a hot meal that night and shared stories of the battle as soldiers often do when the fighting is done. They all slept well… except for Sharon. Many would question what Sharon had done and if the seizure of the pass was necessary, but none would be more critical than Sharon himself.

October 31, 1956 – Sinai Desert, Egypt

Coyle and his Spanish navigator continued their trek north across the Sinai Desert. It was hot and dry. The one bottle of water they carried with them was almost empty. They had been rationing the water, but the dry climate and heat sapped their bodies of moisture and they needed to replenish their fluids continually or risk dehydration.

Coyle knew they would need to find a water source soon or they would be dead by morning – noon at the latest. The problem was that he didn't know where to look and whom they might find waiting if they found it. There were no markings for wells or springs on the map. He figured they would most likely find water in the wadis, the canyons or in the mountains. So far, everywhere they had looked was dry as a bone.

He realized how ill-suited he was for the desert. He didn't like it and it didn't like him. It was his general ignorance that bothered him most. He thought he should know something about the region and the people but he knew almost nothing. "Mira," said the navigator pointing to the horizon.

Coyle looked out. In the distance, he saw something moving on the horizon. He wasn't sure what it was. He motioned for the navigator to crouch low. He did the same. Whatever it was, it was heading in their direction. He could see a cloud of dust in its wake. It was a vehicle. He motioned for the navigator to lay on the ground. He did the same and kept watch as the vehicle approached. He had no way of telling if it was Egyptian or Israeli. He was sure it wasn't civilian. He looked around for a place to hide. There was none nearby. The closest cover was a mountain range behind the approaching vehicle. That did them no good.

Coyle pulled out the knife and stabbed the ground to break up the clay. The navigator saw what he was doing and used his hands to claw the softer dirt and sand below the surface. There wasn't much time. They created two shallow trenches. He motioned the navigator to climb into one. Once inside, he used his hands to cover the navigator with some of the excess dirt from the trench. He could see that there was going to be too much dirt. He threw handfuls away from the trench.

He looked again at the approaching vehicle. It looked like an armored car. He was pretty sure only the Egyptians used armed cars. He had heard from somewhere that the Israelis preferred lower-cost jeeps and trucks. He wondered if they could already see him and if hiding was just a wasted effort. He finished packing the dirt around the navigator and moved to his trench. He threw away as much dirt as he thought was excess of what he needed and climbed into the trench. He pulled the sand and dirt around and over himself as much as possible. They laid flat and still.

As the vehicle approached, he could see that it was actually a small convoy of three vehicles, possibly a reconnaissance patrol. He wasn't sure what side they were on until the vehicles passed and he recognized the decal on one of the doors. They were Egyptian. Their wheels passed within ten feet of their trenches. Coyle and the navigator remained motionless and unnoticed as the vehicles sped away.

They waited until the vehicles were out of sight before climbing out of their trenches and dusting themselves off. They continued walking toward the mountains. Coyle wondered if they should have turned themselves over to the Egyptians. They would have water. It may have been their last chance. He drove the thought from his mind and focused on the mountains. *There has to be water someplace in those mountains,* he thought. *We just gotta find it.*

October 31, 1956 – Mitla Pass

The Israelis kept watch from their defensive positions inside the Mitla Pass. They needed rest after two days of hard travel and fighting. They were receiving regular shipments of food and supplies from cargo aircraft landing on the flat desert to the east of the pass. Sharon approached his radio operator, a young corporal, and said, "Any word from General Dayan?"

"Nothing," said the corporal. "We did get a message about that Spanish cargo plane. Apparently, it was shot down by one of our jets on its way back to the border. He thought it was an Egyptian ally."

Sharon looked concerned and said, "Shit. Any survivors?"

"They don't know. They are sending a patrol out to take a look at the wreckage."

"Alright. Keep me posted and keep this quiet until we know about the survivors. The French woman's boyfriend was the pilot."

"The American?"

"Yeah. There is no need to worry her until we know something for sure," said Sharon, and he moved off.

October 31, 1956 – Mediterranean Sea

The British and French objective was nothing less the obliteration of the Egyptian Air Force before it could attack the incoming invasion force sailing towards Port Said and the Egyptian coastline. The French 33rd Reconnaissance Squadron flew eleven sorties using a mix of Canberra bombers and RF-84F Thunderstreaks to pinpoint the location of the Egyptian planes and airfields near the Suez Canal and coastline.

The three airfields on Cyprus were packed to the brim with French and British aircraft. The only tarmac not occupied with a parked plane were the runways. The congestion made changes in plans a nightmare. Every plane had been placed in a position in order of scheduled take off. The original plan called for an aerial attack on Egyptian positions near the Suez Canal at 4:15 a.m.

October 31, 1956 – London, England

Sir William Forster Dickson walked into 10 Downing Street and was escorted to Eden's office. Dickson held one of Britain's highest military ranks of Marshal of the Royal Air Force. He was responsible for overseeing the air force strategy that was about to unfold in Egypt. He didn't like the idea of being called to the Prime Minister's office just hours before the beginning of the first bombing campaign. *The Prime Minister had a phone just like everyone else. He should learn to use it*, thought Dickson, peeved.

Eden sat at his desk reviewing a schedule of air force sorties which included both military and civilian targets. He believed that by bombing civilian targets, the Egyptian people would be so outraged with their government they would overthrow Nasser and whomever took his place would immediately sue for peace. He had made sure the British and French air marshals had included plenty of targets in Cairo. *We might even get lucky and kill Nasser in one of the raids*, he thought. *That would be fortuitous and bring this whole affair to a quick conclusion.* His phone rang and his secretary informed him that Air Marshal Dickson had arrived. Eden asked that he be sent in immediately. Dickson entered. "Sir William, thank you for coming," said Eden.

"Of course, Mister Prime Minister," said Dickson. "How can I help you?"

"I've been going over this schedule of bombing sorties…"

"I wasn't aware you were included in the distribution of those schedules."

"I wasn't, but I had that situation corrected. That's not important. What is important is the timing of the campaigns."

"The timing?"

"Yes. You have scheduled the first bombing campaign to begin at 4:15 am."

"That's correct."

"You need to change it."

"Excuse me… did you say change it?"

"Yes. It's less than two hours after the deadline for the ultimatum. That is far too soon. Nobody will believe that we were seriously seeking peace with the Egyptians if we drop bombs on Cairo so soon after the deadline."

"With all due respect, sir. We can't just change our bombing schedules. They have been set for days. The attacks were coordinated between multiple armed services. These things don't just turn on a whim."

"Well, they will this time. Reschedule the campaign."

"It's two hours away."

"I don't care if it's ten minutes away. Reschedule it."

"For when, sir?"

"I suppose noon would allow sufficient time."

"A daylight bombing?"

"Oh, well… I guess that would not be prudent. How about just after sundown?"

"Yes, I suppose."

"Very well, then. Please see to it that the other armed services are informed of the change."

"Yes, Mister Prime Minister."

"Well, I am sure you have plenty to do. That will be all, Sir William," said Eden going back to work at his desk.

Dickson left the office stunned. He had just two hours to reschedule the biggest bombing campaign since the end of World War II. Unfortunately, nobody thought to inform the Israelis of the change in plan.

October 31, 1956 – Jerusalem, Israel

Ben-Gurion paced around his office mumbling curses to himself. He was furious. The British and French bombings had not occurred on schedule. Dayan appeared in the doorway and said, "You asked to see me?"

"That son-of-a-bitch Eden has betrayed us just like I suspected he would," said Ben-Gurion just as Dayan entered. "No bombing campaign. The man is a weasel."

"Did you contact the British or the French?" said Dayan.

"Of course not. This whole operation is supposed to be a secret. Now we know why. The British and French planned to leave our forces stranded in the Sinai right from the start. We are strung out over one hundred miles in all directions. If the British and French bombers don't destroy the Egyptian Air Force their jets and tanks will tear our men apart."

"It's not that bad, David," said Dayan trying to calm Ben-Gurion. "We have accomplished many of our objectives and most of our men are well dug in. Our air force can deal with the Egyptians."

"That's wishful thinking, Moshe. We both know the Egyptian Air Force outnumbers our own. And what about their tanks? We cannot destroy their tanks if our jets are tangling with their jets."

"Perhaps. But things could be a lot worse."

"From your lips to God's ear. Watch what you say."

"Of course. Look, until we hear from the British, we can sit tight and keep our heads down."

"No. No sitting. I want our forces withdrawn from the

Sinai."

"David, that's not wise. We paid in blood for the ground we have taken. We can't just turn it back over to the Egyptians."

"Why not? Our whole plan just went up in smoke and Israel's very existence is at stake."

"The Egyptians will think they have won. It will embolden them. Nasser will claim victory and gain power with the other Arab leaders. It's a mistake to give him that power. He will unite the Arabs and attack in force once he does."

"Without the British and the French backing us up we could be facing an attack from the Arab world right now. They can drive us into the sea just like they always wanted."

"We're not going to let that happen, I promise you."

"Promises. I have had enough of promises. I want our men brought back home before our army is destroyed and Israel along with it. That is an order, General."

"Yes, sir. I will see to it," said Dayan.

Outside Ben-Gurion's office, Dayan stopped and took a deep breath. He loved his country and had proven his loyalty multiple times. But now it was time to commit a small treason. He would disobey his commander-in-chief. He knew Ben-Gurion was panicking and angry. There were many reasons why the British and the French air forces could have been delayed. It was war after all. Nothing goes as planned. He made the decision to stall for time. He would drag his feet and ensure that his commanders were slow in carrying out his orders to retreat. He would not give up the ground the men under his command had fought for. Not without a price. Not now. Not ever.

October 31, 1956 – Cairo, Egypt

Nasser refused to sit. He thought better on his feet. He was not a pacer. He preferred to stare out the windows in his office at the garden that surrounded the presidential palace. Amer sat. He preferred to conserve his energy. It also helped hide his unsteadiness from an occasional drink or hangover. "Nothing will happen," said Amer. "It is a ruse just as you surmised. The British are trying to force us to the negotiating table while the Israelis still occupy our land. We can never let that happen. It would be the end of everything you have dreamed of."

"And if we are wrong?" said Nasser.

"Then our troops will drive them into the sea. We have already repositioned the majority of our forces in the Sinai back across the Suez where our men are preparing our defenses for an invasion. We will be well prepared if they come. In fact, it may be a blessing. We can finally show the world what a well-armed Egyptian army can do. But I assure you, Gamal... it is an English bluff. I would stake my life on it."

"Just in case, I think we should put a curfew in place and black out our cities at night. We don't need to give the British and French bombers a clear target if they do come."

"Are you sure that is wise?"

"What do you mean?"

"What will the people think? They may panic if they see you waver. They need to feel your confidence. They need to feel that you are in control of the situation."

Nasser considered the suggestion. The people were everything to Nasser. They were his power base. Amer was loyal and a longtime friend, but he could not control his generals if they decided to remove Nasser from power. The people and Nasser's popularity kept the military in check. "Perhaps you are right," said Nasser.

"Let things play out, my friend. We will react

appropriately when the time comes. Until then, you would do best to get some sleep and relax. You need to conserve your health. The people are depending on you. Egypt is depending on you."

"Sleep? You can't be serious."

"A whiskey might help."

"I don't drink spirits. You know that."

"Perhaps you should start. It will help you sleep."

October 31, 1956 – London, England

U.S. Ambassador Aldrich arrived at 10 Downing Street and was immediately ushered into Eden's office. Eden did not want to antagonize the Americans more than he already had. When this crisis was over, he would need to repair any damage to the special relationship between the two countries that may have occurred. He was a prudent man and did not want to make any more work for himself than was necessary. "How can I help you, Ambassador?" said Eden as Aldrich sat down opposite Eden's desk.

"You can help by calling off this charade," said Aldrich.

"I assure you it is no charade. We gave the Egyptians a chance for peace and they flatly refused. They are bringing this war upon themselves," said Eden. "It will all be over shortly. I assure you."

"I am not here to argue the merits of actions however foolish I may see them. I am here to protect American lives."

"What do you mean?"

"There are twenty-five hundred Americans in Cairo waiting to be evacuated. President Eisenhower would not look kindly on any British bombs or artillery shells that injure or kill American citizens. You have a responsibility to protect foreign civilians if you choose to continue with your actions."

"You can assure President Eisenhower that every

precaution has been taken to ensure that civilians, especially American civilians, will not be harmed from any British military action."

"Very well. I shall forward your assurances to my president. I am sure he will hold Britain to them."

Eden just smiled at the veiled threat and said, "Is there anything else? As you can imagine, it is a very busy day."

"No. Thank you for seeing me on such short notice," said Aldrich rising from his chair.

"I always have time for our American friends," said Eden walking Aldrich to the door.

Eden watched as Aldrich left, then turned to his secretary and said, "Get me the Air Marshal on the phone."

Eden retreated into his office. The phone rang. "Air Marshal Dickson, I know you are very busy, but I had some more thoughts on the revised bombing schedule," said Eden. "I don't think it would be prudent to bomb civilian targets at this point. We should switch to military targets, especially around Cairo."

October 31, 1956 – Mediterranean Sea

On the islands of Cyprus and Malta, RAF English Electric Canberra and Vickers Valiant bombers took off from four airfields. The English Electric Canberra was a two-engine jet built for bombing runs where precision was required. The Vickers Valiant was a four-engine strategic bomber jet capable of delivering a massive payload from a medium or high altitude. The British squadrons headed out over the Mediterranean.

The French had seven aircraft carriers sailing in the eastern Mediterranean. The French navy had only piston-driven Corsairs and Skyraiders. The slower prop planes could not keep up with the British bombers and fighters, so they were assigned sea patrol and searched for Egyptian warships in the Mediterranean. The Corsairs and Skyraiders were also scheduled to provide air cover for ground troops during the invasion landings.

Hawker Sea Hawks and de Havilland Sea Venoms were launched from the British aircraft carriers sailing fifty miles off the coast of Egypt and Israel. The fighters would act as escorts for the bombers as they crossed into Egyptian airspace. The British squadron formed an air armada off the coast of Egypt as the sun set.

The first targets for the British bombers were the Egyptian airfields protecting the canal. The British had built most of the airfields around the Suez Canal during their original occupation. Most had been modernized to endure the fast and heavy landing of jet fighters and bombers. The British Royal Air Force was reluctant to abandon the well-constructed airfields when the time came to leave Egypt. Now it was the job of the British military to destroy what they had so carefully created.

The largest airfield was Abu Sueir, ten miles west of Ismailia, smack in the middle of the canal zone. French intelligence estimated that thirty-five MiG-15s were based at Abu Suier all of which could be used to repel any invasion from the Mediterranean.

Kabrit was another large airfield located at Great Bitter Lake in the southern end of the canal zone. Two squadrons of a combined thirty-one MiGs were based at Kabrit. Both Kabrit and Abu Suier were protected by Czech-built, 20-mm anti-aircraft batteries.

Fayid and Kasfareet airfields were located further to the northwest. Fayid was home to a squadron of fifteen Vampire jets, a squadron of twelve Meteors and a mixed squadron of twenty Vampires and ten Meteors. Kasfareet held all the remaining nine Vampires in the Egyptian Air Force. While the Meteors used two jet engines for propulsion, the Vampires had only one jet engine with a twin-tail boom. Both could carry either bombs or rockets along with their four Hispano 20-mm cannons.

Further inland, the Egyptian bombers were based at the military airfield of Cairo West. Sixteen I1-28 jet bombers were deployed between two squadrons. Ten more of the Soviet-built bombers were based at Almaza airfield just outside of Cairo and another twenty-two bombers were stationed at Luxor airfield in the southern Nile valley.

Although the Egyptian Air Force commanders were making strides toward building an esprit de corps within the squadron, morale was generally low. There was still a serious confidence deficit brought about by the disastrous defeats dealt by the Israeli Air Force during the Arab-Israeli War. Combined with the poor training, the Egyptian Air Force was questionable as a fighting force. There were however individual pilots that fought and flew well.

October 31, 1956 – Suez Canal Zone, Egypt

The Egyptian soldiers at Port Said and in positions along the mouth of the Suez Canal watched in awe as wave after wave of British bombers and fighter jets passed overhead. No Egyptian had ever seen such a fearsome display of air power. As the British and French aircraft moved down the canal zone, squadrons would peel off the armada to attack their selected targets.

Each Valiant dropped twenty-one one thousand pound bombs on its targeted airfield. The resulting explosions created thirty-foot wide bomb craters as deep as the height of a man. While the crater could be filled in within a matter of hours, the Egyptian MIG-15 fighters were heavy and required high speeds to take off. The days of filling in runways and paving over them after a bombing raid were over. Modern runways needed to be stable, durable launch and landing platforms. The earth beneath the runways needed to be compacted and in many cases, concrete needed to be poured and cured-dry before a jet fighter or bomber could land on it. A well-placed bomb crater on the center of a runway could take days, or even weeks, to repair. A dozen bomb craters could put an airstrip out of commission for an entire war.

Putting the runways and airfields out of commission was the main objective of the first mission. The British and French planned on advancing up the Canal Zone quickly and capturing the airfields before they could be repaired and made operational. Even if a few aircraft survived the strafing and bombing attacks, the planes stationed at the airfields would be useless to the Egyptians.

Destroying Egyptian aircraft still on the ground was a bonus for the British bomber crews. The Egyptians left their aircraft in the open instead of parking them in fortified hangers which were expensive to build. They kept them lined up, fully fueled and ready for takeoff at the first sign of trouble. This made the British bombers' job easy. A single bomb that destroyed a fully fueled and armed jet fighter could set off a chain reaction that destroyed an entire squadron.

With the change of target late in the mission, the British sent their squadrons to bomb the military airfield outside of Cairo. The navigators had little time to recalculate their flight paths and one squadron ended up bombing Cairo International Airport and caused significant damage to the buildings and runways.

The Canberra bombers packed a smaller punch with only eight thousand pounds of bombs as their payload. But they were deadly accurate and used to take out strategic targets such as highways and bridges cutting off the Egyptian ground forces.

Before the night was over, the British had bombed the airfields at Almaza, Kabrit, Abu Sueir and Inchas. All four runways were destroyed, and dozens of the Egyptian Air Force's prized jets went up in flames. The casualties were surprisingly light because when the bombs started detonating, the pilots and ground crews ran for cover rather than running to save their planes. They weren't cowards. They just weren't stupid.

October 31, 1956 – Jerusalem, Israel

It was late at night. Dayan once again entered Ben-Gurion's office. "Ah, Moshe. Thank you for coming," said Ben-Gurion.

"Of course, David. How can I help you?" said Dayan.

"The British and French have begun their bombing campaign. Perhaps I was too rash in ordering a general retreat."

"Really?"

"How far have our men progressed?"

"These things take time, as you know. They are just starting their withdrawal as we speak."

"Good. I think we should stay the course and continue our campaign as before. The British and French will deal with the Egyptian Air Force while our jets deal with the Egyptian Armor."

"Alright, David. If you think that is wise."

"I do. I do. Please see to it, Moshe," said Ben-Gurion.

"As you command," said Dayan and exited. He hadn't done a damn thing.

TEN

October 31, 1956 – Rafah, Egypt

Israeli aircraft pounded the Egyptian positions in preparation for the assault on the Rafah salient. French destroyers sailing off the coast in the Mediterranean Sea also shelled the Egyptian positions.

The Egyptians were protected by their extensive network of trenches and bunkers. They took the beating of the bombs and rockets in stride and waited for the attack they knew was coming. The Egyptians were not known for their offense but they knew how to defend a well-built firing position. Their losses were few. Only a direct hit on a position did any real damage. The rest was superficial. Smoke and dust. The Egyptians kept a sharp eye out for the Israelis, but their commanders imagined they would wait until dark before beginning their assault. They were right.

As the sun set on the second day, the French naval bombardment ceased and the Israeli Air Force flew back across the border. Dayan didn't like to combine aircraft with ground forces. The aggressive Israeli pilots were just as likely to attack an Israeli unit as an Egyptian one. The Israeli infantry and armor moved into their final pre-assault positions and waited for their commander's signal.

As darkness fell on the desert, the Israelis advanced on the Rafah salient. The three spearheads moved in unison as Dayan had planned.

The Egyptians opened fire with a thunderous artillery barrage. The Israeli mortars and artillery countered, hoping to take out some of the artillery. The Egyptian Archer anti-tank guns and the Israeli tanks exchanged fire. When the Egyptians fired, they gave away their positions. The Archer gunners could count on heavy machinegun fire and multiple Israeli tank shells slamming into sandbag-protected walls. Explosions and streams of tracer rounds lit up the night sky. The Israelis kept moving forward and the Egyptians kept pouring down fire upon them.

To the Egyptians it seemed like they were being attacked from all sides at the same time. There was confusion in their ranks, with all of their commanders calling for reinforcements to meet the approaching threat. It was the veteran sergeants and small unit commanders that kept the Egyptian soldiers from panicking. The confidence of the platoon sergeant set the tone for the entire unit.

A company of Israeli infantry moved through the middle minefield accompanied by two engineers. In the distance, they could see the battle raging on the hilltops to their front. Flashes from the explosions lit up the pathway and guided their steps. The Egyptians were still unaware of their position and the Israelis wanted to keep it that way as long as possible. A private carrying a light machinegun tripped over a stone outcropping at the edge of the pathway and fell. The machinegun hit the outcropping and rolled off the pathway. Everyone around the private held their breath as the machinegun came to a stop. Nothing happened. The corporal in charge of the fire team scolded the private for being a clumsy idiot and told him to retrieve the machinegun. The private stepped off the pathway slowly. He carefully placed each of his feet near the markings in the sand where machinegun had rolled. He reached down and picked up the machinegun. He grinned at his corporal and said, "Got it." He lifted his foot and heard a small click under his boot. A mine exploded killing him instantly.

Everyone looked toward the explosion with trepidation. It wasn't the loss of one man that horrified them. It was the giving away of their position. Their eyes shifted back to the hilltops. Nothing changed. It was possible that the Egyptians were too occupied to notice the lone explosion. The Israeli company commander ordered his men to keep moving. Ten steps further down the pathway all hell broke loose. Streams of heavy machinegun fire from the hilltop rained down on the Israelis. They instinctively hit the ground. Their commander ordered them up and moving. He knew staying in the minefield without any cover was death for sure. No sooner had they risen to their feet than artillery shells crashed into the ground around them. The Israeli position was bracketed by the Egyptian gunners. Men were hurled into the air, their bodies crushed and shredded. Some Israelis jumped off the pathway seeking cover and were killed by the mines. The Egyptian shells were terribly accurate. The gunners knew the precise location of the pathway through the minefields and had pre-targeted their artillery and mortars. The bombardment was focused and furious. Those Israelis that were brave enough to push forward were mown down by the Egyptians' heavy machineguns. One hundred Israelis died in the minefield that night including their company commander and the two engineers. The Israelis' southern spearhead had stalled.

October 31, 1956 – Sinai Desert, Egypt

It was night in the mountains. Coyle and his navigator were exhausted and dehydrated. They didn't even have the strength to light a fire. They had spent most of the day and evening searching the canyons and valleys within the mountain range for any sign of vegetation that might indicate water. There was nothing. It was just a big dry rock in the middle of a big dry desert. Their water bottle was empty, and that meant death. It was just a matter of time and pain. They had even looked for signs of a passing Egyptian patrol that they could surrender to but there was none. *I am going to die in this god-forsaken land and there is not a damn thing I can do about it,* thought Coyle. *I'm glad Brigitte is not here to see it.*

Coyle was leaning against a boulder in a small level space on a slope when he heard a long grunt in the distance like someone or something was in pain. The navigator heard it too and they exchanged a glance like what the hell was that? They both climbed to their feet and moved in the direction of the noise.

They came to the edge of a cliff and looked down at a canyon below. There was a Bedouin caravan with twelve camels and a small herd of goats. The Bedouins were on foot guiding the camels and goats through the narrow canyon. Several women trailed behind the camels. They were covered head to toe in burqas. Coyle found it strange. He had seen Bedouins before, and while he remembered them having their hair covered with scarves and decorative caps he didn't remember the women wearing full burqas.

The navigator silently motioned that Coyle and he should ask for help from the Bedouins. Coyle motioned back that they should be cautious and follow the caravan to see where they were going. The navigator nodded agreement.

Once the caravan had passed below and was out of sight, Coyle and the navigator climbed down the cliff and entered the narrow canyon. They kept their distance and stayed hidden as they followed the Bedouins.

The Bedouins came to a wide canyon within the cliff walls. To one side of the canyon was a natural spring trickling down the side of a cliff. Coyle once again cautioned the navigator not to make contact yet. They would watch for a while longer.

One of the Bedouin men filled a goat-skin water bag and walked back with it to the women. He handed one of them the water bag. The woman lifted up her hands from beneath her burqa and took the bag. Her hands were tied together with a leather strap. The women drank and shared the bag. The man scolded one of the women for revealing too much of her face when she pulled back her head scarf to drink. He smacked her with the same stick he used on his camel. The woman yelped and pulled the scarf back down covering her face. "Esclavos," whispered the navigator.

"Yeah. If that means slaves," said Coyle. "We gotta be careful. That kinda gang will turn us into the Egyptians for a reward sure as shooting."

"Necesitan libertad."

"You going hero on me? Don't we got enough problems? You do realize there are eight of those guys? And I bet they've got guns or swords or something."

"Las audamos, si?"

"I don't like the sound of that. But I guess you're right. It may not be the smartest move, but yeah... Audamos."

The navigator smiled with a nod. "We'll wait until they are asleep," said Coyle.

"Ellos duermen?"

"Yeah, Duermen bad guys."

Coyle and the navigator waited and watched as the Bedouins set up their camp and prepared their evening meal. The Bedouins slaughtered one of the goats and slide its carcass on a metal spit to barbeque over the fire. The smell of goat cooking over a fire made Coyle and the navigator's stomachs growl so loud Coyle was worried it might give away their hidden position. It had been a full day since they had eaten. The Bedouins talked amongst themselves. Coyle and the navigator didn't understand anything they were saying but by the motions of their hands, their tone and expressions they gathered that they were arguing what to do with the women they had taken captive.

Coyle had no idea where the women were from or what he and the navigator would do with them once they were free. He doubted they spoke English or Spanish. He wasn't sure what the Bedouin men planned on doing with the women but he imagined that it wasn't good whatever the case. But Coyle's biggest concern was the location. They were in a box canyon as far as he could tell. There was only one way in and one way out.

Strategically it was a very bad layout. The camels were on the opposite end of the canyon as far away from the natural spring as possible. They were dirty animals and the Bedouin knew better than to let them anywhere near their water supply. The camel's feet were hobbled with cotton rope to keep them from wandering off in the middle of the night.

The women were kept in the center of the canyon near the fire where they could be watched. It was impossible to reach them without the men knowing. Their hands remained tied and had been further tethered to a stake that one of the men had driven into the ground. The women knew that if they tried to pull up the stake and the men discovered them, they would be beaten. On top of everything, Coyle and the navigator were greatly outnumbered and had no weapons beyond the survival knife and the flare gun. The Bedouins, on the other hand, were armed with pistols, rifles and nasty-looking curved knives that Coyle imagined were kept very sharp. *This is gonna be one tough pickle to get out of the jar,* thought Coyle.

The fire burned down to orange embers and the Bedouin slept. The half-eaten goat carcass sat beside the fire for breakfast in the morning. The Bedouin felt safe within the canyon walls and saw no need to post a guard. They all needed their strength for tomorrow's journey.

Coyle and the navigator emerged from their hiding place and moved quietly into the camp. The women were asleep and Coyle wanted them to remain asleep until the time was right. The navigator picked up several hand-sized rocks and slipped them into his pocket. Coyle and the navigator moved to the camels and carefully removed the rope hobbles from their hooves. The camels didn't like the smell of the foreigners and grunted their displeasure. Coyle looked over at the Bedouin, concerned they would wake at the noise, but the Bedouin were used to the camels complaining and thought nothing of it.

Coyle and the navigator removed the last hobbling rope from the camels and moved back to their hiding place among the canyon walls. Coyle removed the flare gun from his rucksack and slid in a cartridge. He took aim and fired a shell into the rock wall above the camels. The magnesium burst into a bright star like a meteor. It bounced off the rock face and landed at the camels' feet. The frighten animals bolted. The Bedouins woke, unsure of what was happening and startled by the bright light. The women were also frightened. The camels took off down the narrow trail toward the mouth of the canyon. The Bedouins chased after them and ran past Coyle and the navigator without noticing them hiding behind a small inlet of rock. The leader ordered two of the men to stay behind to guard the women and the camp. The rest of Bedouins disappeared around a canyon wall to chase down the camels.

"Shit," said Coyle under his breath.

The navigator motioned that it was okay and that he would take care of the problem. He retrieved one of the rocks from his pocket and peeked around the corner. The two guards were stomping on the flare trying to put it out. The navigator wound up and threw the rock like a baseball pitch. It hit the closest Bedouin square in the back of the head. He collapsed unconscious. The other Bedouin saw him collapse and knelt by his side to see what had happened. He touched the back of his head and felt blood. He picked up the rock beside him and inspected it. He pulled out his pistol and moved to search the canyon.

As the Bedouin turned toward the natural spring, the navigator stepped out from behind the rock cliff, wound up and threw another rock. The Bedouin heard the noise and turned. The rock hit him on the side of the nose, breaking it, but not knocking him out. He collapsed to his knees with blood pouring out of his broken nose.

Coyle peeked out from behind the rock and saw him. The navigator prepared to hurl another rock. Coyle pushed him out of the way and ran straight at the Bedouin. The Bedouin saw him and reached for his pistol on the ground. He raised the pistol toward Coyle and pulled the trigger. The gun's hammer jammed from too much sand. Coyle jumped into the air feet-first. He hit the Bedouin in the face with both his boots, knocking him out. Coyle landed with a thump.

The women stared at him, surprised. He was white. "Howdy," said Coyle with a smile.

The women exchanged curious glances with each other, then nodded back to the white man. The navigator ran over to the other guard near the fire and removed his pistol and knife. Coyle grabbed the pistol and knife from the Bedouin he had knocked out. They cut the women's bonds. They were free. They grabbed everything that looked useful, including the water bags, the half-eaten goat carcass and three of the rifles the Bedouins had left behind along with spare ammunition in the pockets of the camels' saddle bags. Coyle motioned for the women to follow them. They were hesitant. They didn't know these two white men and weren't sure if they were slavers too. Coyle shrugged and said, "You wanna stay? Stay."

They again exchanged looks as if they were voting as a group. Their facial expressions demonstrating what was on their minds to each other like a silent conversation. They turned back to Coyle and nodded. "I guess that means you're coming with us. Vamanos," said Coyle moving toward the canyon trail.

Coyle knew the situation. He had played it out in his mind. If the Bedouin were still in the canyon or returning with the camels, then Coyle, the navigator and the women were probably dead. He believed the Bedouin would not ask a lot of questions before shooting. Coyle and the navigator would put up a fight with the guns they had taken but the Bedouins were known for shooting long distances with amazing accuracy. There was a possibility they would be taken prisoner and sold as slaves like the women. Coyle didn't like the sound of that either. He and the navigator would fight to the death if it came to it.

They moved to the mouth of the canyon and looked out. Nobody was in sight. Coyle found that strange. At the very least the Bedouin should be running after the camels across the desert. But there was nothing. No camels. No Bedouin. *Spooky*, he thought. One of the women knelt and studied the footprints in the sand. She pointed south. "Best news I've heard all day," said Coyle.

Another woman pulled a small dried up bush from the ground by the mouth of canyon. She motioned for everyone to step in the direction of the Bedouin footprints mixing the footprints together. They followed her instructions, then stepped backwards to their starting point. As they walked away from the canyon in the opposite direction of the Bedouin she brushed the sand to hide their footprints. She had a real knack for it like she had done it before. The sand looked natural and undisturbed.

They moved north along the edge of the mountain until they were out of sight of the mouth of the canyon. Coyle was sure the Bedouin would chase after them. What he wasn't sure of was how long they would pursue them until they gave up. They walked for four hours straight and there was no sign of the Bedouin following them. *The woman's trick with the bush might have worked,* thought Coyle.

The three women stopped. "We ain't got time for a potty break right now," said Coyle. "We've gotta keep moving."

One of the women pointed east like that was the direction they were headed. "You're leaving?" said Coyle.

The woman nodded. She looked at the rifle Coyle was holding. He handed it to her. "Sure. Why not? Probably a better shot than me anyhow," said Coyle.

They divided up the supplies, ammunition and guns. The women motioned their thanks with a bow and took off across the desert toward the east. Coyle and the navigator headed north again.

October 31, 1956 - Abu Ageila, Egypt

In the predawn light, Colonel Avraham Adan commanded the 82nd Armored Battalion of the 7th Armored Brigade as it made its way toward the hidden gap that Frischman and his men had found. Adan wondered if the whole thing was set up as a trap by the Egyptians. Once his Battalion of eighty halftracks was single-file in the narrow gap, it would be almost impossible to defend them if the Egyptians attacked. There was also the possibility of bombing by the Egyptian Air Force. A thousand ways to die came flooding into his mind. It wasn't so much that he was afraid of death, he just didn't want to look like a fool while dying. It all just seemed too easy and convenient. A secret gap through the Hedgehog was discovered at the exact moment the Israeli forces needed it? *Come on,* he thought. *We ain't that lucky.*

His men knew what they would be up against if the Egyptians attacked. They kept a sharp eye out for any signs of an ambush. If Adan's battalion made it through, it would be followed by a battalion of tanks and artillery. Together they would assault the village of Abu Ageila and then, God willing, the slope up to the Ruafa Ridge on the western side of the Hedgehog. At the same time, another armored battalion would attack up the Umm Qataf Ridge on the eastern side of the natural fortress. The Egyptian commander would need to divide his forces. Hopefully, one of the two Israeli fronts would make a breakthrough. The plan was complicated. Adan didn't like complicated. *If something can go wrong, it will go wrong,* he thought. *The only question is what?*

Keeping a battalion of halftracks quiet was a hopeless task. Adan made sure the treads and gears on his vehicles were greased up before they left. It didn't help much. The engine noise was enough to give them away. If that didn't give away their position, then the series of tremors created by a column of nine-ton halftracks would surely do the trick. Stealth was not his battalion's strongpoint.

As the battalion approached the mouth of the gap, Adan took a deep breath. The walls were steep and the path was narrow. Frischman's platoon had done their best to clear the way but Adan had borrowed an engineer platoon to ensure that the gap was passable. He also ordered two heavy machine gun fire teams and an anti-tank gun squad to join the first group through the gap.

He studied the entrance to the gap. He didn't like it much. He ordered one of his companies to dismount. They would go in on foot. If it was a trap, the Egyptians would probably shoot down from the heights. His halftracks were unprotected from overhead fire. His men would stand a better chance on foot where they could seek cover if there was any.

He knew it was stupid to lead the mission himself. If he went down, they all went down. He had confidence in his company commander and the platoon leaders. But he also knew that if the shit hit the fan, he was the most experienced commander in the brigade and would likely be the best officer to help his men get out of a tight situation. It was worth the risk.

Frischman already had men positioned all the way through the gap, but Adan knew that the Egyptians would wait for bigger fish before they attacked. He and his men were the bigger fish. If the Egyptians were going to attack Adan wanted them to do it before his armor entered the gap. In many spots, there was no place to turn around if the Egyptians blocked them. The tanks and half-tracks would be sitting ducks. Better his men on foot took the brunt of any attack. They could retreat quickly if need be, although they would probably take heavy losses. It was a shit-sandwich no matter how he looked at it.

The company's scouts moved into the mouth of the gap. Adan and the rest of the company followed, keeping their eyes on the heights above.

They moved into the canyon where the Egyptians had blown up the bridge. They were leapfrogging all the way as they advanced – one platoon moving up, taking defensive positions, then followed by another platoon that would do the same, all the time watching both the path in front of them and the heights above. "They don't even need bullets or grenades. They can just drop rocks on us," said a platoon sergeant.

Adan was going to tell him to shut up but he knew the soldier was just stating the obvious. He pushed his men further into the narrowing gap. The walls were sheer cliffs of sand and stone. A small rockslide grabbed everyone's attention. He ordered his men to take cover wherever they could find it. All weapons pointed upward. There was no movement beyond the sand and small rocks tumbling down to the ground. He ordered several of the engineers to stay behind and clear the way. The company moved on.

It took twenty minutes to move through the gap. Adan could see the mouth on the northern side of the canyon and the open space beyond. They had made it… so far.

He ordered his men to take up defensive positions at the mouth of the canyon. The fire teams set up the heavy machineguns and anti-tank gun facing outward from the canyon. An Egyptian attack was most likely to come from the direction of the village. They kept close to the walls to hide their positions.

Adan took out his binoculars and scanned the village to the north. He could see a half-dozen Archer anti-tank guns and several heavier artillery guns in reinforced defensive positions. Ruafa Dam was to his right. It was even more heavily armed than the village and the defensive positions were higher giving them greater advantage against any attacking force. Adan would need to take out both the village and the dam before he could advance on the Hedgehog from the western side. *One at a time,* he thought. *Be patient and most of your men just might live through this.* Patience was not easy for Adan. He was aggressive and understood the need to keep the Israeli advance moving forward. But in this case… patience.

There was a second problem with the layout at the mouth of the gap. There wasn't much room. Once his half-tracks exited the gap, they would be in range of the Egyptian guns from both the dam and the village. He decided to bring up all the vehicles into a tight formation inside the gap like a compressed spring. It was a risky move. It could be what the Egyptians above were waiting for before they revealed their positions and attacked. But moving the vehicles out of the gap one by one was also very risky. He had the element of surprise and he wanted to keep it as long as possible while deploying his forces.

Adan also had a big resupply problem once his forces cleared the gap. Only tracked vehicles could make it over the rough ground through the defile. All his trucks carrying ammunition, food, water and engineering equipment were stuck on the opposite end. Anything coming through the gap had to be hand-carried. They could use a half-track but he needed all his half-tracks for the assault. That made resupply for the two battalions difficult until they could secure an alternate supply route.

Even with all the challenges, Adan knew the Israelis would be in a far better position to assault the Hedgehog if his task force could secure the second front by taking the Egyptian positions in both the village and dam.

During the early morning hours, the Israeli armor moved into a tight formation inside the gap. Adan held his breath and wondered if he would have a heart attack from the stress. When a vehicle moved into its pre-attack position it turned off its engine and the crew caught whatever sleep they could muster before the attack. They would need their strength and would remain sleepless until they either won… or lost the battle.

As the sun cracked the dawn, the Israeli drivers started their engines and the soldiers chambered rounds into their guns. Adan took one last look at the village that he would attack first. It was still except for a few people milling around. He gave the signal and the tightly packed vehicles sprung out of the gap as fast as possible. Everyone had strict instructions not to fire or even turn toward the village until the last tank was out of the gap or the Egyptians opened fire. Adan hoped for the former. With a little luck, the Egyptians would think the Israeli forces were Egyptian and pay little heed. *And why not?* thought Adan. *They aren't expecting an attack from that direction. Just a little luck. That's all we need. A little luck.*

Luck met the Israelis halfway. All of Adan's half-tracks made it out of the gap before the Egyptians realized that they were about to be attacked and opened fire. The tanks were just starting to appear through the western mouth of the gap when the first shell exploded nearby. Adan cursed but he knew he had tickled the dragon and had no right to expect more than he had received from fate. The Israelis returned fire with everything that was available. It would take the armored battalion thirty minutes before all their tanks were in position and available to support the attack.

Adan chanted the mantra, "Patience," under his breath as the battle intensified. Ten of his half-tracks were hit by Egyptian anti-tank gun shells and exploded into flames. "Fuck it," said Adan to nobody.

With only half of the tanks available, Adan ordered his men to advance on the village. The other tanks would just have to join the battle as they emerged from the gap. The Israelis were being torn to shreds and Adan saw little to be gained by delaying his attack. A long line of half-tracks followed by tanks sped toward the village. The treads kicked up a thick cloud of dust that acted as a smoke screen but caused the Egyptians to focus their fire on the half-tracks leading the charge because they were the most visible. Shells rained down from the village in their front, while shells from the dam positions rained down from the Israeli right flank. It didn't stop them. Stopping meant sure death. They had to make it to the village and overrun the Egyptian positions. Adan wasn't sure what the Egyptians at the dam would do once the Israelis entered the village but something inside told him they would continue their shelling even though it meant the lives of Egyptian civilians. It was war after all. Friendly fire and collateral damage were inevitable.

As the Israelis drew closer, the anti-tank guns from the village became more accurate and intense. Every ten seconds another half-track exploded, killing its driver and passengers. *Doesn't matter,* Adan told himself. *It is God's will.* But it was a lie. It did matter. Those were his men. He would mourn their loss later.

As the Israeli half-tracks approached the Egyptian positions in the village, the Egyptian gunners abandoned their guns and ran for their lives. The Egyptians were pragmatic. They had fought the good fight, but little would be gained by their deaths. If they lived, they could fight the Israelis again. So, they ran through the village and into the desert. Many took off their boots and discarded them so they could run faster on the sand.

The Israelis captured the village and quickly dispatched any pockets of resistance that were brave enough to face them. Just as Adan had thought, the Egyptian artillery and guns from the dam continued to fire. At least now, the Israelis could use the buildings for cover until they consolidated their position.

The last of the Israeli tanks exited the gap and roared toward the town. As they did, Israelis scouts reported that an armored column from the north had appeared and was advancing on the village from the rear. The Israeli tanks shot past the village and continued to meet the Egyptian threat. The tank battle that followed was short and violent. The Egyptians thought they were only facing dismounted troops and were not prepared to face the tanks racing towards them. The two sides clashed head on. The Israeli aggression surprised the Egyptian tank crews. With tank turrets twisting hard in opposing directions, each side lost several tanks from close-up shots. At close range, it got down to who fired first. The Egyptian commander heard a report over the radio that a squadron of Israeli jets had been spotted heading toward their position. In reality, the Israeli jets were heading toward the Mitla Pass on a mission to defend the paratroopers and had no intention of attacking the Egyptian armored column. But reality mattered less than fear in this case. The enemy line broke and the Egyptian tanks retreated going back the way they came. Running low on ammunition and fuel, the Israelis did not pursue the fleeing Egyptians. The Israelis didn't understand what had happened but were grateful that the battle ended when it did. They were victorious twice in one morning. That was enough and they returned to the village to join the rest of the task force.

The Israelis spent the rest of the day repairing their vehicles, resupplying their ammunition and fuel and tending to their wounded and dead. Those that could, slept even as Egyptian shells continued to rain down on their positions within the village. Their day was still not done. It would be a long night.

October 31, 1956 - Abu Ageila, Egypt

The sun was setting as the Israelis moved out from their covered positions within the village and lined up in a column. In the fading light, Egyptians shells continued to rain down and explode. Sometimes they found their target and destroyed it. Sometimes they found dirt and sand, kicking it up into the air, causing a smoke screen-type effect.

Adan ordered his task force forward. The half-tracks once again took the lead creating clouds of dust that protected the tanks. As they approached the slope leading to the dam, the Israeli column broke and formed a front. The half-tracks kept up a barrage with their machineguns on the Egyptian positions. The Egyptian tank guns fired at close range, destroying one half-track after another. Only when the Israeli tanks moved up into positions did the half-tracks stop exploding, the Egyptians diverting their fire to the larger threat. The Israelis advanced up the slope toward the dam.

Even as the last of the daylight disappeared, the Egyptian fire was accurate and murderous. Every single one of the Israeli tanks suffered a hit from the Egyptian artillery and anti-tank guns. Fortunately, many of the shells did only superficial damage when they exploded against the tanks sloped armor. The Israelis kept moving up the hillside, taking their beating and giving it back to the Egyptians.

As night fell upon the battlefield and tracer rounds lit up the sky, the Israelis reached the dam and the Egyptian positions. Some of the Egyptian gunners began to flee. Other held their ground and continue to fire their guns. And then the unthinkable happened. The resupply problem caught up with the task force and the Israelis tanks ran out of ammunition. On the verge of winning, Adan encouraged his men to keep fighting. Their main guns and machineguns empty, the Israeli tank commanders opened their hatches and hurled grenades into the Egyptian positions as they overran them. When the grenades ran out, the tankers used their rifles and sidearms. The last of the Egyptians broke and fled. The Israelis let them go. The dam was theirs.

As the last Egyptian soldier disappeared over the horizon, the Israelis climbed from their tanks and half-tracks and fell to the ground exhausted. They had given their all.

The Israelis were still in a precarious position. The Egyptians could counterattack and the Israelis had little with which to fight them off. Adan told his commanders that in the event of a counterattack, the Israelis would use whichever of the anti-tank and artillery pieces had not been spiked by the Egyptians before fleeing.

With both the   and the village captured, the Israelis would open a new supply route. It was just a matter of time before they were resupplied and could continue their attack on the western side of the Hedgehog.

October 31, 1956 - Abu Ageila, Egypt

After only a few hours' sleep, the Israelis in the 7th Armored Brigade woke and got to work. There was a lot to be done. All of the Israeli tanks had been hit at least once and those still viable needed to be repaired. The resupply of ammunition was slowly arriving. The fighting positions left by the Egyptians were in the wrong locations and new positions needed to be dug facing Katef Ridge on the western side of the Hedgehog. It was at that moment that the Egyptians counterattacked.

Archer tank destroyers came from the western ridge of the Hedgehog supported by the Egyptian artillery on the Shinhan Ridge to the south. The shore of the dam exploded in violence. The Israelis ran to their fighting positions at the top of the slope. They had little with which to fight back but were determined to show the Egyptians their resistance. If the Egyptian tank destroyers reached the crest of the dam, the badly damaged Israeli tanks and artillery would be at their mercy.

The night sky flashed bright from one explosion after another. Israeli trucks with ammunition arrived as the Egyptians approached the Israeli positions. The Israelis formed lines to pass shells from the trucks to their tanks and artillery. Israeli tanks shells were fired within seconds of being unloaded from the trucks. Israeli machineguns sprayed the Egyptian infantry accompanying the tanks up the slope, slaughtering some, driving others to ground. The Egyptian tank destroyers finished off three more Israeli tanks and their crews. The Israelis fought back giving everything left inside their exhausted bodies.

The Egyptians broke and withdrew from the dam leaving thirty-eight dead along with four of their precious Archer anti-tank guns burning in the night. The battle had consumed most of the night and the rest that the Israelis so desperately needed. No sooner had the Egyptians left the battlefield than the Israelis again collapsed from exhaustion. Those with anything left to give unloaded the ammunition from the trucks and carried it to the remaining Israeli tanks. Then they too fell on the ground and slept. In the morning, they would be expected to fight again.

October 31, 1956 – Washington D.C., USA

Eisenhower was just sitting down to a State Dinner honoring the President of Mexico, when he was handed the message that Britain and France had begun bombing Egyptian positions. He kept his emotion in check and exchanged pleasantries with the people sitting near him at the head table. Inside, he was boiling mad, but not surprised.

It was as he thought. Britain and France had every intention of attacking Egypt right from the start. They were carrying through with their plan. He would need to wait to see what their endgame would be, but he already had his suspicions. He suspected they would give Egypt a good drubbing, then negotiate a ceasefire that left them in control of the canal zone perhaps alongside some sort of

U.N. peacekeeping force. But Britain would have the real control over the canal. It was no longer about revenue. It was about security and reflecting power. They would destroy Egypt's military and political aspirations. It would be the end of Nasser.

Eisenhower was no fan of Nasser. He understood Nasser's complaint about the French and British imperialists. He agreed with him. But Eisenhower didn't see the logic in egging on the Western nations to enhance his personal power. Sure, it was good politics for any Arab leader to stand up against the Westerners but it was also risky. Eden was not wrong to think that Nasser had brought all this upon himself. But that didn't make Eden right. There was little Eisenhower could do except smile and sip his soup.

ELEVEN

November 1, 1956 – Cairo, Egypt

It was early morning. Francis Powers was again tasked to take reconnaissance photos of strategic locations in Egypt. Eisenhower wanted to keep a close watch on what was happening on the ground. The U2 was flying at seventy thousand feet when it passed over the West Cairo military airfield. The planes and buildings were clearly visible. The runway looked like it was still in good shape and absent of any bomb damage. Powers didn't personally care one way or the other. It was above his pay grade to figure out the mess unfolding down below. *That's Ike's job,* he thought. He pressed the record button on his camera controls and took a series of high resolution photographs of the airfield and surrounding area.

He had orders to take photos at a minimum of two different angles so the analysts could compare any questionable photographs. The U2 was an unwieldly beast and wasn't the kind of aircraft that would turn on a dime like a jet fighter. He performed a slow arcing turn and circled back around. It took almost ten minutes to complete the full turn and reposition the aircraft for a second reconnaissance run. When he flew over the airfield again he noticed that things had dramatically changed. Most of the buildings and aircraft were burning and the runway had huge craters in it. He thought for a moment, then realized that while he was making his turn, British or French bombers had attacked the airfield below. He looked around for any sight of them. The sky was clear except for the black smoke rising from the airfield. He hit the record button again and photographed the damage. *This will be a great story that I can tell my grandchildren,* he thought. *They'll probably be bored to tears.* He slowly turned his aircraft for home.

November 1, 1956 – Suez Canal Zone, Egypt

French reconnaissance planes combed the Suez Canal and the surrounding area for potential targets and to keep tabs on Egyptian troop movements. The pilot of an F-84 Thunderstreak was flying over Lake Timsah when he saw two tug boats pushing the Egyptian Navy's *LST Aka* toward the narrow channel at the southern end of the lake.

The *LST Aka* was three hundred and twenty-eight feet long and weighed over sixteen hundred tons. She was a big bruiser and ideally designed for her new purpose as a blockship. Originally built as a military landing craft for tanks and vehicles, the *Aka* was being pushed into the main channel by the two tug boats. Her hull had been filled with cement and debris. Once scuttled, she would be difficult to raise. If she landed upright on the bottom of the channel, she was tall enough to prevent all commercial vessels from traveling through the Suez Canal unless they were willing to risk their hulls being ripped open by the *Aka's* bridge tower and loading cranes.

The pilot radioed back his findings including details of the ship's current position, speed and direction. It wouldn't take long before the *Aka* had been moved into position and scuttled. There was no time to waste if the British were going to stop her. The Thunderstreak flying overhead did not have any bombs loaded on the hardpoints under its wings. It was on a reconnaissance mission and needed to conserve as much fuel as possible. The most it could do was strafe the ship with its machineguns which wouldn't cause any real damage but might give the crew of the tug boats a good scare. He checked his fuel gauge and decided against it. He was running low on fuel. He banked his aircraft hard and headed back to his base on Cyprus.

November 1, 1956 – Mitla Pass, Egypt

Brigitte joined an Israeli reconnaissance unit sent to scout the area between the Mitla Mountains and the Suez Canal. The Egyptians were retreating to the west and crossing over the canal. Sharon wanted to know what was out there and if the retreat was real or just a ruse. He had strict orders from Dayan not to move his brigade any farther west than its current position. Sharon did not believe that meant he was to remain blind. He instructed his reconnaissance units to keep out of sight and to avoid all enemy contact as they traveled west. They were to observe only and maintain radio silence. At the first sign of trouble they were to return and report.

Sharon still had not heard any news of the Spanish cargo plane crash. He didn't know if Brigitte's American pilot was dead or alive. He considered telling her about the crash but decided against it. He had grown to like the sassy French journalist. She was doing her job and telling her would only hurt her. He wasn't sure how she would respond and he didn't need a weeping woman while fighting the Egyptians. The time would come when he could not hold back the truth anymore, but for now his silence was merciful.

Brigitte boarded one of the three jeeps, and the reconnaissance unit took off down the mountain. She had seen the carnage from the last Egyptian ambush and was feeling anxious as the jeeps snaked their way down the mountain road into the valley below. She was surprised at the complete absence of Egyptian soldiers. The pass was clear. The three jeeps drove out into the valley and toward the Suez Canal, unmolested.

November 1, 1956 – Mediterranean Sea

A flight of four British Hawker Sea Hawks was already armed and ready for takeoff on the *HMS Eagle* aircraft carrier sailing in the eastern Mediterranean when the message came in from French intelligence. The aircraft were immediately retasked to sink the *Aka* in Lake Timsah before she entered the main channel. The jets launched, formed up and headed inland at maximum speed.

November 1, 1956 – Suez Canal Zone, Egypt

The three reconnaissance jeeps from the 202nd Paratrooper Brigade pulled to a stop behind a small hill. The Lieutenant in charge of the unit pulled out his binoculars and exited the jeep. Brigitte followed him to the top of the hill where he laid down. In the distance was the Suez Canal. Brigitte laid down next to him and said, "Why are we stopping here? Why not go all the way to the canal?"

"I suppose we can if you don't mind being shot at. The Egyptian army is on the opposite bank. If they spot us they might decide to take a few potshots with their artillery and mortars. We can see everything we need to see from here," said the Lieutenant. "That alright with you?"

"Sure. I'm in no hurry to die," said Brigitte pulling out her own set of binoculars and peering at the canal.

Just as the lieutenant had said, she could see Egyptian forces on the opposite bank. There were two tanks with their gun barrels pointed toward the eastern bank of the canal. "Can they see us?" said Brigitte, alarmed.

"No. Not unless they are really looking for us. I doubt they know we are here."

Brigitte relaxed. She trusted the lieutenant even though he was young. There was something about him that made her feel safe like when she was around Coyle or Bruno. She scanned the horizon and spotted the *Aka* being pushed by the tug boats. "Looks like someone's having engine trouble," she said.

The lieutenant turned his binoculars to see what she was seeing. "I don't think that's it. I think it's a blockship."

"What's a blockship?"

"Nasser threatened to block the canal if any foreign army set foot in Egypt. He fills old ships with heavy debris from demolished buildings and floats them into the center of the canal. When the time comes, he blows out their hulls and sinks 'em."

"You think that's what they're doing?"

"Probably. Most of the ships are headed for salvage and their engines are caput. They have to be towed into position."

"Mind if I ask you a few personnel questions?"

"No. Go ahead and ask. I just don't promise I'll answer."

"Fair enough. What's it like living in a country where all your neighbors want you wiped off the face of the earth?"

"More boring than you would expect."

"Really?"

"Yeah, well… our commanders drill the possibility of complete annihilation into our heads so much we kinda become numb to it. Most of our time is spent waiting around for the apocalypse. It's times like these when we can actually go out and do something about it that are exciting."

"Interesting."

"Probably not but it is the truth. I've had a target on my back my whole life, yet one day pretty much looks the same as the last."

"The idea of millions of armed Arabs doesn't scare you?"

"Sure. A little… but we're well trained and I'm told we have God on our side."

"You don't believe in God?"

"I don't believe and I don't not believe. I just don't know and frankly I don't think it matters."

"And yet you fight for Jews?"

"I fight for the survival of my people and my country. Religion has nothing to do with it."

"I think there are a lot of both Jews and Arabs that would disagree with you."

"And I think you'd be surprised if you really knew what was in people's hearts."

"Maybe."

"At the end of the day war is a test of wills. They fight for revenge. We fight to survive. Now who do you think is gonna win?"

The lieutenant stopped talking as if something had caught his attention. He looked toward the sky. "Listen… jets," he said.

"Egyptian or Israeli?" said Brigitte feeling very vulnerable on a hill with no cover in sight.

The lieutenant spotted the incoming aircraft and peered through his binoculars to get a closer look. "Neither. They're British. Sea Hawks, I think."

The British aircraft reached the Egyptian vessel as she was about to enter the mouth of the narrow channel at the southern end of Lake Timsah. The first two Sea Hawks swooped in for an attack as the other two kept overwatch in case any Egyptian fighters showed up. The first two Sea Hawks were armed with four five-hundred pound bombs each. It was not the ideal weapon to attack a ship like the *Aka* but there had been no time to switch out the armament before takeoff. As they flew over the ship, the pilots released their payloads.

One of the bombs hit one of the tug boats and blew it apart killing the crew. Another bomb hit the *Aka* just in front of the bridge and blew a ten-foot hole in the deck. The damage looked a lot worse than it was since the cement and debris packed into the cargo area prevented the explosion from reaching the bottom of the hull. The *Aka* was pouring out black smoke but still moving toward the channel with the help of the remaining tug.

The pairs of Sea Hawks switched places and the second set of aircraft swooped in to attack while the first set kept watch. One of the aircraft in the second set had been armed with sixteen 127-mm unguided rockets designed to take out heavily armored vehicles such as tanks and mobile artillery. The first aircraft dropped its bombs with little effect. The second aircraft swooped in low hugging the water surface. As it approached within five-hundred yards it fired all sixteen rockets in a matter of seconds and pulled up into a hard climb to clear the ship's masts. One of the rockets struck the *Aka's* hull and punched a hole at the waterline.

The *Aka* started to take on water. It was sinking, but slowly. The Egyptian tug captain pressed his vessel to maximum speed and pushed the *Aka* deeper into the channel. The *Aka* had been rigged with explosives at the bottom of the cargo area but they proved unnecessary. The *Aka* stayed afloat just long enough to move into perfect position before sinking. It settled upright on the bottom of the main channel.

On the hillside, Brigitte watched. She couldn't help but think of the irony of what had just transpired. It was the first time in eighty-seven-years the Suez Canal had been blocked and it was the British that sank the blockship. The whole point of the French and British invasion was to keep the canal open and now it was blocked. *This is gonna make a great story,* she thought.

The *Aka* was the first of many.

November 1, 1956 – Suez Canal Zone, Egypt

In retaliation for the British and French airstrikes on Cairo, Nasser had given the order to block the Suez Canal. If Egypt wasn't allowed to control the Suez Canal, it would be closed to the entire world until the world saw reason.

Forty blockships were towed out into the shipping channels of the Suez Canal. Each ship was placed in a strategic position in an area of the canal to achieve maximum affect. The Egyptian engineers lit the fuses to the explosives in the hulls and ran for the waiting tug boat to carry them away to safety. The explosions were spectacular and caused small earthquakes in the villages and cities near the canal. Egyptian spectators along the shores of the canal cheered as each ship exploded, sending geysers of water into the blue sky. Some ships cracked in half and others tipped their bows up for a final salute before sinking. Each ship sank until it came to a rest on the muddy bottom of the canal. Although some of the ships were completely submerged, many still had their steam stacks and masts visible above the waterline.

The destruction was complete. Any commercial or military ship that dared to navigate the wreckage was risking having its hull torn open and sinking, causing even more blockage. Insurance companies refused to insure any shipping company attempting to use the canal. The Suez Canal would be blocked from all shipping traffic for over a year until the sunken ships could be cut into pieces by divers and the pieces removed by tugs and tractors. The canal was the very reason nations were fighting and now it was completely useless. Egypt would miss out on millions of dollars in tolls and construction of their dam project would be delayed once again for lack of funds.

The Suez Canal, one of mankind's greatest engineering achievements, was nothing more than a very long and narrow swimming hole in the middle of a desert.

November 1, 1956 – Washington D.C., USA

It was very early in the morning in the White House. Eisenhower was asleep when his personal butler opened his bedroom door and entered. The butler walked over to the bed and gently shook Eisenhower's arm until the president awoke. "Mr. President, Director Dulles would like to see you. He says it is urgent," said the butler.

"Of course. What time is it?" said Eisenhower.

"Two-thirty, Mr. President."

"Alright. Give me a moment. I'll meet him in my study," said Eisenhower.

The butler left and Eisenhower rose and put on his robe and slippers. With luck, he would be able to go back to bed and get a few more hours of sleep before starting the day. He walked through the bedroom doorway and into the hallway. His personal study was just two doors down. He entered. Allen Dulles was waiting. "I'm sorry for waking you, Mr. President," said Dulles.

"No, you're not. It's your job. Out with it."

"We just received word... Nasser has sunk thirty to forty ships in the main canal. It's completely impassible. The canal is shut down to all naval traffic."

"Well, I can't say I'm surprised. When a lion is backed into a corner it fights back. How long before it can reopen?"

"We won't know until we get a better look at the damage. We are sending a U2 to take reconnaissance photos."

"Alright. Let's wait and see where we stand."

"Should I have waited until morning?"

"No. I've grown used to it. I'd rather be informed than awake and chirper."

"Are you heading back to bed?"

"Yeah. I won't get any sleep but I think better horizontally."

"Yes, Mr. President."

"Ya, know, Allen... this may not be all bad news."

"How's that, Mr. President?"

"Britain and France just shut off most of their oil supply, along with the rest of Europe. They'll deplete their reserves within a week or two."

"You think there may be an opportunity?"

"Perhaps. I'll think on it. You do the same. Let's rendezvous at breakfast. Good night," said Eisenhower moving toward the door.

"Good night, Mr. President."

Eisenhower went back to bed and surprisingly… slept.

November 1, 1956 – Sinai, Desert

Coyle and the navigator continued their trek across the wasteland of the Sinai. They had dodged several Egyptian patrols over the last two days. The farther north they moved, the more panicked the retreating Egyptian forces seemed to be. They even saw a group of twenty soldiers crossing the hot desert barefoot and weaponless. Coyle thought about stopping them using their pistols, but he figured they probably didn't have any water or food. The Egyptians were in worse shape than they were.

Coyle and the navigator stopped for a moment and shared the remaining water in the goat-skin bag. "Well that went fast," said Coyle tossing the empty bag to the ground.

The navigator picked up the empty bag and slid it over his shoulder. "I like your positive attitude. That's great if we find water but it's gonna slow us down. Even empty it's heavy," said Coyle.

"Esta bien," said the navigator.

"Suit yourself," said Coyle continuing to walk in the same direction. "I suppose it ain't gonna matter much anyhow if we don't find some water soon. Then your bag's gonna come in real handy. Whoopi."

The navigator followed, silent.

November 1, 1956 - Abu Ageila, Egypt

The 7th Armored Brigade was given the mission of

preventing Egyptian forces from escaping the Hedgehog and fleeing north to Al-Arish. They would be the anvil. The 10th Infantry Brigade commanded by Colonel Shmuel Goder would be the hammer and assault the Hedgehog from the eastern side. Without any armor, the 10th Infantry Brigade was not well-suited to assault the well-defended Hedgehog. With only three infantry battalions, a jeep-mounted company and a heavy mortar company, the 10th Brigade was no match for the Egyptian anti-tank guns, artillery, and heavy machine guns dug into the ridge. To make matters worse, it was an uphill battle for the Israelis and they were attacking a well-prepared defensive position. It spelled disaster from the start.

The Israeli Defense Forces commander Moshe Dayan was an infantry-man. He believed that his infantry brigades were the best for almost any situation. Infantry was flexible and could be easily mobilized if required. They could climb the roughest terrain. They were more dependable than his armor brigades which were always having problem with breakdowns and required large amounts of fuel to keep going. He ensured his infantry brigades were well-armed to take on armor when encountered or any other mission they were tasked with. Few politicians agreed with Dayan but he was the man in charge and would have things his way. Dayan wanted infantry to take the Hedgehog.

As their jeeps rode over the desert, 10th Brigade began their assault. It didn't take long before the Egyptians responded with a ferocious barrage of artillery and heavy machinegun fire. The Israelis abandoned their jeeps which were easy targets for the Egyptians. It was safer to approach on foot so the Israelis could use the terrain as cover. Even a shallow slope or wadi offered some protection against the Egyptian machineguns.

The Egyptians were using up their ammunition at an alarming rate as they poured shells and bullets into the approaching Israelis. They were acting as if they had an infinite supply of munitions, which they didn't. The Egyptians had been cut off from resupply when the village of Abu Ageila was captured by the Israelis. But either they hadn't realized that fact or they just didn't care. They were determined not to let the Israelis get any kind of foothold on the eastern front of the Hedgehog.

Adan and his men attacked from the western side up the Katef Ridge. Their job was not to take the Egyptian positions on the ridge but to give up enough of a fight that the Egyptian commander would split his forces in two allowing the 10th Infantry to successfully assault the ridge on the opposite side of the Hedgehog. It was a feint but it had to be believed. The Israeli tanks, now repaired and resupplied with ammunition, fired on the Egyptian positions from the base of the slope while the Israeli infantry fired their anti-tank guns and heavy machineguns from the top of the dam. The Egyptians were taking a beating from both sides of the Hedgehog, but they held on.

Just after noon, the Israelis on the eastern side broke off their assault. They had suffered heavy casualties and lost most of their jeeps. They were stuck and unable to make any progress against the Egyptian positions. It was hopeless without armor to support their advance. It didn't matter what his commanders believed. Infantry alone was not going to make it up the slopes of the Hedgehog. Goder finally pulled the plug on the operation and ordered his men to withdraw back down the slope.

November 1, 1956 - Southern Israel

Dayan was furious when he received word that 10th Brigade had withdrawn from the battlefield. He refused to believe that the ridge could not be taken with infantry. He decided to visit the battlefield and confront Goder directly.

November 1, 1956 - Abu Ageila, Egypt

Dayan arrived by small aircraft in the early afternoon and reviewed the situation for himself. He railed on Goder for not properly preparing the battlefield before the attack. He was especially adamant about the lack of a preparatory bombardment of the Shinhan Ridge where the Egyptians had been using their artillery to support their defensive positions on the eastern side. Goder reminded Dayan that his brigade was not equipped with artillery or armor. The one heavy mortar company that he did have at his disposal focused its attack on the Egyptian positions on the ridge his men were assaulting.

"Why did you withdraw?" said Dayan.

"My men were unable to advance. They were being slaughtered," said Goder.

"You know to expect some losses."

"Some losses, yes. But if we had stayed much longer my entire brigade would have been wiped out."

"Shmuel, we have to take the Hedgehog. If we could go around it, we would. It's just not possible without exposing our supply lines."

"I understand the need for the mission. But I will not just sit back and watch my men get slaughtered without at least a hope of success."

"You are the commander. You create the hope. You create the opportunity for success."

"I tried, Moshe. The Egyptians wouldn't budge."

"Then you eliminate them one by one."

"Of course, if we could find them. Our intelligence reports have been worthless. They showed the Egyptian guns in one position and when we arrived they had shifted to another. Lives wasted capturing dirt and sand."

"Then you should have kept going until you found them."

"We tried. My men took a terrible beating."

"They're soldiers. It's their job to take a beating when on a mission."

"Sir, now that they've taken the dam and opened the road, 7th Armor is receiving supplies. The Egyptians in the Hedgehog are cut off. It is only a matter of time before they run out of ammunition and supplies. They'll be forced to surrender. We don't need to sacrifice Israeli lives to take the Hedgehog. It will fall on its own."

"That's wishful thinking. They could counterattack and retake the village cutting off our supply lines once again."

"And if they do, we can take the Hedgehog and rain fire down upon them. They will surrender. Our men shouldn't be asked to give up their lives for nothing. No man should."

"It's not for nothing, Shmuel. If we don't win this war soon, the Egyptians will consolidate their forces and counterattack. If they are successful at driving us back, I doubt they will stop at the border. Our country is at risk. Our intelligence reports that the Egyptians are at the point of collapse. We just need to push them."

"Moshe, 37th Armor will arrive this evening. With their tanks we can combine forces and take the Hedgehog."

"We cannot wait. I am taking over operational control."

"What?!"

"I am sorry but your mission is too critical to the overall strategy. You have become soft and indecisive, Colonel. I am taking over."

"I see."

"You will attack within the hour."

"In broad daylight?"

"Yes… in broad daylight. That is an order."

"Yes, sir," said Goder offering a lackluster salute and moving off.

November 1, 1956 - Abu Ageila, Egypt

The Israeli Infantry lined up, some riding in the remaining half-tracks. Colonel Goder said, "I hope everyone got some sleep. No naps are allowed during the assault."

His men chuckled at their commander. They all knew what they were facing and few were in the mood for humor. Many prayed in the last moments. Goder glanced at his watch. It was time. The Israeli artillery opened fire.

The ridge above them exploded in cascades of rock and sand. It would do little good. The Egyptians were dug in like ticks. They would keep their heads down and wait for the attack they knew was coming. Some looked forward to it. Another chance to kill Jews.

Goder felt terrible ordering his men up the long slope leading to the ridge top. He had his orders and he would obey them. He knew he needed to display confidence for the sake of his men. "Advance," he shouted in the strongest voice he could muster. The Israelis moved forward.

The Egyptians waited until the first half-track reached the base of the slope before opening fire with their Archer anti-tank guns. Three Israeli half-tracks were destroyed and their crews killed in the opening ten minutes of the assault. More Israeli infantry fell as Egyptian machineguns raked their lines and artillery shells tore into the hillside. Some Israelis took cover behind groups of boulders only to have 120-mm mortar shells rain down on them. The Egyptians had pre-targeted any position that looked like it could offer cover. Their aim was deadly.

The Israelis fought back, targeting the Egyptian positions with their light machineguns and ordering in artillery and mortar strikes. It wasn't much, but it was something. Each time the Israelis attacked they chipped away at the Egyptians who were unable to receive replacements or resupply. They had what they had and it was enough to hold off the Israelis once again.

The assault lasted less than an hour. The Israelis didn't even get close to the top of the ridge line. It was the Israeli platoon sergeants that finally called for their men to retreat. They were the bravest of the brave, but they knew when a mission was beyond hope. They didn't care about the consequences. They could not watch their men die for no reason. The company commanders said nothing and let the sergeants' orders stand.

Goder ran out to meet the survivors. Most were wounded. Every half-track had been hit by at least one Egyptian shell spraying the driver and riders with hot shrapnel. "I'm sorry. I'm so sorry," he said to the men in his brigade as they limped past him. He knew he was done as their commander. Dayan would be furious at the brigade's failure to take the ridge. Goder didn't care. He could not order his men to attack the ridge again. It was too much to ask.

Goder was right. Dayan relieved him of his command and replaced him with a more aggressive colonel experienced in infantry tactics.

November 1, 1956 – Sheik Zuweid, Egypt

In the early afternoon, the Israeli vanguard rolled into the Egyptian outpost of Sheikh Zuweid about six miles west of Rafah. It was empty and every building was a smoking ruin. Israeli Ouragan and Mystère jets had caught the Egyptians forming up in a convoy to abandon the outpost and head toward the bridges over the Suez Canal. The destruction was complete. The Egyptians had removed their dead and wounded but it was clear from the burning armored cars, jeeps, and trucks, that the air attack had been devastating. It was an eerie demonstration of mankind's perfection of warfare. The Israelis were silent as they moved through the wreckage.

The Egyptians were retreating to the western bank of

the Suez faster than the Israelis could advance. The Israelis had mixed emotions learning about this development. It meant little resistance, but it also meant that significant Egyptian forces were escaping destruction and could be used in a counterattack later in the conflict or in a future war.

November 1, 1956 – Jeradi Pass, Egypt

The Egyptian rearguard, an infantry company, had taken up a blocking position at Jeradi Pass. The mountain range holding the pass was the last natural obstacle between 27th Armor and Al-Arish. The gap in which the pass was located was narrow with high cliffs making a flanking attack all but impossible. It was a strong position for the Egyptians.

Colonel Barlev considered going around the pass. After all, it was only a company of riflemen and a few artillery pieces. They wouldn't create much of a threat of attacking the Israeli tanks from behind as they assaulted Al-Arish. Besides, they would probably just surrender once the city fell. The problem was his supply lines. If the Egyptians were stubborn and didn't give up, they could harass his supply convoys. He decided the pass had to be taken.

There was a minor road that rounded the southern part of the mountain range, but it would take time to get a company in behind the Egyptians. Barlev was already behind schedule. He chose brute force over tactical maneuvers to root out the Egyptians. He sent several of his AMX tanks south to get a better angle of attack on the Egyptian positions. The Sherman tanks in his brigade had thicker armor in front than the light AMX tanks. They would become his battering ram. Like his boss, General Dayan, Barlev didn't like mixing the Israeli air power with ground assaults because of the risk of friendly fire from the overzealous pilots. But Barlev was cautious and requested a squadron of prop-driven Mustangs armed with rockets to be on standby as his armor attempted to take the gap on their own. The Mustangs flew in huge circles nearby like vultures hoping for a meal.

Israeli artillery and mortars joined the AMX tanks firing from a distance. Israelis shells pounded the enemy positions, forcing the Egyptians to keep their heads down while the Shermans advanced up the road into the gap. As the Shermans approached, the Egyptians opened fire and destroyed the lead tank, which blocked the narrow pass. There was no way to clear the wreck without risking several more tanks and men. Barlev cursed like a sailor and called in an airstrike.

The Mustangs flew in high from the east and dove on the Egyptian positions. As prop-driven planes, they were slower than jets, but that made them ideal air-to-ground fighters. Their rockets were deadly accurate and took out several of the Egyptian artillery pieces and machineguns. With their rocket launchers empty, each Mustang took its turn diving down using its six 50-cal machineguns. Eighteen hundred rounds from each plane tore into the Egyptian soldiers killing over a dozen.

Barlev watched and waited as the Mustangs finished their attack. As the warplanes headed back to their airfields across the border, Barlev ordered his tanks to advance once again. And again, the Israeli artillery, mortars and AMX tanks fired a heavy barrage of shells from a distance, pounding the Egyptian positions.

The Egyptians had finally had enough and broke. They fled back through the gap. They bypassed the city of Al-Arish and fled toward the safety of the west bank of the Suez Canal. The Israelis secured the pass, setting up defensive positions facing the city in case the Egyptians changed their minds and counterattacked. They didn't.

November 1, 1956 – Mitla Pass, Egypt

Brigitte returned in the jeeps with the reconnaissance team. She was tired from the long drive but wanted to make some more notes on the sinking of the *Aka* before grabbing some shuteye.

"You made it," said Sharon approaching.

"I did and I have one hell of a story to tell," said Brigitte.

"That's good I suppose."

"So where do you go from here?"

"Nowhere. We stay put. The British and French have issued an ultimatum. We must keep 10 miles from the canal."

"Yeah, I know."

"You do?"

"I heard one of the men discussing it."

"I see," said Sharon wondering if Brigitte knew more about what was going on than he did.

November 1, 1956 – Suez Canal Zone, Egypt

A flight of six Egyptian MiG-15 prepared for take-off on an airfield near the shores of the Suez Canal. Their mission was to attack advancing Israeli ground forces in the northern Sinai. Once in the air, the MiGs were fast and maneuverable. They could compete with any of the Israeli jets. However, the Egyptians were no match for the Israeli pilots.

The Soviets had sent experienced instructors and technical advisors to train the Egyptian pilots and ground crews in the use of the technically-advanced aircraft. Unfortunately, none of the instructors or the advisors spoke Arabic. Each training session had to be painstakingly translated by an interpreter. The interpreters provided by the Egyptians knew little about flying and many of the technical terms were misinterpreted, confusing the pilots and ground crews.

Many of the Egyptian generals that commanded the air force had never fought in combat. They were political appointees with family connections. They did not understand the need for training and were reluctant to spend their yearly budgets on the fuel, spare parts and ammunition required for a robust training program. Live fire exercises were particularly scarce and many of the Egyptian pilots fired their first shots at the Israeli planes and tanks during a battle. Experience in the cockpit made a much bigger difference in air battles than technical advancements. The Israelis shot down seven Egyptian jets for every one jet they lost themselves.

When the pilot of the first MiG rolled onto the runway, he looked toward the horizon on the opposite end of the runway and saw eight British Sea Venoms flying at maximum speed toward the airfield. He radioed the flight commander to report as he throttled up his engine. He knew his only hope of surviving was to get into the air where he could fight or run. Considering the enemy's advantage, running was the most appealing option. He released his wheel brakes and roared down the runway. The anti-aircraft guns protecting the airfield opened fire at the incoming enemy jets.

Halfway down the runway, the lead Sea Venom dropped a one-thousand-pound bomb directly in the MiGs path. The explosion blinded the Egyptian pilot and created a hole in the concrete runway the size of a bus. The MiG was moving too fast to stop or even veer out of the way. Its landing gear hit the edge of the crater and the nose of the jet tipped downward. The aircraft smashed into the opposite side of the crater. Its fuel tank and munitions exploded killing the pilot and creating an even large crater in the runway.

The other MiGs were trapped. With the runway destroyed the pilots could not take off and there was nowhere on the airfield to hide their aircraft. Some of the pilots abandoned their cockpits and ran for their lives, while others simply said their final prayer to Allah and waited for the inevitable.

The pilots of the Sea Vemons still had to deal with the anti-aircraft guns blazing away at the edge of the airfield. They were flying fast and low making it difficult for the electrically-powered guns to swing around as they passed.

One of the British Sea Vemons firing on the airfield took a direct hit, killing the pilot. The burning aircraft slammed into the desert floor and cartwheeled, sending flames and wreckage into the air.

Seeing his friend die, the pilot of a Sea Vemon dropped his entire payload on an anti-aircraft gun crew and their gun. The resulting explosion left little evidence that the gun ever existed. The pilot swung back around and used his Hispano 20-mm cannons to strafe the MiGs still on the airfield. Three more MiGs along with their munitions blew up killing their pilots and destroying the remaining anti-aircraft gun. With the anti-aircraft guns silenced, the Sea Vemon pilots took their time and destroyed every aircraft, vehicle and building on the airfield. They left the enemy airfield burning out of control and headed for home out in the Mediterranean.

November 1, 1956 – Cairo, Egypt

Amer and the Egyptian generals were in a conference room with maps marked with the British and French air strikes. Nasser was in a panic. The Halloween bombing campaign had shocked him and his generals. "How is this possible?" said Nasser. "The British and French have destroyed half of our air force in less than twenty-four hours."

"They have been incredibly lucky. Our pilots and air defenses were overwhelmed," said Amer. "The British and French have committed a large part of their fleets and air forces to this campaign."

"A campaign that you assured me was a bluff," said Nasser.

"As you said, what the British and French are doing doesn't make sense. They will enrage the Arab countries and lose all credibility in the Middle East."

"Not if they win. I will be made the fool."

"They cannot win as long as we fight. Our Arab brothers will join our struggle and we will drive the British and French into the sea if they dare set foot on Egyptian soil."

"I want all of our armed forces across the Suez now. Everything. We must be prepared to repel their invasion when it happens. We must protect the heartland. We must protect Egypt."

"Of course. It is already being done."

"I want the rest of our aircraft out of harm's way. Move our bombers to the Sudan or even Russian if you need to. I can't lose those bombers."

"I will see to it personally," said Amer. "Time is precious. Perhaps you should let me take care of the redisposition of our forces. Your time may be better spent coordinating with our allies and the Russians."

"Yes. Yes. There is much to do," said Nasser.

Nasser left the meeting and called the Arab leaders of neighboring countries. At first, he demanded their help as part of the defensive pact they have formed. When that didn't work, he pleaded for their help as fellow Muslims, declaring Jihad against the Western countries. Whatever his argument, it didn't matter. Nobody showed any interest in taking on the Israeli, French and British armies. They did however wish him luck and would offer prayers to Allah for his protection. *Cowards*, he thought. *How would they react if their country was being invaded? They will be reminded of this moment when the shoe is on the other foot and they call Egypt for help.*

Nasser's only hope of surviving the coming onslaught was the United Nations and the Soviets. He called his foreign minister and instructed him to plead Egypt's case to the United Nation general assembly. He knew the U.N. moved like a river of honey and it would take days or even weeks of debate before they could come to any conclusion to help Egypt... or not.

Nasser's next call was to the Soviet Communist Party Leader, Nikita Khrushchev. Khrushchev was a poorly-educated metal worker that had worked his way up the political ladder to become one of Stalin's closest advisors. He had been brutal during the Great Purge and had personally ordered the arrests of thousands of Soviet citizens that were eventually executed. He was respected by the military and won the struggle for power that followed Stalin's death to become the leader of the Communist Party. It was in the Communist Party where the true power of the Soviet Union lay. It was as the leader of the Communist Party that Khrushchev rejected Stalinism and opted for a more liberal society. Many of his policies, especially in agriculture, were well-meaning and intended to help the average Soviet citizen. Unfortunately, most failed and drove the Soviet Union deeper into stagnation and, in some cases, famine. Even with these failures, Khrushchev was one of the most powerful leaders in the world. He had nuclear missiles and wasn't shy of threatening their use when required to achieve his objectives.

Both Nasser and Khrushchev used translators on the call which made communication laborious and slow. Khrushchev listened as Nasser laid out the situation and predicted the invasion of British and French troops that was about to be unleashed on Egypt. "You say that you want the Soviet Union to be a friend to the Arabs. This is your chance to prove it. We need your help in defending ourselves from Western aggression and we need it now," said Nasser.

"Of course. Of course, we will help in your struggle against the capitalist swine. But there are practical limitations to what we can do militarily," said Khrushchev.

"What type of limitations?"

"Moscow is almost three thousand kilometers from Cairo. It could take weeks or even months for our troops and equipment to reach Egypt. That's assuming we could obtain the required permission from all the countries in-between our two nations and that is highly unlikely. Turkey would be especially difficult."

"What about ships? You have a Navy."

"Yes, but we do not have any ports that would allow us quick access to the oceans. Even if we did, the French and British would likely blockade Egyptian ports and the ports of its surrounding neighbors."

"Fine. Your air force can surely reach Egypt. Your jet fighters could destroy the Western air forces and your bombers could drive the British and French landing forces back into the sea."

"True. But we still need permission to fly over neighboring countries. That will take time to negotiate. And even if we are successful, I doubt the Americans would sit idly by if they saw Soviet fighters and bombers heading toward the Middle East. We are not yet prepared for a military confrontation with the Americans, not to mention NATO. We are still building our nuclear arsenal. We cannot risk all-out war. Not yet."

"There must be something you can do," said Nasser exasperated.

"Yes. Of course. We have a great deal of influence in the international community and powerful allies. We can put a great deal of pressure on both the British and the French."

"Pressure? You offer pressure?"

"Do not underestimate our influence. Politics got you into the mess and politics can get you out. As a member of the Security Council, Russia also has veto power in the United Nations. If the U.N. attempts to pass any resolutions against Egypt I assure you, Russia will stand by you and use its veto."

Nasser was crestfallen. After delivering the bad news, Khrushchev asked Nasser to keep him informed on the situation and that he would make himself available at any time if Nasser needed a sounding board for any possible solution. Nasser thanked the Soviet leader but secretly cursed him in his mind. The Soviets would be of little help. Egypt was on her own. He promised to remember this lesson when searching for allies in the future.

November 1, 1956 – Al-Arish, Egypt

Before the Israelis was a long, wide plain leading to the city of Al-Arish, the largest city in the Sinai. It was getting late in the day. Barlev decided to keep pushing his forces forward while he still had sunlight. The company of AMX tanks sped ahead toward the outskirts of the city. The Egyptian forces were in disarray and scrambling back and forth as they prepared to move back across the Suez Canal.

With Egyptians literally running across the desert trying to find safety, the Israeli had to be careful not to attack their own units. Friendly fire from tanks and aircraft was turning out to be more costly than enemy fire. Israeli 7th Armor had formed an ambush for the fleeing Egyptians and accidently fired on a company of Sherman tanks from Israeli 37th armor. Before they realized their mistake eight Sherman tanks from the 37th had been hit and their company commander along with several other Israeli soldiers were killed.

Again, the Egyptians set up a blocking force on the eastern outskirts of the city to buy time for the rest of

Egyptian forces as they escaped the Israeli advance. When the AMX column came into range, the Egyptian rearguard opened up with an earth-shattered barrage of artillery. The Egyptian shells rained down and exploded *en masse* churning up the main road, cratering the path to Al-Arish. Barlev called off the attack. The Egyptians were in full retreat. There was no need to risk his men's lives. By morning the city would be in Israeli hands with little effort. He would leave the remaining Egyptians for the Israeli Air Force and the British and French ground forces landing at the mouth of the Suez Canal.

November 1, 1956 - Abu Ageila, Egypt

The Israeli 37th Armor Brigade arrived at the eastern edge of the Hedgehog as the sun set on the Sinai. The brigade Colonel Shmuel Golinka in command, it consisted of two armored battalions and two motorized infantry battalions with half-tracks. The motorized infantry battalions arrived with Golinka while the two armored battalions lagged behind.

Golinka had heard of Goder's fate and had no desire to succumb to Dayan's temper. After looking at the intelligence reports, Golinka, like Dayan, was convinced the Egyptians were ready to break and run. When he received a report that his tanks were still hours away from the battlefield, Golinka grew impatient. He ordered his infantry battalion commanders to get ready to attack. What remained of 10th Infantry would act as their reserve during the assault.

Golinka decided to lead the attack himself using one of the half-tracks as a mobile command post. He ordered the drivers to turn on the lights on their half-tracks. He believed the Egyptians would be intimidated when they discovered that two full battalions were attacking their position.

It was just before midnight when Golinka ordered his men forward. They were well-rested after a few hours' sleep and eager to get at the enemy.

The Egyptians were surprised to see the headlights on the Israeli half-tracks still on and wondered it was some sort of ruse. They opened fired with their Archer anti-tank guns destroying more than a dozen of the Israeli vehicles. Twenty Israelis died and sixty-five were wounded. Golinka was among the dead. His half-track had been hit by multiple anti-tank shells. The Israelis retreated once again into the night. The half-track drivers, defying their dead commander's last order, turned off their headlights.

TWELVE

November 2, 1956 – Sinai Desert, Egypt

It was just past midnight. Coyle and the navigator had walked as far as they could during the early evening when it was cooling off. Exhausted, they had made camp in another outcropping of rocks. Their faces were drawn and blistered from the sun. Their lips were cracked and bleeding. A fire burned brightly. They didn't care if the Egyptian patrols found them.

Coyle held up the water bottle from the aircraft. He swirled it around. A small amount of water sloshed inside. It was the last of it. Coyle and the navigator longed for a drink, but they had agreed to wait until morning to finish it off. Then… it was just a matter of time until they died.

They laid by the fire. Talking took too much energy. It was cold. *Not supposed to be cold and dry,* thought Coyle. *One or the other but not both. It ain't hardly fair.* Coyle closed his eyes and tried to sleep. It wasn't easy with a parched throat and lips that felt like they were covered with paper cuts. Finally, he dozed off.

Coyle and the navigator slept. The fire burned down. A snake emerged from underneath a boulder and glided across the sand toward the warmth of the fire. It was a Red Spitting Cobra with a salmon-colored body and a black band near its head. It was nocturnal. It was rare to see one this far north. They preferred the savanna closer to Cairo and bordering the Nile valley where they could prey upon small birds and amphibians.

The cobra had no interest in Coyle or the navigator beyond the heat of their bodies. Certainly, it did not see them as food. Laying down, the size of the humans was not intimidating to the snake. It moved past Coyle's head.

Coyle's eyes opened a little. They were unfocused and only saw that something long was moving past his face. He jerked back instinctively.

The snake was surprised by the sudden movement and immediately went into defense mode, curling up in a coil and raising its head facing toward the threat. That was what Coyle was... a threat. The snake's head fanned out and flattened. Coyle watched wide-eyed, unmoving. The snake's head was less than two feet away. There was no way it would miss him if it struck. The snake hissed.

The navigator stirred and opened his eyes. He saw the snake in front of Coyle's face. He reached for his pistol. He could easily shoot the snake coiled up just six feet from the end of his pistol's barrel, but the bullet would most likely go through the snake and into Coyle. He slowly slipped off his flight jacket. He kept the pistol trained on the snake. He used his jacket as a whip, whirling it above his head. He brought his sleeve down into the upper body of the snake. The snake went flying and landed near the navigator's feet. The snake coiled up again. Coyle reached for his pistol. He could see the snake was ready to strike at the navigator. He didn't hesitate and pulled the trigger. Coyle's pistol fired at the same moment the snake spit venom at the navigator's face. The bullet blew the snake's head off. The venom landed in the navigator's eyes. He jerked back and screamed in pain like it was acid. Coyle grabbed the water bottle and sloshed the last of the water into the navigator's eyes. They were already swelling and turning red as their blood vessels burst. The navigator had saved Coyle's life but if he didn't get help soon it could cost him his eyes. He moaned in agony.

November 2, 1956 - Abu Ageila, Egypt

When morning broke, the rest of 37th armor brigade arrived and their tanks were unloaded from their transports. Dayan ordered his two new brigade commanders to attack once again. 37th Armor took the lead followed by 10th Infantry. The men were exhausted and morale was low. The Israelis moved forward and approached the base of the slope. They expected the Egyptian artillery to begin its bombardment once they started up the slope. They were surprised when nothing happened. They kept moving up the hillside with caution wondering when the Egyptians would unleash their Archer anti-tank guns and heavy machineguns, but still nothing happened.

When the first Israelis reached the top of the ridge they looked out at the empty defensive positions. The Egyptians were gone. The Israelis were stunned. Many fell to their knees and offered prayers of thanks to their Hebrew God.

Unbeknownst to the Israelis, the Egyptians had run out of water. They always had control over the dam and its abundant supply of water. It never occurred to the Egyptian commanders to store extra water on the Hedgehog in case the dam was overrun. After two days of battle, the Egyptians were dying of thirst. They spiked their guns and stole away on foot in the early morning before sunrise. They headed northwest across the desert toward Al-Arish and away from the Israelis.

Goder wept when he heard the news.

Dayan was relieved. With the Hedgehog now firmly in their possession, the Israelis controlled the center of the Sinai. The Egyptians could not attack the Israeli border without taking back the Hedgehog or risk having their supply lines cut off. Israel's southern border was safe for the time being. This allowed the Israeli forces to reposition their troops and vehicles to the front and continue their advance. There was little risk of attack from behind or to their flanks which were now protected with overlapping forces.

November 2, 1956 – Rafah, Egypt

The northern spearhead of the 27th armored brigade started toward their objectives on the Rafah salient just past midnight. The mechanized infantry battalion riding half-tracks took the lead. Egyptian artillery bracketed their positions and unleashed a heavy barrage. Archer anti-tank guns positioned on the hilltops joined in the massacre pouring rounds into the Israeli vehicles. Most of the Israeli half-tracks were hit and destroyed before they ever reached their objectives and over one hundred riflemen were killed riding in back.

While the Egyptian guns were busy picking off the mechanized battalion, the armored battalion of AMX-13 tanks raced forward. The AMX-13's were lightly armored which made them susceptible to anti-tank and artillery fire. But the light armor also made them fast, reaching speeds of 37 mph across the flat terrain. They were hard to hit while moving. Using the main road they raced parallel to the Egyptian positions, then pivoted and charged up the small hills on the northern flank of the salient launching their smoke grenades to cover their advance. The AMX tanks 75-mm main guns took a heavy toll on the Egyptian Archer anti-tank guns and heavy machine gun positions. Within three hours the Israeli armored battalion overran the hilltop positions and sent the Egyptians fleeing across the desert.

Once the Israelis captured the hilltops on the northern flank they could pour fire into the nearby Egyptian-controlled hilltops assisting the other two spearheads in their advance. The Egyptians collapsed and fled their defenses. The salient was captured and the nearby crossroads were secured.

The city of Rafah fell in a matter of minutes under an

overwhelming Israeli assault. The northern Egyptian forces were in full retreat.

The Israeli now had two objectives. The first was to push their advance forward toward the coastal city of Al-Arish, considered by Dayan to be the most important city in the Sinai. The second objective was the destruction of the Fedayeen in the Gaza Strip. With the Egyptians gone, the Fedayeen guerilla fighters didn't stand a chance against the well-trained and well-armed Israelis forces. Most of the Israelis in the northern infantry and armored brigades had family members or friends that had been killed by the Fedayeen over the years of cross-border attacks. The operation that followed the capture of Rafah was designed to decimate the Fedayeen forces, but for many Israelis it was time for revenge.

Colonel Givli's 1st Infantry was put in charge of the clean-up in Rafah and anchoring the Gaza Strip operations while Barlev's 27th Armored raced toward Al-Arish in hopes of capturing the city by nightfall.

27th Armored was divided into three spearheads. The first was a vanguard battalion made up of a dozen AMX-13 tanks backed by a mechanized infantry that would use the main road to form the tip of advance. The second and third spearheads were made up of mixed armored battalions of Sherman, Super-Sherman and AMX tanks accompanied by motorized infantry battalions. They would follow and then spread out to protect the flanks of the vanguard whenever they made significant contact with enemy forces. Dayan had allotted them six hours to cross twenty-five miles of desert. It wasn't much time.

November 2, 1956 – Sinai Desert, Egypt

The navigator moaned in pain as he walked. His eyes were wrapped with a cloth torn from Coyle's shirt. The sunlight was excruciating. He kept his hand on Coyle's shoulder. He let his hand drop. Coyle stopped and turned to check on him. "We have to keep moving," said Coyle.

"No mas. No puedo," said the navigator. "Dejame."

"I don't know what that means but I ain't leaving you if that's what you're babbling about."

"Dejame!"

"No. No dejame!"

"Entonces, tirame," said the navigator reaching for his pistol.

"I ain't gonna tirame either," said Coyle pushing his hand away from the pistol. "You're gonna make it, damn it. Even if I have to carry you."

"No mas. No puedo."

"Yes, puedo. Now get your ass in gear and let's go."

The navigator collapsed to the ground. He wasn't budging. "Shit!" said Coyle. "You are a stubborn Spanish bastard."

"Me dejas," said the navigator.

"No, dejas. Not without you."

"Me dejas por ayuda," said the navigator.

Coyle knew what he wanted. It was the smart move. Coyle could move much faster without him and return with help if he found it. If he didn't find anyone, they both were gonna die anyway. He looked around. In the distance was another low hill with a rock outcropping. There was little chance there of a water source but it could provide shade. Coyle used all the strength he could muster and picked up the navigator in a fireman's carry. He set out for the rocks.

It took five minutes to reach the rocks but Coyle thought it was the longest five minutes of his life. The navigator had gone limp half way to the rocks. Coyle was worried he might have died but he heard him still breathing with a kind of raspy-wheezing. He set the navigator down in the shadow of a large boulder. It was getting late in the afternoon and Coyle was tempted to stay with the navigator and set out again in the early morning while it was still cool. He gently shook the navigator awake. "Listen. Listen. I go for help. Ayuda. Like you said. I will come back. I promise... unless I'm dead," said Coyle removing the navigator's pistol. "You're not going to need this. You can't see anyway. Probably end up shooting me when I return if I leave you with it."

"Okay. Okay. Ayuda."

"Yeah. I'll get ayuda. You stay alive. Deal?"

The navigator grunted and passed out again.

"I'll take that as a yes," said Coyle. "Hang in there, amigo."

Coyle left his rucksack beside the navigator and headed north once again.

November 2, 1956 - Gaza, Palestinian Territory

The Israelis saw the Gaza Strip as a bridgehead for the Egyptians. As long as the Palestinians controlled the Gaza Strip, the Egyptians could build up ground forces in the northern end of the strip and strike deep into Israel. Gaza was also a sanctuary for the Fedayeen that plagued the Israeli settlements near the border with raids.

Now that Rafah had fallen and the Gaza Strip was cut off from the Egyptian forces that protected it, the Israelis were free to attack the Palestinians and any remaining Egyptian forces within Gaza from the bottom up. The Israelis had closed the box and there was no escape.

Colonel Givli's 1st Infantry Brigade was in Rafah on the Egyptian side of the border at the southern end of the Gaza Strip. 1st Infantry acted as a block for any Egyptian or Fedayeen forces attempting to escape Gaza.

The Gaza Strip had two major population centers, Gaza City in the north with its fifty thousand inhabitants and Khan Yunus in the south. Dayan planned to focus his assault on both, starting with Gaza City then working his way down to Khan Yunus.

Gaza City had an Egyptian brigade of three thousand five hundred National Guardsmen and several mortar detachments protecting the city. There was also a motorized border patrol company that acted as a reconnaissance and cavalry unit for the Egyptian forces. The city was surrounded by fortified hills including Ali Muntar where British forces fought the Ottoman in a protracted battle during WWI. It was here that the Egyptians placed most of their artillery and heavy machineguns. The hill had a series of deep trenches and the Egyptians had placed mines on its slopes. It would be a tough nut to crack for any infantry-based force.

The six Sherman tanks in the 37th Armored battalion led the Israeli attack just past dawn. 11th Infantry followed close behind the tanks. The Egyptian mines were designed for infantry and were not powerful enough to take out a tank. The Israeli infantry stayed back as the tanks sped up the slope and ran over the mines triggering their explosives and launching shrapnel against the tanks' heavy armor. The tanks trampled the barbed wire protecting the Egyptian trenches, clearing a path for the Israeli infantry. The Israeli tanks rolled right through the Egyptian defenses and only stopped for a moment when they found a worthwhile target such as an artillery gun or mortar position. They continued toward the city. The Egyptians were powerless to stop them. They had their own problems as the follow-on Israeli infantry reached the top of the ridge and attacked the surviving Egyptian National Guardsmen. Just before noon, the hills and the city were secured by the Israelis. Those Egyptian National Guardsmen that survived, fled throwing down their weapons and removing their boots.

37th Armor and 11th Infantry pivoted south and headed for Khan Yunus, only twelve miles away. The city of Khan Yunus was protected by three battalions of Palestinian 86th Infantry Brigade that had formed a perimeter around the outer boundaries of the city. The Egyptians also had several batteries of heavy mortars and artillery to support the infantry battalions. These were strategically placed to provide supporting crossfire should any of the positions be overrun. Unlike the Egyptian National Guardsmen in Gaza City, the Palestinians were fighting to protect their homes and families. They were much more stubborn and many of the soldiers defended their positions to the death. While the area had few hills from which to fight, the Palestinians had dug deep trenches and surrounded themselves with mines and multiple layers of barbed wire.

The Israelis met light resistance on the road to Khan Yunus but elected not to attack as they took up positions around the Palestinian defenses and night fell. The commanders in Jerusalem were concerned that many of the Palestinians might escape if the Israelis overran their positions during the night. Both the Palestinians and the Israelis were impatient to get at each other and exact revenge for past grievances.

THIRTEEN

November 2, 1956 - Bay of Aqaba, Egypt

Colonel Yoffe and his 9th Infantry Brigade had been given orders to sit tight after their victory at Ras an-Naqb. Dayan was concerned about Egyptian air and naval assaults on the brigade as it made its way south. The Egyptians had been ravaged but they still had a bite.

The British and French had ignored the timetable in the Sèvres Agreement and delayed their air attacks on the Egyptian airfields for eleven hours. The 9th was ordered to wait until air superiority had been achieved. Yoffe was one day behind schedule and was getting antsy. There was nothing the men of the 9th could do in the meantime but clean their gear and sleep. If there was one thing Yoffe was sure of, it was that he needed to keep his men occupied to keep them out of trouble. The same traits that made them good fighters made them ornery as badgers. Yoffe was also concerned that the more time he was forced to wait before advancing down the coastline, the longer the Egyptians had to prepare for his brigade's assault.

When Yoffe finally received permission to move out, he thought it came none too soon.

The journey down the eastern side of the Sinai was difficult. There were no roads suitable for a force the size of the 9th Infantry Brigade. The jeeps and trucks that carried the men were forced to travel off-road through rugged terrain of almost two hundred miles. Flat tires and broken wheel rims were common and slowed the brigade's progress. There was a cool breeze coming off the Gulf of Aqaba making the high temperature more bearable.

Israeli warships sailed down the coast protecting the 9th Brigade with their four-inch guns. The soldiers of 9th saw little action. After Nasser gave the order for a withdrawal from the Sinai, most of the Egyptian forces had fled toward the Suez Canal or down to the port of Sharm el-Sheikh for evacuation by sea. It took sixty hours for the men of the 9th to reach their next objective – Ras Nasrani.

November 2, 1956 - Mitla Pass, Egypt

Brigitte was finishing the last of the goodies that Coyle had brought her. She watched as six Dakota troop transports landed on the desert and pulled to a stop. The Israelis had created a temporary airfield by clearing away any large rocks that might damage a plane's landing gear and marking the landing strip with piles of rocks on both sides. It was primitive but it worked well for the air resupply shipments that were coming regularly now.

Brigitte wondered if they were carrying food and water. She wasn't hungry at the moment but she always liked to plan ahead, especially when it came to eating. The crews of the transports opened the door and unpacked the planes. Among the boxes of ammunition and rations were two hundred parachutes. She immediately realized the implications of such a sight. The 202nd Paratroop brigade was preparing to move south toward the city of Tor. The parachutes meant Sharon was going to send an advanced element into the city. *That's where I will find the story*, she thought. Brigitte went in search of Sharon.

She found Sharon talking with a battalion commander. They were going over the last-minute details of the mission. "Colonel Sharon, do you have a moment?" said Brigitte.

"Not right now," said Sharon.

"If you're planning a jump. I'd like to go," said Brigitte not listening to him.

"How do you know what we are planning?"

"I saw the Dakota crews unloading the parachutes. My guess is an advanced para element into Tor. Two companies based on the number of parachutes."

Sharon grunted. He liked to keep his plans secret and Brigitte nosing around wasn't helping. He understood she was just doing her job, but these were life and death situations.

"I know how to stay out of the way," said Brigitte, risking his wrath.

"Have you every jumped into battle before?" said the battalion commander.

"Six times. No seven times... I forgot one."

"You've jumped seven times into battle?"

"Once in Dien Bien Phu. That one was a bit of a hair-raiser."

"Most of my men don't have seven combat jumps," said the commander to Sharon. "Can she shoot too?"

"I think she prefers to type," said Sharon. "But she can be just as deadly."

Sharon still hadn't told Brigitte about the downing of the Spanish cargo plane. He knew she would be of little use once she got the news. Besides he still didn't have any information on the survivors at that point. Sharon and his battalion commander exchanged a look. "She's qualified," said Sharon reluctantly. "You want her, you got her."

"Get your gear," said the commander.

Brigitte thanked them with a smile and ran off.

November 2, 1956 – Mitla Pass and Tor, Egypt

It was late in the afternoon when the two companies of Israeli paratroopers took off from below the Mitla Pass and headed for Tor.

Inside the lead Dakota, Brigitte sat next to the battalion commander. He wanted to keep an eye on her and, if he was being honest, he wanted to be the focus of her story. Military exploits and politics went hand-in-hand in Israel and he had political aspirations when he retired from the army. Brigitte had on her jumpsuit and was wearing a parachute like the paratroopers. Her hair was up in a tight bun so it wouldn't get tangled in her parachute's lines. She had learnt that lesson the hard way during parachute training when she failed to listen to her French instructor. She got so twisted up in the parachute lines, she had to use her pocket knife to cut off a large chunk of her hair after she landed.

The Israeli paratroopers glanced at her, wondering why a French civilian was being allowed on such an important mission. They had no problem with her being a woman. They had fought beside many women in the Arab-Israeli war and found them to be reliable and surprisingly aggressive – a trait they admired. But she was French and while the Israelis liked the French, they didn't necessarily trust them. In fact, they trusted few foreigners. The Israelis had learnt to be self-sufficient and fight their own battles. Help was always welcomed from western nations, but rarely offered.

The flight didn't take long. The pilot warned the commander that they were coming up on the landing zone and the jump indicator box turned red. The jump master gave the command to stand up and hook up. The paratroopers and Brigitte hooked up their parachute release straps to the wire running through the center of the cabin and moved toward the door making a tight line. The idea was to jump as close together as possible so they all landed in the general vicinity of each other. A platoon of paratroopers could get spread out over two miles if they weren't careful. That was not an effective way to fight if the landing zone was hot. The Israelis were well-trained in battle jumps and every soldier knew what was expected of him. The light flashed green and they headed out the doorway one after another, about one to two seconds apart. Brigitte was the last to jump as she followed the battalion commander out the open door.

Her chute deployed and she felt the familiar slug-in-the-crotch as the harness straps snapped tight. She floated down. She could see the other parachutes below her and more chutes opening above her from the other planes. The sun was setting. The desert below was beautiful in the orange light. She didn't see any gunfire coming from the city but that didn't mean they were in the clear. The Egyptians could be waiting before springing their trap.

Fortunately for the Israelis, most of the Egyptian soldiers were offering their evening prayers when the planes were spotted. Many chose to finish their prayers knowing it may be their last. They collected their weapons and went to their trenches to meet the Israelis.

As battles go, Tor wasn't much of a fight. The majority of the Egyptian units had already headed west to cross the Suez Canal. What was left was a token force to show the Egyptian people in the town that their leader had not abandoned them. It wasn't much of a force.

The Israeli paratroopers landed one mile out from the city without incident. Surprisingly, nobody broke an ankle or leg which was expected in a jump this size. Brigitte landed and rolled as she had been taught. She was lighter than the men, so her chute slowed her descent considerably and made her landing less traumatic. She released her harness, gathered her parachute and placed it with the others to be collected later. She moved to the commander's side and listened as he issued his orders. It was to be a frontal assault of the city. The Israelis didn't have much time. The rest of the 202nd Brigade had departed for Tor as the jump task force had taken off. It wouldn't take them long to arrive unless they ran into resistance, which wasn't expected since the Egyptians were retreating.

The Israelis formed a skirmish line and advanced toward the outskirts of the city. The Egyptians had surprisingly little in the way of weapons. Most had been taken by the units that had already left. Mortars and light machineguns were the biggest problem for the Israelis.

The terrain around the city was flat and there wasn't much in the way of cover. The paratroopers kept down and crawled their way forward. Many were excellent marksmen and picked off any Egyptian that raised his head above the trench line. Once the Israelis closed in on the Egyptian trenches, they used grenades. The Israelis had been trained to release the grenade's spoon starting the timer then wait for a short time before pitching them into the trenches. The Egyptians had no time to pick up the grenades and toss them back out. Instead, they died or were badly mauled by the grenades' shrapnel.

The battle for Tor lasted less than thirty minutes before the Egyptian commander surrendered along with sixty-two of his soldiers. Twelve Egyptians were killed with another twenty-three wounded. Two Israelis were killed and eight wounded. The disparity in losses was due to training, leadership and aggression. The Egyptians were no match for the Israelis.

With the fighting stopped, Brigitte moved up with the commander and took photos of what she saw. She would use the photos later to jar her memory as she wrote the stories of what had happened in the battle. A few key photos would end up in the magazine alongside her writing. She was impressed with the Israeli paratroopers. They were a tight group and fought well. Their esprit de corps was on par with the French paratroopers with whom she had so often jumped. Both the Israelis and French had fought multiple wars since the end of World War II. As terrible as the wars were, they kept the soldiers in their militaries experienced and well-trained. Nothing prepares a soldier to do battle better than battle itself. They knew how to fight because they continued to fight and win. This gave them an edge in both morale and experience. It was a sad truth.

A few hours later the rest of the 202nd Brigade rolled into Tor. Resistance had been light, mostly small Egyptian units that were on their way toward the Suez Canal and had no interest in fighting the Israelis. The two sides ignored each other as they passed. The 202nd needed time to regroup, resupply and prepare for the next phase of their operation – the assault on Sharm el-Sheikh. Many of their vehicles had been badly damaged from Egyptian artillery and warplanes. The tank and half-track crews needed time and parts to repair them before they could be used again in battle. Tor had an airfield that the Israelis had captured. It would make resupply and reinforcement safe and easy for the Israeli cargo planes. The Israelis were still concerned about an Egyptian counterattack. It was true the Egyptians were retreating across the Suez Canal but they could turn at any time and attack the Israeli forces.

Brigitte was grateful for the rest and looked forward to the full eight hours' sleep that would get rid of the dark circles under her eyes. She wanted a bath and a chance to clean her clothes. She also needed to organize her notes. If she could find a phone that still worked she would call her editor and give him a couple of articles she had written while in the field. Most of the phone lines in the north had been cut by the Israeli planes but there was a chance that the Egyptians had repaired a few lines so their commanders could communicate with headquarters in Cairo. She thought it was worth a shot anyway. She might even be able to place a call to Coyle who she was sure was back in Algiers or Paris drinking a beer and eating his favorite sandwiches. If the phones didn't work, she might be able to send her articles by radio. Sharon had been very stingy about giving her radio time. She hoped he would loosen up a bit if she dropped a hint that one of her articles was about him.

Brigitte looked for Sharon. She found him standing near a café talking with one of his battalion commanders. She approached him from behind. He didn't see her as he dismissed the battalion commander. Sharon's radio operator approached and said, "Colonel, I just got word from the patrol sent out to examine that plane wreckage. The American was not among the survivors," said the radio operator. "I thought you'd want to know right away."

Sharon heard the quiet steps behind him and turned to see Brigitte. Her face said everything when she heard the news. He wasn't sure what to do. He could command a brigade of paratroopers, but he knew little about women.

"Yes, yes. Give me the details later. You're dismissed," said Sharon to the radio operator attempting to mask the news.

"An American? What plane crash?" said Brigitte afraid to ask.

The radio operator realized his mistake and moved off sheepishly. "I was going to tell you once we knew for sure what happened," said Sharon.

"Tell me what?" said Brigitte with panic welling up inside. "What happened, Colonel?"

"The Spanish cargo plane piloted by your boyfriend was shot down on its way back to Israel. It crashed in the desert."

"Oh, my god," said Brigitte, her legs giving out from underneath her.

Sharon reached out and grabbed her to keep her from falling. He wasn't sure what to do. He let her down slowly in one of the café's chairs. He reached for his canteen thinking that water would somehow help. "I'm sorry. I just wanted to be sure before telling you," he said.

"Tom," said Brigitte crying. "What have I done? This is my fault. He never would have come if I wasn't here."

"You don't know that," said Sharon trying to comfort her.

"But I do. He was always trying to save me from myself and I finally got him killed. It's my fault," said Brigitte weeping uncontrollably.

November 2, 1956 – Luxor, Egypt

By nightfall, Egypt's air force had been decimated and was ineffective as a fighting force. Over eighty percent of the MiG-15s and Meteor fighters and over seventy percent of the Vampires had been destroyed. Nasser had ordered his precious I1-28 bombers out of harm's way. He sent twenty-one of the Soviet-built bombers to Saudi Arabia along with a small number of MiG-15s where they would wait out the war. He sent another twenty-one to the valley of Luxor in hopes that the British and French wouldn't risk damaging the ancient capital of Egypt. As the ground invasion approached, neither the British nor the French were inclined to let the bombers remain a threat to their troops no matter the cost. They made their plans to destroy the airfield in Luxor.

A miscalculation on a level attack could carry a load of bombs hundreds of yards or even miles off target and destroy the ancient buildings all around the city. Instead, the British bombers would dive-bomb the Egyptian aircraft parked on the airfield. While dive-bombing was more difficult and dangerous there was less chance of any of the bombs going astray. They would also use high-explosive one-thousand pound bombs for the attack to ensure that even a near miss would destroy or at least badly damage the targeted aircraft.

The initial attack destroyed three of the Egyptian bombers but most of the bombs landed wide of the airfield. While no ancient buildings were destroyed, the fleet of bombers were still a very real threat to the invasion.

November 3, 1956 - Gaza, Palestinian Territory

The Israelis waited until morning before attacking the city of Khan Yunus. Once again, the Sherman tanks took the lead followed by the infantry in half-tracks. The tanks and half-tracks raced across an open plain toward the Palestinian perimeter. The half-tracks strafed the trenches, forcing the Palestinians to take cover while the tanks unleashed a barrage of cannon fire and advanced. The tanks' 75-mm shells blew holes in the barbed wire providing a channel for their infantry. Israeli 120-mm mortar shells rained down on the enemy artillery positions destroying many of the Palestinian guns.

The Palestinians held their ground and kept fighting but their rifles and machineguns were useless against the Sherman tanks. The gunners in the Shermans would sight an enemy position, destroy it with a high explosive round, then move on to the next enemy position. Once the Shermans ran out of targets, they moved on toward the city using their machineguns on anyone foolish enough to stick their head above the top of a trench.

The Israeli infantry moved in and attacked the Palestinians inside their trenches by tossing dozens of grenades over the edges. It was too much. The Palestinians were being slaughtered. Their lives wasted. The Palestinians broke and fled the outer perimeter toward the city. Fleeing Palestinians mixed with the advancing Israeli tanks as they approached the city. It was mayhem.

Israeli infantry cleared out any stragglers and wounded from the trenches, then took up position in the trenches facing the city in case the Palestinians mounted a counterattack. But the Palestinians were too busy manning their secondary line of defensive positions within the city. They would fight the Israelis block by block, house by house.

The Israelis used their tanks and half-tracks to comb the city streets and take out pockets of resistance. The Palestinians had abandoned their artillery in the outer perimeter and had nothing with which to fight the armored vehicles. One by the one the streets fell as the Israelis advanced and overran the Palestinian positions. It took less time than either side imagined. By nightfall, the last of the Palestinian forces surrendered and the Israelis secured the city. The battle for the entire Gaza Strip took just fifty-eight hours. The Palestinians fought bravely but lost decisively.

November 3, 1956 – Sinai Desert, Egypt

Things had calmed down. The last of the Egyptian units had either made it across the Suez and rejoined the main body of the army or had entered Sharm el-Sheikh in the southern tip of the Sinai where they hoped to be extracted by boat. The Israelis finished digging in and preparing their defensive positions.

November 3, 1956 – Nile Delta, Egypt

The Gamil Bridge connected the only road leading from Port Said and the Nile Delta. Any Egyptian reinforcements would need to cross that bridge to reach the garrison at Port Said. It was the British Navy's job to make sure that didn't happen. But it wasn't a simple task. The bridge was made of concrete and had eleven supporting columns.

In the Mediterranean, *HMS Eagle* turned into the wind and launched a mixed squadron of Sea Hawk jets and Westland Wyverns, turboprop fighters. Each Sea Hawk carried four five-hundred pound bombs while the Wyverns carried six five-hundred pound bombs. But it didn't matter.

When the British fighters swooped down and dropped their payloads on the bridge they found that their bombs did little more than blow large chunks of concrete from the columns and roadway leaving the structure still standing. There was much cursing when the pilots returned to the *Eagle*.

On the second raid, the fighters changed the configuration of their bombs to thirty-second delay fuses. This time the bombs hit the support columns and penetrated the concrete like darts into a board. When the bombs detonated, the force of the explosion was enhanced by the confined space surrounded by concrete. The columns shattered and the bridge crashed into the water below. The mood of the pilots greatly improved on their return to the *Eagle*.

November 3, 1956 - Gulf of Aqaba, Egypt

It was just before sunset when *HMS Crane* - a British Black Swan Sloop - patrolled the entrance to the Gulf of Aqaba. The 192-man crew had been involved in little action since the start of the war. Most were inspections of commercial vessels in the area. There were the occasional sniping incidents from shore which were quickly ended by a barrage from the *Crane's* 50-cal machineguns.

The crew watched from a distance as Israeli and Egyptian forces slugged it out for control of the coastal cities. The British vessel could not be seen as taking sides and did not participate in any of the battles between the two belligerent armies. The crew simply watched at the guard rails making bets on who would win. The odds were usually against the Egyptians who were seen as inferior fighters to the Israelis. It was only when the Israelis were vastly outnumbered that the contest became interesting but even then the odds rarely improved beyond evens.

Commander Jack Hodges was hungry as he sat in his captain's chair on the bridge. He was thinking about the lamb chops he had requested for dinner. That was one of the perks of commanding his own ship – he decided what was for dinner and he really liked lamb chops with mint jelly. He could see a flight of five Israeli jets attacking Egyptian positions on shore. They were mostly using their machineguns to strafe the Egyptian soldiers which he thought strange because the jets were also armed with both rockets and bombs. *A well-placed bomb or rocket would end any argument,* he thought.

He would need to wait until the Israelis were finished before he could make his entry in the ship's log and head to dinner. He watched through his binoculars. The Israeli jets looked like hawks swooping on field mice running from hole to hole. The attack ended and the Israeli jets rose into the sky to form up and head for home. But they didn't head for home… they headed toward his ship. They swung around to the west high above the British vessel. "See if you can raise those Israeli jets and make sure they know we are British," said Hodges to his communication officer.

It was too late. The jets moved fast and lined up in a single-file attack formation. "Oh, shit. Sound general quarters," said Hodges to his executive officer. "And get us underway. Head out to sea. Evasive maneuvers."

The *Crane* started to zig-zag but there wasn't much room to maneuver while it was still in the gulf. As the first jet started its dive, the ship's anti-aircraft batteries opened fire. The Israelis were attacking from the west so the setting sun was in the eyes of the ship's gunners, making it difficult to spot their target. The first jet dropped two five-hundred pound bombs. Both missed, exploding in the water next to the ship. The pilot finished his dive with a fusillade of machinegun fire that ripped into the deck.

"Why in the hell haven't they responded to our radio calls?" said Hodges.

"I don't think they understand us. They seem to be speaking in Hebrew," said the communications officer.

"Christ all mighty," said Hodges.

The next jet started its dive toward the zig-zagging ship. The ship's anti-aircraft were well-trained and knew how much lead to give a jet versus a propeller-driven plane. The jet screamed toward the ship and fired its rockets. One of the rockets slammed into the forward deck, exploding and creating a six-foot hole in the thick steel plating. As the jet pulled out of its dive, the anti-aircraft gunner on the port side lined up his stream of 20-mm projectiles so the jet flew right into them. The jet exploded killing the pilot before he could eject. The crew cheered.

Black smoke poured out of the hole created by the Israeli rocket. Something was burning below deck. The crew of a warship didn't fear the sea. They feared fire. The *Crane's* fire brigades ran towards the fire with their hoses and poured on the water. The ship was made of steel and seemed invincible but there were still plenty of things to burn below decks. Fuel and ammunition were the biggest concern. Fire in the wrong compartment could mean a deadly explosion. It was a race to keep the fire from spreading.

The third Israeli jet started its dive toward the ship. The pilot had seen the explosion of his friend's aircraft. He knew there was no survivor. He could only offer his dead friend revenge. His jet dove into the streams of anti-aircraft fire. He fired his rockets. One punched through the top deck and out the side of the hull.

Inside the ship an engineering compartment flooded. The men inside all got out except for one. He was too far back in the compartment to reach the door before a warrant officer commanding a fire team ordered the water-tight door shut to prevent further flooding. The compartment filled with water. The engineer searched for pockets of air to breath. The bow of the ship rolled up the front of a wave and popped up when it reached the top sending the stern of the ship deeper in the water.

The flooded compartment finished filling with water pushing out the air from most of the pockets. The engineer took a deep breath as the last pocket filled up with water. The ship's bow slammed back down and the stern of the ship rose.

As the stern of the ship rose up, the water in the flooded compartment emptied pouring out the hole in the hull and carrying the engineer with it. He was severely cut by the jagged edges of torn steel as he tumbled out of the hole and into the sea. He was bleeding badly from multiple wounds.

One of the crew members on deck spotted him. There was little he could do beyond tossing him a floating ring. The ship's captain was fighting for the life of his crew and ship. There would be no stopping to retrieve any sailor washed overboard until the battle was over. The engineer swam toward the floating ring but lost consciousness from loss of blood and slipped under the water. He was gone.

The Israeli jets continued their attack until their munitions were expended. One more jet was hit with anti-aircraft fire but only suffered damage to one of its tail stabilizers. The jet would limp back to base guarded by the other three remaining aircraft.

The *Crane* had received several more rocket hits and one bomb exploded on her aft deck but caused surprisingly little damage and no casualties. The strafing fire from the jets took the biggest toll and chewed up the steel plating on most of the top deck and bridge.

In the following weeks and months both the Israelis and the British would make no mention of the incident. Friendly fire was never looked upon fondly by either side.

FOURTEEN

November 4, 1956 - Ras Nasrani, Egypt

It was approaching sundown when the men of the 9th came to the outskirts of Ras Nasrani in the southern Sinai. The artillery pieces that they had lugged with them down the coastline were moved into positions overlooking the city. Black smoke rose from burning buildings and houses. The Israeli Air Force had bombed the city relentlessly for the last three days hoping to reduce resistance when the Israeli ground forces arrived.

Israeli reconnaissance patrols moved toward the city and found it abandoned by the Egyptians. The civilians were hiding in their homes and businesses and watched the Israelis through the cracks in their shutters. It was eerie that the Egyptians had left an entire coastal city unguarded. Even the 6-inch naval guns that overlooked the Straits of Tiran were silent and unmanned.

When the reconnaissance team reported back to Yoffe, he ordered the men of the 9th to advance into the city. They'd captured another city and a major gun installation without so much as a shot being fired. They were on a roll and morale was soaring.

Twelve miles to the east, Yoffe watched Sharm el-Sheikh through his binoculars. Even from that distance he could see Egyptian vehicles moving artillery and troops into position on the outskirts of the city. It was the most fortified city in all the Sinai. He had no illusion that the Egyptians would give up Sharm el-Sheikh without a very big and mean fight. But for the moment, he would let his men celebrate. He needed them confident for what they were about to face. Sharm el-Sheikh was the last major objective in Operation Kadesh. To the Israelis Sharm el-Sheikh meant freedom. If the city fell, Israeli ships could be assured access through the Straits of Tiran and could open trade routes to eastern Africa and Asia.

The Israelis had superior numbers and were well-led. The Egyptians had strong defensive positions with trenches, minefields and barbwire. The Egyptian soldiers were well-armed with artillery, heavy machine guns and anti-tank guns. As small units in defensive positions, the Egyptians fought well.

Operation Kadesh called for Yoffe and the Israeli soldiers of the 9th to attack Sharm el-Sheikh first from the east. The Israelis wanted the Egyptian commander to reorient his forces to face the threat coming at them from the eastern side of the city and port. While the Egyptians concentrated on the east, Sharon and the 202nd would attack from the west and smash through the enemy positions to overrun the city. Once Sharon and his men were in the city and attacking the enemy from the rear, the Egyptian commander would have no choice but to surrender or die.

The terrain between Ras Nasrani and Sharm el-Sheikh was flat as a pancake and offered little protection for the attacking force. It made Yoffe and his men a tempting target for the Egyptians. The 9th's attack needed to be convincing. Yoffe send a company around the city's outskirts to attack from the mountains to the north.

November 4, 1956 - Tor, Egypt

Sharon was careful not to make any movements toward Sharm el-Sheikh. He wanted the Egyptian commander to believe that he and his men were getting ready to head west toward the Suez Canal and had no orders to attack the southern-most city. If the Egyptians felt threatened by Sharon and his brigade they would not consolidate their forces to the east and the 202nd's assault could be stalled. The road from Tor to Sharm el-Sheikh went along the eastern coastline of the Sinai and was mostly flat until it reached the southern mountains that towered over the city's northeastern side. The 202nd would travel fast once they launched their attack from their staging area in Tor. It would give them the element of surprise over the Egyptians. The Egyptian commander was blind beyond the horizon because of their lack of reconnaissance aircraft.

November 4, 1956 - Sharm el-Sheikh, Egypt

Even the Israeli Air Force was careful to only bomb and strafe the Egyptian defensive positions on the eastern side of the city so it looked as if that was the side of the planned assault. Israeli fighter-bombers pounded away at the Egyptians for three days straight depriving them of sleep and shattering their nerves. While the warplanes had little effect against the well-protected Egyptians, their bombs and machineguns were demoralizing and created a large number of desertions from the inexperienced soldiers.

Colonel Raouf Mahfouz Zaki commanded the Egyptian forces at Sharm el-Sheikh. He had ordered the abandonment of Ras Nasrani once he received reports of a large Israeli force approaching the city from the north. He knew he could not defend both Ras Nasrani and Sharm el-Sheikh with the two battalions under his command. The two cities were far enough apart that they could not support each other with their artillery batteries and Zaki had no tanks under his command. He decided that the deep-water port and the airfield at Sharm el-Sheikh were more important strategically than the costal guns that protected the Straits of Tiran. Sharm el-Sheikh had substantially better prepared defensive positions than Ras Nasrani.

Zaki had also been told by his superiors in Cairo that

he and his men were to be picked up by the Egyptian navy as soon as transports became available. He needed the port facilities to load his equipment and men. Sharm el-Sheikh was the obvious choice to defend. In the meantime, he and his men were ordered to defend the Straits of Tiran.

Zaki was in a black box. Without aircraft, he could not see out to know what was coming. He had reconnaissance patrols, but many were destroyed or captured by the Israelis before they could report back on their findings. He didn't know from where the Israelis would arrive or what was the size of their force. He could only wait and see how the battlefield unfolded. He suspected that Israeli paratroopers would most likely be dropped on his flanks forcing him to divide his forces even more. It was a hopeless situation. He was biding his time, hoping the sealift would arrive before the Israelis.

Zaki was disappointed when he saw the first Israeli units occupy Ras Nasrani at noon on November the 4th. He was going to have to fight to save his men and his honor. He wasn't afraid. There was too much to do to be afraid. He just didn't want to make a mistake that would cost Egyptian lives. Other than that, he and his men would do their best to fend off the Israelis. He realized he was in a strong defensive position and he planned to make the Israeli pay dearly when they tried to capture the city.

It was dark on November 4, 1956 when Yoffe and the men of the 9th arrived on the outskirts of Sharm el-Sheikh, the last major strategic position held by the Egyptians in the Sinai. The Egyptians had been shelling the Israelis with artillery ever since they left the outskirts of Ras Nasrani. Egyptian fire teams had kept up a continuous harassment of machinegun fire the entire ten miles of the Israeli advance. The Egyptians would set up, fire on the Israelis forcing them to hit the ground, then abandon their position and fall back before the Israelis could overrun or flank them. Once they were out of danger, the Egyptian fire teams would set up the next ambush. Hit and run. Hit and run. It was old school guerilla warfare.

Yoffe could see that his men were tired but he decided to push the attack. He needed the Egyptians to reposition their troops before Sharon and the 202nd arrived. The Israelis advanced and met stiff resistance from the Egyptian trenches. Tracer rounds from the machineguns streaked across the desert and lit up the sky.

The battle lasted four hours. At one point, it looked like the Israelis would overrun the western Egyptian positions, but Zaki sent in his reserves at the last moment and drove the Israelis back.

The Israelis were exhausted. Yoffe ordered his men to fall back into the desert. The Egyptians kept up their artillery fire, determined not to the allow the Israelis to regroup. Yoffe ordered his men to dig in and wait until morning, when they would attack again.

November 5, 1956 - Sharm el-Sheikh, Egypt

At dawn, the Israeli Air Force arrived at Sharm el-Sheikh. The warplanes proceeded with a massive bombardment that included Napalm and rockets. The Egyptians were driven from their forward trenches and forced back into the city where they took up defensive positions in the buildings and houses.

During the predawn hours, an Israeli battalion had swept around the northern side of the city using the mountains to obscure their movements. Yoffe's main force remained at the eastern edge of the city. When the air force let up, the Israelis attacked from two sides and tore into the Egyptians with everything they had.

It was too much. Within an hour, Zaki and his men surrendered. Sharm el-Sheikh fell to the Israeli 9th Infantry Brigade four hours before Sharon and the 202nd

Paratrooper Brigade arrived. Yoffe had unknowingly stolen Sharon's thunder and Sharon would never let him forget it.

Operation Kadesh ended in victory once again. The Israelis had completed their part of the Sèvres Protocol. Now it was time for the French and British to complete their end of the bargain. Operation Revise was about to begin and the world was about to become a much more dangerous place to live in.

November 5, 1956 – Sinai Desert, Egypt

It was early in the morning, a few hours before sun up. The fighting had calmed to a lull in the northern Sinai. The Egyptians were in full retreat back to the Suez Canal and fire fights involving stray soldiers were sporadic. The Israelis had strict instruction not to advance any further than their current positions. They were allowed to defend themselves, but there was a sort of self-imposed ceasefire. The Israelis did not chase after the Egyptians. They had beaten them badly and Dayan was anxious not to see any more Israelis die when it wasn't necessary to achieve his objectives. They had won a great victory for Israel and that was enough. They were in a strong position to negotiate when the peace process finally started.

As part of their defense, the task forces had placed dozens of outposts throughout the desert. Any change in the Egyptians retreat would be immediately detected and the Israelis would respond. In the meantime, it was boring guard duty for the Israeli troops. A far cry from the excitement they had faced in the last five days.

The desert sky had already started to lighten and was now a dull grayish-blue with the stars fading. Two Israeli soldiers manned a light machinegun overlooking a section of the desert toward the south. "I hope I get a promotion after this. I really need a raise," said a private. "Chana and I are getting married as soon as I get back."

"You don't want to get married," said a corporal. "You're both too young."

"I'm too young to get married?" said the private kneeling behind the machinegun. "I'm risking my life and fighting a fucking war in case you hadn't noticed."

"One has nothing to do with the other."

"Like hell it doesn't. When did you get married?"

"That's irrelevant."

"Why is that irrelevant?"

"It's about maturity, not age. I was far more mature than you when I was your age."

"But you said I was too young, not immature."

"You're both. Look... I'm not saying it to be mean. I just don't want to see you making a mistake and ending up in a divorce."

"We're in love with each other."

"Irrelevant. Shit happens. People change."

"We're not gonna get a divorce."

"You say that but you don't know."

"Nobody knows the future. Except God. God knows the future."

"Don't go getting religious on me. We're just talking here. No need to bring God in on the conversation."

"Hey. I think I saw something."

"Where?"

"Out there," said the private pointing. "Two hundred meters."

The corporal looked out in the direction the private was pointing. "I don't see anything."

"That's because you can't see shit at night. I'm telling you I saw something."

"So, what the hell was it?"

"I don't know. A guy I think."

"You saw a guy? You mean like a soldier?"

"I don't know. It didn't look like he was carrying anything. A soldier would be carrying a rifle, right?"

"Maybe. The Egyptians have been tossing their weapons so they can move faster."

"You think he's Egyptian?"

"I don't know. I didn't see him. But who else would be roaming around the desert in the dark?"

"You think he's gonna attack?"

"I doubt it. Most of the Egyptians are running for the Suez. He probably just got lost."

"But you don't know that?"

"No. Not for sure."

"So, he could be a sniper or something?"

"I suppose."

It was Coyle. He was wandering. He had lost his sense of direction. He was dehydrated and exhausted. His mind was not working right. He was just putting one foot in front of the other. It was all he could think to do. He hadn't slept in two days and was starting to hallucinate. He saw Brigitte. His cracked lips smiled. "Brigitte, you're here." The ghostly image said nothing in return. "Are you mad at me?" said Coyle concerned.

The image shook its head and reached out with both its arms. Coyle smiled again. He was with Brigitte. He was safe and could sleep now.

"It's definitely a man," said the private, staring into the darkness.

"What's he doing?" said the corporal also looking out but not seeing anything.

"He's walking toward us that's what he's doing."

"That can't be good. He's closing his distance."

"I'm going to fire a burst."

"Alright. I suppose it couldn't hurt."

The private squeezed the trigger on the machinegun. The burst of fire lit up the surrounding area and Coyle as he collapsed and hit the ground. "Oh, now I see him," said the corporal. "Nice shot."

"I'm not sure I hit him," said the private.

"What do you mean? He fell."

"Yeah, but he fell just as I fired. I'm not sure it was me that did it."

"Well who else would it be?"

"I don't know. People fall sometimes."

"We can't just leave him out there if you're not sure you killed him."

"Yeah, well… I ain't sure."

"Go check him out."

"Me?"

"You shot him… or didn't shoot him. Go check him out. He's your kill. You'll be fine. I'll cover you."

"What if he's still alive?"

"He's an Arab. Shoot him."

"Alright," said the private picking up his rifle and walking out into the desert.

He walked over with his gun pointed at Coyle. There was no movement. He poked Coyle's side. Coyle grunted. "He's still alive," he yelled back to the corporal.

"So, shoot him," said the corporal.

The private took aim. Coyle groaned and rolled over. The private looked down at his face. He was Caucasian. "I don't think he's Egyptian," yelled the private.

"Well what is he?"

"English, maybe French."

"Oh, shit," said the corporal. "Don't shoot him."

"I wasn't planning on it. What should I do with him?"

"Take him prisoner."

"Prisoner?"

"Yeah. Until we know where he's from. But don't shoot him."

"I'm not gonna shoot him."

The private knelt down. He saw the pistol in Coyle's waistband and took it. "Hey, wake up," he said. "Ya gotta wake up."

Coyle stirred. He looked up at the private. "Israeli?"

"Yeah. You?"

"American."

"No shit?"

"No shit. You got some water?"

The private took his canteen and gave Coyle some water. Coyle drank and coughed as the water hit his parched throat. "How the hell did you end up in the Sinai?" said the private.

"Plane crashed. Got shot down."

"Egyptian?"

"Israeli."

"Oops."

"Yeah… oops. There are survivors. They need help."

"Alright."

"I also have a friend. My navigator. He needs help."

"Where is he?" said the private.

Coyle motioned in the direction he came. "Alright. We can send a patrol out to find him. Let's get you to the medic first, okay?"

"No. Send help first."

"We're gonna send help but you gotta show us where he is on a map. The plane crash too."

Coyle nodded. "Can you walk?" said the private.

"I don't know. I think so."

The private helped Coyle to his feet and they walked back to the outpost together.

Three hours later, an Israeli patrol with three jeeps rode across the desert. Coyle was in the passenger seat of the lead vehicle. He spotted the rock outcropping where he had left the navigator and led the driver to it.

Coyle climbed from the jeep and moved to the boulder. The navigator laid motionless with his back to Coyle. "Wake up. I brought help just like I said I would. I've got water and a medic," said Coyle.

The navigator did not respond. Coyle was afraid. Coyle gently rolled him over. It was too late. The navigator was dead. "God damn it you stupid Spaniard. You weren't supposed to die. I brought help just like I said I would. I kept my word," said Coyle. "I wish I could remember your name."

Coyle wept. The Israelis covered his body with a blanket and placed him in the jeep.

November 6, 1956 - Sharm el-Sheikh, Egypt

Sharon was writing a report while sipping his morning coffee in a café by the ocean. He was pissed that his brigade had not captured the city of Sharm el-Sheikh. He tried to convince himself that it didn't matter which brigade took the city but it did matter... a lot. His radio operator approached sheepishly. "What is it?" said Sharon, curt.

"The American. They found him," said the radio operator.

"You mean they found his body," said Sharon.

"No. I mean they found him. He's alive. I must have gotten the message mixed up or something. He wasn't dead. He just wasn't among the survivors. He had gone for help."

"So, where the hell is he?"

"In a Mash unit in Arish. He was pretty banged up."

Sharon jumped up, kissed the radio operator on the forehead and went off in search of Brigitte.

November 6, 1956 – Sinai Desert, Egypt

Coyle laid on a bed in a medical tent. There were dozens of wounded Israeli soldiers around him. An IV dripped fluid into his arm rehydrating his body. He had slept for twelve hours. He had nightmares of the cobra striking again and again. He finally woke and stared at the ceiling of the tent. It was hot and the smell in the tent was foul – a mixture of formaldehyde and urine.

Brigitte entered the tent. She saw him and ran to his side. They hugged and kissed. The kiss on his cracked lips was painful but Coyle didn't care. He was just happy to see her again. "Are you okay?" she asked.

"Yeah. I'm fine. Just a little dehydrated," said Coyle.

"I came as soon as I could. I had to bribe my way on to a transport plane."

"How'd you do that?"

"You don't want to know."

"I suppose I don't."

"You were shot down?"

"Yeah. One more crash landing for my log book."

"You poor dear. They found the wreckage and the survivors."

"I heard."

"You saved their lives."

"No. I didn't. They found them before they found me. Good thing too. They wouldn't have lasted much longer."

"I was told two men went with you into the desert."

"Yeah. They were Spaniards. Part of my crew. They died."

"Oh God. I'm so sorry."

"Ain't your fault. I'm the one that couldn't save them."

"But you tried, right?"

"They were my responsibility and I failed."

"I know you. You did your best."

"I did what I could. It wasn't enough. They were good men."

"The doctor said you're gonna have to stay in bed for a couple of days."

"Yeah. They wanna poke me and prod me some more. Makes 'em feel useful."

"I can't stay long. The French and the British are

preparing to invade."

"What in the hell is that about?"

"I'll explain everything when it's all over. In the meantime, you rest."

"Are you going to find Bruno?"

"If I can, yes. I think he's on Malta with his brigade."

"Tell him I said hello."

"Of course. You know you have nothing to worry about with Bruno and I."

"I'm not worried. You're just good friends," said Coyle, lying.

"That's right. Just friends. I feel safe with him."

"Then I say stay close to him. He'll protect you. When do you have to go?"

"I still have a few hours."

Coyle smiled and said, "Good. I missed you."

"Me too," said Brigitte kissing him on the forehead. "We should take some time when we get back to Paris… to talk."

"That'd be nice."

Coyle was relaxed and dozed off. Brigitte watched him sleep. They were safe… for now.

THE END OF PART ONE

LETTER TO READER

Dear Reader,

I hope you enjoyed Sèvres Protocol as much I enjoyed writing it. The next book in the Airmen series is "Operation Revise."

In the meantime, if you are so inclined, I would really appreciate a review of Sèvres Protocol. Loved it, hated it, I'd benefit from your feedback. It makes me a better writer and, honestly, if it's a positive review, it helps promote the book. Reviews are hard to come by these days and now more than ever, potential readers use them in their decision-making process. You, the reader, have the power to make or break a book.

Just click on the cover of Sèvres Protocol on Amazon and you will find the reviews button under the yellow stars. Once you land on the reviews page you can select the Write a Customer Review button and you are ready to write your review. It's pretty simple. And if you want to write a review on a different site, like Goodreads, well that is appreciated too. Thank you for your consideration and I hope to hear from you.

In gratitude,

David Lee Corley

AUTHOR'S BIOGRAPHY

Born in 1958, David grew up on a horse ranch in Northern California, breeding and training appaloosas. He has had all his toes broken at least once and survived numerous falls and kicks from ornery colts and fillies. David started writing professionally as a copywriter in his early 20's. At 32, he packed up his family and moved to Malibu, California to live his dream of writing and directing motion pictures. He has four motion picture screenwriting credits and two directing credits. His movies have been viewed by over 50 million movie-goers worldwide and won a multitude of awards, including the Malibu, Palm Springs, and San Jose Film Festivals. In addition to his 23 screenplays, he has written three novels. He developed his simplistic writing style after rereading his two favorite books, Ernest Hemingway's "The Old Man and The Sea" and Cormac McCarthy's "No Country For Old Men." An avid student of world culture, David lived as an expat in both Thailand and Mexico. At 56, he sold all his possessions and became a nomad for four years. He circumnavigated the globe three times and visited 56 countries. Known for his detailed descriptions, his stories often include actual experiences and characters from his journeys. He loves to paint the places he has visited and the people he has met in both watercolor and oil. His paintings make great Christmas presents, though his three children may beg to differ.